CITY OF TRIALS

SHELLY JARVIS

Thus hath the candle singed the moth. O these deliberate fools!

THE MERCHANT OF VENICE WILLIAM
SHAKESPEARE

CONTENTS

Chapter 1	1
Chapter 2	12
Chapter 3	21
Chapter 4	28
Chapter 5	38
Chapter 6	47
Chapter 7	52
Chapter 8	60
Chapter 9	71
Chapter 10	80
Chapter 11	90
Chapter 12	98
Chapter 13	109
Chapter 14	116
Chapter 15	127
Chapter 16	135
Chapter 17	146
Chapter 18	156
Chapter 19	164
Chapter 20	171
Chapter 21	180
Chapter 22	185
Chapter 23	192
Chapter 24	202
Chapter 25	212
Chapter 26	220
Chapter 27	233
Chapter 28	240
Chapter 29	247
Chapter 30	253
Epilogue	260
About the Author	267

CHAPTER
ONE

If I'm fast, I will make it to the next hiding place in less than an hour—quicker if not for hauling all this weight behind me. After one last survey from my hiding spot, I rise and head off through the grasslands. The ropes of my skiff bite into my shoulders, but I can't stop for that. I'm too exposed and need to keep moving.

I wince at the thought. The goods I've collected from the homesteader are my offering to the Raiders, my people. Or, at least, the people I *want* to be mine.

Even after living with them for a dozen years, I remain an outsider. It is my own fault. They found me when I was a young girl, barely eight years old. They clothed me, cared for me, trained me as one of their own; all they've asked of me is one simple task, which I have been unable to complete. Now I am of age, and my opportunity will soon come to an end. If I cannot return with a capture, a new person to become a Raider and add to our family, I will be banished.

I shiver, try to shake away the thought. Despite my best efforts to ignore the inevitable, solstice approaches; I can't avoid my fate much longer.

A howl stops me in my tracks, cutting through all other thoughts. I drop to the ground, letting the tall grass surround me, and slip the skiff's makeshift harness from my shoulders. My fingertips itch as I move them towards my knife, aching for speed when I desperately need stealth. My blade is not a fine thing—no gems or precious metals, no ornately wrought handle—but it is mine, and it is sharp, and that is enough.

The grasses sway, wind breathing life into the dry weeds, while I watch for the tiniest movement in the hopes that I might take meat home for my family. Then I see it: a coyote. It is beautiful. Silver fur glinting in the moonlight, every step steady and sure. We are both hunters, hungry and alone, away from our packs. It is a shame that I must kill it, but killing is what Raiders do.

In the empty grasslands to my right, a stranger appears as if from nowhere, a phantom in the night. I blink, unsure of what I'm seeing. The coyote's eyes have shifted to him as well, so at least I know I am not hallucinating.

Perhaps he is from another band of travelers, one of the worshippers of the mountain gods who dwell nearby. If the sun were still up, I would be able to see the faces of the carved gods on the distant Mountain of Ushmor. But no, he doesn't dress like any Raider I've seen, and none I've met would stand exposed in the middle of this place where anyone or anything could attack.

I glance between the man and the coyote. The stranger still hasn't seen the beast who stalks ever closer to him. My heart surges in realization of the gift I've been given. A beast and a man in one place—all I have to do is reach out and take them.

For a second, the man seems to flicker in and out of being. My breath hitches in my chest, fear arresting my heart. But it is not the shimmer in the air around him that worries me, nor the way he vanishes for a half a second before reappearing; no, the panic surging through my veins, pulsing in my heart, is the realization that this stranger is my only hope. I must take him to the Raiders or find a new road to walk, alone.

My eyes dart to the coyote to check his location, then shift back to the man as he drops to the ground, appearing to wrestle with something. He rolls in the dirt, spitting curses in a language I don't know. Finally, he grabs a rock and smashes it against his arm.

The coyote and I both watch this happen, and for a moment I think the beast and I share a conspiratorial look as we question the sanity of this man or ghost or whatever he is. But the stranger's madness passes and he rises, brushing off dirt and tufts of grass from blue-black skin. He's bare to the waist, his thin frame taut with twitching muscles; his dark eyes drink the night, white teeth glinting in the moonlight as he breathes open-mouthed and quiet, listening for a sound that doesn't come—the sound of my approach.

I slip behind him, my steps feather-soft. The Raiders have trained me well in this, making me as stealthy and dangerous as they are. Once I would've been sick at the thought of being like them, but now pride fills me and I revel in the way I can slink over the savannah unseen.

Up close, he is taller than I thought. I couldn't tell from my hunting spot, but now I am so close I can smell the salt of his skin. I stand a chin above most of the Raiders, but he is bigger still. I tilt my head, sizing him up, marvelling at his unknown vulnerability. I could kill him if I wanted. I've killed others before, those who could not be captured. Dangerous people. Violent people. People who wanted to kill me. But I was faster and stronger and better.

This stranger does not seem like the others. My mouth goes dry at the thought of killing him simply for being here. The dagger feels heavy in my grip as I weigh this decision, pondering who this man is and whether he belongs with my family. The metal begs to sing through the air, to bite into flesh and pour crimson into the night.

My dagger has won this battle before, striking out a killing blow instead of taking home a prize. But not this night. I don't know why my hand stills instead of slicing his throat. Perhaps because I need him. I've never felt the desperation I do now.

Or maybe it is his beauty, for he is beautiful. Possibly it is the way he moves through the night on quiet feet as if he, too, were a Raider. Whatever the reason, I will not sink my blade into him no matter how sweetly it sings; instead, I will add to our patchwork family and be known as a life-bringer instead of only a death dealer.

My heart hammers through my chest as I close the gap between us. His head twitches so slightly I almost miss it. I stop, frozen in place, certain he hears me. I count in my head, as Rego taught me, until my heartbeat steadies and I am surrounded by calm. I am silent as the wind, I am the night. He hasn't heard me.

Then I realize my mistake.

The man swivels away from me as a blur of silver crashes against him. The coyote, so patient and stealthy, seems to have given in to the hunger panging through him.

I spring, fast as a chigerbeast, diving against the coyote's side just as his teeth snap towards the stranger's throat. I scramble away from the gnashing teeth and bury my blade into the beast's side, aiming for the knot-like heart. I rip out the knife and jab it back in, over and over, levering it back and forth until blood gushes from the coyote's side. When the snarling jaws cease and the creature shivers into death, I turn my attention on the stranger in front of me.

His eyes are black pits, absorbing all the light around him. He stares down at me as if he's never seen another person. Maybe he's never seen another person like me.

A tentative smile tugs at the corners of his mouth. He looks as if he wants to thank me, but thinks better of it, as if he isn't quite sure whether he would have been safer with the coyote. I bare my teeth at him, a warning that I am just as dangerous as the bloody beast.

He takes a step back, a tiny thing, but enough to remind me that I can't let him escape. I dive towards him, toppling him to the ground and pinning his arms and legs with my body. My hands dance across his legs in the seconds before he bucks against me, throwing me off and jumping to his feet. He is more of a challenge than a half-starved coyote and I laugh, thrilled with the hunt, joyful that he fights. He will make a grand addition to our ranks.

He tries to run. He didn't notice my quick hands, didn't feel my rope as it coiled around his ankles. He falls to the ground, understanding crossing his face. He struggles still, but I make quick work of tying his hands and gagging him. I retrieve my skiff from its hiding spot. I built this sled myself, curved and sanded the wood until it resembled a small boat with runners on the bottom. It's full of bartered goods to give to the Raiders, but I shove them all aside and roll him onto it. The man squirms when I drag the coyote over and press it in beside him, but I don't worry that he'll get free. My knots are strong; he will not escape.

WE LEAVE THE GRASSLANDS, TREKKING OVER DESERT FOR A DAY AND A half before I spot one of my people. Ukaru, another of the hunters, lumbers over the dunes wrapped head to heel in layers of loose-fitting indigo robes. He angles towards me so our paths will intersect.

There's a jolt in my chest. He will be the first to recognize that I am a life-bringer. For some, the title means little. But for me, it is everything. Becoming this stranger home to become one of us signifies that I have met my part of the bargain and am ready to accept my permanent place with the Raiders. I will no longer have to live along the outside of this patchwork family, feeling like a drain on them despite my contributions, dreading the day they would cast me out.

"Nova," Ukaru hails, throwing a hand into the air. "Where has your light shone today, Little Star?"

I stop to bow my head. He waves his hand dismissively. He is less formal than the others and treats me kindly. The others are not unkind, but my status as an outsider does not afford me much in the way of gentleness, despite the many years I've hunted and lived at their sides.

"I've captured a beast, Nova," he says, his toothy smile bright against his head cloth. Ukaru steps aside to show his skiff, clearly proud of his haul. A colossal hornhoof lays there, its thick hide gashed from Ukaru's spear.

"A fine capture," I say, returning his grin.

He puffs out his chest for a moment, but deflates and grows quiet when he leans near me and asks, "What does the old tongue say?"

I search his eyes. Ukaru has never asked me to speak in the old tongue with him. But there is only kindness in his amber gaze. "Antelope," I reply.

"Antelope," he repeats, stretching out the unfamiliar word. We laugh together at his clumsy attempt before he turns his eyes to my skiff. "What have you returned to us?"

Now it is my turn to be proud. I whip back the cover with a dramatic gesture. I turn back to Ukaru with a smile, but his face has paled. He steps back, putting distance between us as he carves an X in the air in front of his eyes.

I look back to my haul. The coyote doesn't offer much meat, but the prisoner should warrant celebration. The man is asleep, or at least pretending to be, but I don't see what could cause such fear in Ukaru. I drop the skiff's rope and step towards Ukaru with an outstretched hand. He recoils, refusing to let me touch him.

"Ukaru-du, why do you turn from me?"

"You have cursed us, Little Star," he whispers. "You have brought the eyes of the gods upon us."

I shake my head, furrowing my brows. "N-no," I stammer, confused at his words. "I've returned with a new Raider. With him I become a life-bringer."

Ukaru curses. "You are no life-bringer, Nova. Death walks at your side."

"I don't understand."

"You wouldn't. You weren't among us the last time a cursed man fell from the stars. We ran from him then, but still we were punished, losing two dozen of our warriors. And now you haul the curse back to our doorstep."

My whole body chafes at the words, but I speak them anyway: "I could release him."

"It is too late for that."

He spits at my feet and turns, grabbing the reins of his skiff and marching away. I stare after him until he's crossed the next dune and disappeared. My jaw still hangs open. I can't imagine what I've done to warrant such a reaction. I've never heard a tale such as his, not even when the others would share frightening stories around the fire.

Tears linger at the corners of my eyes, but I will not cry. I can't afford to lose the moisture.

With a sigh I turn back to my skiff. This offering must be accepted or I risk losing the only family I've known. My gaze drifts to the man—the man who isn't there. I jerk my head up and my eyes dart across the empty landscape. If he ran, I return with shame and an insufficient offering. But how will I be received if I return with him?

From behind, rope passes over my head, tightening against the soft flesh of my throat. He pulls so it digs into my neck. I try to slip my hands between the cord and my skin, but it tightens even more, burning across my flesh. I flail, throwing my arms and legs behind me, but I can't make contact.

My vision darkens at the edges and my body loses its strength. I gasp, drawing in as much air as I can. Fading much too quickly, I throw my head back. It connects with his face, rewarding me with a sickening crunch. He jerks back, his grip loosening enough for me to pull away. I spin to face him, my knife at the ready before I've even thought to withdraw it.

His eyes are wide and wild as he casts about for an escape. He's afraid. I can see it on his bleeding face, in the slump of his shoulders. But like a cornered beast, his actions grow more frantic.

In his eyes, I see the thought flicker into being, like a lantern lit on the darkest of nights. He will run.

Half a second later he darts towards me. I sidestep rather than plant my feet, missing his attack but losing my footing as I scramble out of his way. He is propelled by the ferocity of a man with nothing to lose, and I know he would have injured me if I had tried to stop him. In the seconds it takes me to gain my feet, he's made it to the closest dune and is fighting the cascading sand as he tries to crest it.

I grab the rope he used to choke me and scurry after him. He's made little headway in the sand, clearly unused to walking on it, and he's only just reached the top of the dune when my hands grasp his ankle. He kicks down at me, trying to break free, but I hang on for dear life. He tries to shake me loose, but I cling to him, climbing farther up his leg and using my weight to pull him down. Though he hasn't realized it yet, every time he stamps his foot at me, he loses ground on the sand. Soon, we have slipped back down the sand and his escape has all but failed.

Releasing his leg, I drop into a crouch. With my knife in one hand and my rope in the other, I stare at the man, ready to pounce. The stranger is strong and fast, but he does not have the stamina of a Raider. Not yet. His panting, labored breath tells me that he will not run again, because he can't. Instead, he settles on the ground before me, sighs, accepts defeat.

I slip the tip of my dagger under his chin and raise his eyes to meet mine. My breath catches at the strange, dark gaze that settles on me as if he knows me. I whisper, "Not again. Next time I will hurt you."

I sheath my dagger. The metal whines, angry that I've denied it yet again. But I don't kill him, though if Ukaru is to be believed, I probably should.

I tie him up again. He doesn't fight. When I march him back to the skiff, he gets in willingly. Kneeling before me he says, "You'll regret this."

"Not today," I say, tossing the tarp over him.

I march forward, dragging my prize. My mind reels, turning the past few minutes over in my head. Ukaru's reaction was painful and his words still linger. My throat hurts when I swallow, thanks to the stranger, and his words...his words were spoken in the old tongue.

I drop the rope and throw off his cover. This time he doesn't pretend to sleep but glares up at me. I glare right back and ask, "Who are you?"

He leans over the skiff and spits at my feet in answer. I jab my finger against his bleeding nose and he yelps in pain. I ask again, but he does not speak. His eyes are full of anger. When he sees my fist clench, threatening to catch him in the nose again, he growls, "Krew."

"Krew," I repeat. "Where are you from?"

He clenches and releases his fists. "The station."

Station? I think. I don't know what this word means, but I refuse to tell him as much. Instead, I get to the question I've wanted to ask all along: "How did you come to speak the old tongue?"

His brows wrinkle as confusion crosses his damaged face. "This is the language I was taught from birth."

I squint at him, unsure if I believe him. In the twelve years I've lived with the Raiders, through the many lands we've traveled, I've never met another fluent in the old tongue. None, except Aunt Rachel.

I wince at the thought of her, my mind darting through faded memories. A campfire, figures moving through darkness, running, separating...

"You lie."

I throw the cover over Krew and return to my harness. This boy will not revive the memories I have worked so hard to forget. He is for my new family, the Raiders who took a frightened child and turned her into a warrior. With his life, I become one of them—not just in name, but in spirit. I will live my days with them without fear of being cast aside. I become Nova-du.

THE CHIEF IS WAITING ON THE DUNE OUTSIDE THE PERIMETER WHEN I reach camp. Her dark eyes are ringed with white paint, stark against her sun-browned body.

"Eija-du," I say, bowing my head.

"Hello, Little Star," she says, her voice softer than I expect.

"I brought a gift," I say. I don't smile. I can see on her face that Ukaru has already told her.

She nods. "Show me."

I pull back the cover, revealing Krew. She inhales sharply. Eija takes a step towards my skiff, kneeling to run her finger over the soft skin on the back of his arm. He jerks, turning his face so his black eyes meet her brown ones.

"Don't touch me," he growls.

She tilts her head, watching him. Eija does not know the old tongue, but his meaning is clear. Still, she withdraws her hand slowly to show she is not afraid, but I see the fear in the press of her lips. Something about Krew scares the Raiders, and though I don't understand, it's starting to scare me, too. Like Ukaru, Eija marks her eyes so as not to have seen him before she turns away.

I reach out, grabbing her shoulder. She stops, her head angling towards my hand, and I remove it with haste. "Forgive me, Eija-du."

"Not this time, Nova," she says, her voice barely a whisper.

"I don't understand," I press. "I have brought life. I have fulfilled my promise to become a Raider in earnest."

Eija shakes her head. "No, young one, this man is not life. He is cursed. As are we if we keep him."

"But Eija—"

"No," she interrupts. "For once in your life, you cannot talk your way out of this." I open my mouth to argue, but the fire blazing through her eyes silences me. She says, "You will stay with us until this matter is decided. But if he is sent away…"

She pauses, and for a moment I see a glimmer of hurt in her eyes. Eija has watched me grow for a dozen years. Though we've never been close, I have been a student of the Raiders and she has been my chief.

Before I can gather my words around the lump in my throat, she says, "You will take him to the council tent before you find your rest. Understand?"

I nod. I don't understand, but I dare not say so. I watch her stalk towards camp, her long braids swaying behind her with each step. When she's gone, I do as she said and drag Krew to the tent. Ukaru is there, alongside Sadhi and Nukiki. They stare at the unmoving tan cover over my skiff as if it holds the mysteries of the world.

Before I turn to leave, I look to Ukaru but he won't meet my eyes. My face sours despite my best attempt to remain calm. I am angry at Ukaru, angry at Eija and even Krew. More so, I'm angry at myself for not understanding what I've done wrong.

CHAPTER
TWO

The scream wakes me. It chokes out, silenced by the daylight, by my waking. I still see the teeth, snapping at me.

It's nothing, I think, willing myself to let the image die.

I often wake myself this way. Memories to dreams, dreams to nightmares. Always biting. Though I haven't dreamed of the gnashing teeth in quite some time, it's clear why they've returned to me now.

Krew, I think, then shake my head to dislodge his name from my mind. Maybe he is part of it, reminding me of a past that is better left unremembered. But I'm sure the coyote is really what my brain is projecting this time. I hope that is all.

I gaze over the pile of sleeping bodies, some entangled, others alone. There are just over a dozen of us in the unmated tent, a mixture of women, men, and mazulla—those beyond the confines of gender. Some are both, some are neither, some move between gender like the motion of a river. All are Raiders, all are loved.

Fatboy kicks weakly at me, shushing. I glare at him, jealous of his untroubled mind, before scrambling out of the tent into the morning sun. It is bright, too bright for my night-trained eyes, and I shield my face with my hands to fight the discomfort.

Rego is watching today, staring through his spyglass towards the horizon. I scramble up the dune beside him and sit on his blanket, enjoying the sand beneath as it heats through my robes.

"Can't sleep?"

I shrug, not wanting to go into it, though I know he already knows. He always knows.

"Another dream of your Rachel?"

I smile at the way Rego's lips stretch around the unfamiliar name. I've been teaching Rego the old tongue for many months, but he still finds some words strange to say.

"Same dream," I say with a sigh. "It's always the same."

Rego presses his lips flat, dipping his head. My eyebrows raise, surprised by the gesture. This signal of sympathy is rarely used among the Raiders.

Rego's tanned cheeks burn red, embarrassed by his own action. His gravelly voice is quiet when he says, "Someday you will sleep without dreams, missing these days when your heart still mourns her."

"I don't think I will ever miss the dreams, Rego. They hurt."

"I know, Nova-du."

I gasp. Turning quickly, I check to make sure no one is near enough to hear us. I push against Rego's arm and ask, "You blaspheme openly?"

Rego shrugs. "You brought a new one to us. You are worthy."

"Guard your words, Rego. They do not count me a life-bringer yet."

"Pah," Rego scoffs. He picks up a handful of sand and throws it into the wind. "We are scattered, like the sand. All people are our people, lost. You were returned to us, now you return others. You are the circle, *du*, complete."

His words are wrong, but they comfort all the same. I curl against him for a moment, thankful for his kindness. He pats my hand before shooing me away. I obey, sliding down the dune and making my way to the council tent. I don't know why I go, or at least I tell myself that.

I peek inside. Krew is in the corner, chained to a post. He leans against it, unable to lie down. A surge of anger runs through me at such cruelty. I slip in, quiet enough to sneak past his guard. The chain is easy to loosen, and I move the links through the catch so that he has enough room to rest.

When I turn to leave, he is watching me. His dark eyes question me, unsure why I have done him this small kindness. I bite my lip, unsure how to answer his unspoken question. I whisper, "This is not who we are. You should've been welcomed."

He shakes his head and says, "I should have been left alone."

His words sting in their rightness. He is a prisoner here because of me, because of the desires in my heart. He should not be here.

But I don't say these words to him. I can't. Instead, I turn and skulk away, ashamed for what I've done, but too proud to admit it aloud.

———

THE AIR OUTSIDE THE COUNCIL TENT IS STIFLING, OPPRESSIVELY HOT; combined with my shame, it is hard to find my breath. I stumble away, gasping, trying to put distance between myself and Krew though it likely won't help.

I scurry between two tents and come out by the dune opposite where Rego keeps watch. The sunlight beating down on the dune gives me sandblindness and for a moment I don't see the figure in front of me. Thoa. The Bonecutter.

The sight of him sends a chill through me, despite the heat. He stands there basking in the sun, dressed in his killing leathers. He does not wear the robes most of the Raiders favor. I don't understand how he manages the sun as he does, how he seems to thrive in the heat. But I don't ask. I don't speak to Thoa. No one does.

Though we are close in age, we haven't spoken since we were

children. He was taken from our learning circle and made a hunter before I got to know him. Now I think that I could no more know him than I could know the stars above.

He looks up from sharpening his blade. When our eyes meet, I fight the urge to run. He slowly sheathes the weapon at his side, his eyes never leaving mine. He saunters towards me. I am acutely aware of the sweat beading on his tattooed chest as it rises and falls mere inches from me.

"Little Star," he growls, his voice dark and dangerous.

I dip my head. "Forgive me Thoa-gra. I did not mean to intrude."

He laughs, a rumbling sound. "This is not my desert, Nova. You are free to walk where you will."

I look up at him, surprised by the gentleness of his words. He speaks my name as if we are friends. Perhaps we are. I gaze into blue eyes that shine like polished stone. I want to look at them longer, but I dare not. I nod a thanks and step away from him, retreating to the shadows of the tents.

———

At dinner we feast on the hornhoof Ukaru brought home, as well as the gamey meat of a slimneck prancer. I catch eyes with Ukaru as he takes a bite of the prancer and I wonder if he is silently asking me the name of the beast. *Antelope*, I think. The word feels foreign, even to me.

After the meat we have stone fruit gathered by another of the hunters. Her gift is sweet, the nectar dripping down my chin as I bite into the flesh of the mango. I breathe in the aroma of the fruit, trying to memorize the details as I hold it to my face. When we roam, we sometimes go many moons before we find such a treat again, and I am grateful that Caita returned with it instead of another beast.

Krew is seated at a table for one. None may eat with him. I scan the room and see many cross their eyes and turn away from him. He is a curiosity they can't stop looking at, just as I can't stop looking. Krew does not return our stares, looking at his plate instead. The meat sits upon it untouched, though he must have eaten the fruit and nuts already, and I wonder why he does not partake of the beasts.

Leer sits beside me and I'm grateful for his company. Many of the others are distant from me; some because of Krew, but most because even after twelve years with them I am still an outsider, a token of bad luck.

"How was the homesteader?" Leer asks as he tears into the hornhoof flesh.

"Kind," I say. "She made smallclothes for the children and new babes, fine things. Sturdy."

"That bodes well for the coming seasons."

"Aye, it does." I lower my voice and say, "She made something special for you. It's hidden in my bedroll."

Leer's eyes go wide but he keeps his voice quiet. "A real binder?"

I nod. "I've never seen it's equal. You will no longer have to fight with those cloth strips you've been using."

He fights his smile. "This is a true gift. How can I repay you?"

"Think no more about such things. I am happy she was able to create it before we journey again."

After the meal, Eija calls us from the tent and we follow her outside to the fire. It is her grandfather who greets us, warm eyes and open smile. He was chief before Eija, before her father, and he is old enough to remember the days when his own grandfather was chief, and his before that, generations ago, before the world split.

Papa-du motions for us to circle the fire, as we do every solstice. "Tonight, we honor the sun who gives us the day, who withdraws so we may have night. Like the sun, we give ourselves to whom we choose as we share the right to wed. Like the sun, we turn away as we desire, offering instead a period of rest."

He shakes his walking stick in the air. Beast teeth and beads scrape together, creating a strange music in the quiet of the circle. Papa-du turns his stick to Eija and she steps forward. She walks around the fire and looks at each face. When she stops in front of Nukiki, she smiles and holds out her hands, saying, "Will you walk with me through sunlight until the solstice marks the end of our path?"

The woman smiles and joins her hands with Eija. "Let the sun guide us, Eija-du."

The women leave the circle and walk towards Eija's tent. Papa-du shakes his stick, pointing to Leer. He chooses Danika, as he's done for the last three solstices. They leave for their tent and I know he will not come for his binder tonight.

Papa-du points to another and another. Many leave to return to their tents, honoring the sun by offering their bodies to their new mates. Some are refused but remain in the circle while the other names are called. This is the fifth solstice I have been old enough to join the circle, but I have never felt the hands of a mate. No one chooses me, and I choose no one.

Thoa has been called. I have never known him to have a mate. He circles the fire, but many duck their eyes, afraid of his gaze. I watch as he prowls—for that is what he does, like the very beasts he kills—and I find my eyes drifting over his broad shoulders, his scarred skin. He is not smooth and unmarred like Krew, but he is still beautiful. His beauty comes from his strength, the power exuding from him, the silent mystery in his gaze.

I look up into his eyes, surprised to find them meeting mine. He holds his hands out to me. I stare at them, unblinking. I turn my eyes back to his face. His lips are moving, but I cannot hear him over the rush of blood pounding through my ears.

Without thinking, without words, I turn my back to him.

The seconds tick by in silence as I stare into the black night, away from Thoa, away from the light, into the nothingness beyond. When Papa-du says my name, I turn back to the circle.

Heat creeps up my neck and I'm thankful no one can see it in the dim firelight.

I look up to see every eye upon me. I realize it is my turn to choose. My eyes flicker to the tent where Krew is chained, and I wonder what my choice would be if he were accepted as one of us.

From the corner of my eye, I see Thoa's face harden as he turns from the circle and stalks away. He is angry with me, but I can do nothing to change that. With a sigh I walk the circle, but I keep my eyes down. When I reach Rego I stop in front of him. I look into his eyes and force a smile. Holding my hands to him I say the words. Rego smiles in return and puts his hand on my cheek before he turns from me. It does not hurt when I stare at his back; Rego is in love with a ghost, watching the horizon every day for the return of a husband who does not come back.

I return to my place in the circle and stand in silence until all have chosen. When Papa-du dismisses us, I slither away into the pre-dawn light, eager to find a quiet place in the unmated tent to wrangle the thoughts roiling through my head.

***

It is the ninth day. Krew is brought before the Raiders and I stand to offer his life to my people. Captivity has not been kind to him and he looks thinner than when I returned with him. I try to convince the Raiders of his worth, citing his strength when he escaped and fought me, but they balk at the thought.

"If he were strong, you would be hurt, or scarred," Sadhi says.

The others murmur in agreement. When Ukaru stands, I cringe. He says, "I do not know if he is strong. It is the curse upon him that worries me."

"He is not cursed," I say. "He is just a boy. We can make him a Raider, a man."

Ukaru scoffs. "You do not know, Little Star. You have not lived long enough to see the mark of the gods." My eyes follow his pointing finger to the boy's wrist where a thin silver bracelet presses into his flesh. I lift Krew's wrist to view the thing closer, eliciting gasps from the assembly.

It is a fine thing, so well-made I cannot see the clasp. It rests against his skin so tight it seems to be part of him. I run my finger over the bracelet until I feel a bump. It glows as constant as the sun, as red as the dawn. I drop his wrist and look to Ukaru. I ask, "Jewelry. You fear him for this?"

Ukaru barks a bitter laugh. He points up to the sky, to the dark ring that circles the world. "He is marked by the gods. Others have come before, others will come after, but we do not interfere with those who ride upon the stars. His people will send for him and we cannot have him when they do. He shall not be one of us."

"You do not decide that," I say, anger flushing my face.

Eija stands and raises her hand for silence. "No, he does not. But Ukaru is not wrong. The cursed ones have come to us before. Each time, they have brought nothing but destruction to our people."

"That doesn't mean Krew is like them."

There is muttering at the mention of his name. At first, I wonder if I have done something wrong by saying it. Then I realize they simply do not wish to know it, because it makes him less of an *it* and more of a *him*.

"This decision belongs to all the Raiders. Our lives are intertwined, binding us to one another, and all must decide. To accept this man as one of us, stand with Nova. To cast him out, stand with Ukaru."

Eija doesn't move, doesn't side with either of us, but the others are in motion as soon as she stops speaking. Rego joins me, and to my surprise, so does Nukiki. Leer stands between each group, looking shamed when his wife draws him to Ukaru's side. I do not blame him. The tide turns against us.

With brow furrowed as if it pains him to do so, Thoa also joins us at the front. I am surprised by this, since I turned from him and since all the other Raiders side with Ukaru. His eyes meet mine for only a second, and I hope it is long enough for him to see that I am grateful.

Rego puts his arm around my shoulders as Eija moves to stand in front of me. "Your life offering is refused, Nova. In the morning you will release his blood to the sun. After, you will leave the Raiders and never return."

I turn to look at Krew. His eyes dart around the room as he tries to follow what is going on, but he doesn't speak our language. When his gaze finds mine, a sob rises in my throat. My tears slip past my lashes to trail down my cheeks, silent and shameful.

I am banished. I have failed. But one last task before I go.

Tomorrow I will kill Krew.

CHAPTER
THREE

The sun peeks over the edge of the earth as they bring Krew out of the council tent. Rego withdraws his comforting hand as Eija approaches. I must face this alone.

They place him on the ground before me. He is dreary-eyed and frail, not the sharp boy I took from the grasslands. *Good*, I think. His weakness makes it easier to kill him; not because he will not fight me, but because I cannot love a fragile thing.

Eija says, "Death returned nine days past, bringing gifts of beast and fruit, grains, hides, and water. We consumed it with haste, as death commands." The Raiders' heads nod in agreement, their murmurs urging her on. "Life takes time, demands it of us. And we give. Nine days of life have been given to this man, this gift from Nova."

At these words they hiss and spit, their eyes flickering to me. I stand straight, my back and shoulders unbending under the heaviness of their gaze. I will not be shamed for my offering, not by them. It is only Krew's eyes that harm me. When he stares up, his eyes pulling all the light from the world into their heady darkness, that is when I feel shame, pain.

My blade is heavy in my hand. Krew shudders, realizing what

I'm about to do. I want to step behind him so I don't have to watch when life ebbs away, but I do not. I owe him the courtesy of looking in his eyes while I slit his throat.

His thick black curls tangle in my hands as I hold him in place while placing my knife against his throat. My hand shakes. I take a deep breath, steady myself. Krew whispers, "Please."

There are no other words. I shake my head. I want to apologize, tell him I regret bringing him here. But it doesn't matter to either of us. It is done and this is the consequence.

My knife bites at his skin, drawing a drop of blood. I clench my fist around my knife until my knuckles whiten, draw back, and—

"Stop."

Thoa's voice roots me to the spot. He walks through the Raiders, coming towards me. When he reaches us, his blue eyes linger on mine, but I do not understand the question he asks without words. Finally, he turns to the others and says, "Little Star will not become Nova-gra. Not today."

Ukaru stands, his eyes flashing in anger. I do not know how I once thought him kind. He says, "It is decided. We will not have the boy as ours."

Several murmur in agreement, but when Thoa raises his hand they fall silent. They fear him, the Bonecutter, but they respect him as well. "He will not be ours, in life or death. If the eyes of the gods follow him as you say, and you fear their ire if we give him life, we should not have his death upon our hands either."

Heads nod. His words are wise and many see his way. Eija says, "Your words make sense, Thoa-gra, but what would you have us do? Return him to the grasslands?"

Thoa shakes his head. "He is weak. Returning him to the grasslands is the same as killing him."

My hand trembles as I slip my knife back to my belt. I release Krew's hair and he shuffles back from me, crawling on tied hands and feet. I forget myself and put my hand on Thoa's arm to turn him to me. I ask, "What do we do with him?"

Thoa's eyes look to my hand and I withdraw it, my cheeks going hot. He stares at me, his jaw clenching and unclenching before he says, "Take him to the City of Trials."

I gasp along with the others. I shake my head and say, "You cannot mean that."

"I do," he says. "Let the gods follow him there and we will be rid of them."

Ukaru's voice rises above the whispers. "Nova should take him. It was she who brought this curse upon us."

"Nova is banished," Rego says through clenched teeth.

"Her banishment has not begun. Let her redeem herself in this," Thoa says. "She will return this man to the gods, and when she returns, she will bring a new life with her to become a Raider."

Ukaru's lip curls. "That is not our way."

My knife sings Ukaru's name, but I dare not draw it. Too many agree. I don't speak against it, knowing it is useless. It was decided as the words left his lips.

Thoa asks, "Are you so eager to lose a good hunter, Ukaru-du?"

After a quiet moment where Ukaru doesn't answer and no one else dares do more than breathe, Eija says, "Nova can't make this trek alone. She will need help."

Rego steps forward. "I will go."

I smile. Rego is more than double my age and his days with blades have long passed. But he is wise, with a swift tongue that knows when to speak and when to still. I am grateful for him.

Nukiki steps forward and says, "I will go."

Eija's eyes are round with fear. She reaches for her wife, stopping her from joining us. "If you go, so do I."

"No," Papa-du says, walking forward through the parting crowd. "You will not go. Your duty is to your people."

"My duty is to my wife," Eija says, steel in her voice.

I have seen her in the hunt, alive with fire dancing in her bones, sparking from her skin. I have heard her roar, seen her bare her teeth as she takes down a beast double her size. I have wiped blood from her skin, hers and not. Yet I have never seen her look as fierce as she does right now.

Papa-du does not cower in her rage as the rest of us do. He stands his ground, saying, "The Chief will stay. Her wife will go."

Eija growls, more frightening than any beast I've heard. When she stalks from the assembly, none dare follow. Instead Papa-du turns to the others and said, "Are there any others brave enough to join Little Star?"

They will not look at me, shuffling feet and staring into the distance. Their silence speaks more than any word could. Beside me I hear Thoa say, "I will go, Papa-du."

I fight the urge to embrace him. He saved Krew with his words and now he volunteers to take him to the edge of our world. There is no reason for him to do this, no reward in his actions, but he does it anyway. For his people. And, maybe, for me.

Papa-du nods. "We prepare today. At nightfall, you leave. Now go, find your rest."

I DON'T KNOW HOW I AM TO REST, KNOWING I WILL SOON BE traversing the desert with my motley crew. Fatboy snores beside me in the unmated tent, but I do not envy his blissful slumber today. He will stay here with the same people, the same chores, while I go across the land on an adventure.

I test the word on my lips: *Adventure.* It sparks something inside me, sending my stomach spinning. I have been on the hunt for days at a time, but I have never ventured away from camp without an inkling of when I might return. *If* I might return. I fear I will not see this place again.

I find Rego tightening his bedroll. He ties it to his pack and tests it on his back. I worry for him, for what this journey may do to his body. As if reading my thoughts, he says, "I'm fine, Nova. I would not have volunteered if I thought I couldn't handle it."

But I know he's lying. He would've volunteered even if he were resting against death's arm. He loves me.

"I know," I lie in return.

Nukiki sticks her head inside the tent. "Ready?"

I nod, giving her a tight smile. I do not know her well and I'm not certain why she has agreed to join us. Though I want to believe it is from kindness, I am no fool. Raiders do not make decisions because of kindness.

We join Thoa at the edge of camp. We each have a pack, but Thoa also has a skiff. I lift the tarp to find Krew tied and gagged inside. He stares up at me, but his eyes are glazed over. I cover him again, but there is worry inside me.

Eija whispers with Nukiki, though I do not hear the promises they make one another. She is the only one who comes to see us off. Though it hurts, I am not surprised. Aside from Nukiki, we are each unmated, outcasts in our own way. The Raiders will miss Rego's bird-eyed watch, but there are other watchers; they will miss Thoa's hunts, guaranteed to bring food to the camp, but there are other hunters.

I offer nothing for them to miss.

Still, I thought perhaps Leer would be here to say goodbye. He is the closest thing I have to a friend in this place, aside from Rego, who has become my family over these long years. But Leer has a wife to worry about, and being friends with me is a fast way to lose her. Everyone knows I am bad luck.

Rego pries Nukiki away from her wife and we set off across the dunes. Thoa carries his own pack and the skiff with Krew in it, but he still marks a brutal pace and we trail after him. We walk in silence for many miles, each lost to their thoughts, unable or unwilling to break the quiet.

The heat is fading but the night is without wind, cool, but comfortable. My copper-colored robes are movable, made to allow airflow while keeping moisture in, but without the wind the cotton feels heavy. When Thoa stops and signals a break, I lift the robes and tie them over my hair, leaving only my thin shift underneath.

Nukiki tilts her head, her lips quirking up in a smile. "Your robe is the same color as your hair."

I nod, but it is Rego who speaks. "It was my husband's robe."

"Forgive me," Nukiki says, pressing her lips flat and dipping her head. "I did not mean to invoke his memory."

"Nothing to forgive, sweet girl. My memories of Jasper are a blessing," Rego says. He smiles at her, for the gesture of sympathy. A small thing to her, maybe, but Rego's eyes have softened when he looks at her. Her action has gained her favor.

I turn to Thoa and see him several yards away giving water to Krew. He leans over him, speaking in low tones. I approach slowly, unsure where I stand with either of them. When I'm near to them I say, "He doesn't understand our language, Thoa."

"Yes, Nova, I know," Thoa says. He speaks in the old tongue.

My brows raise as surprise covers my face. He takes pleasure in surprising me; I can see it in the way his lips curl, how he looks up at me in an almost sheepish way. His accent is not as heavy as Rego's, though he hovers on the last syllable of each word as the Raiders do.

I smile in return and say, "I did not know you spoke the old tongue."

He stands and takes a step towards me. Heat from his bare skin simmers against mine as he says, "There is much you do not know of me, Little Star."

My breath catches in my throat, but he pushes past me, brushing my shoulder with his as he goes. I want to turn and follow him with my eyes, to trace the movement of his body in the moonlight, but I do not. Instead I move closer to Krew and kneel by the skiff.

He's hunched over a handful of figs, his back to me. I watch for a moment as he greedily eats and notice that a bit of life seems to have returned to him. I take a step closer and watch as his shoulders tighten. Slowly, slowly, he slides down the skiff away from me.

"Krew," I whisper. I hear the pain in my voice and wonder if he does as well. From the way he winces at the sound of his name on my lips, I don't think so. I say, "I'm sorry for what happened."

His fingers move to the scab on his neck where my knife bit his skin. His black eyes are so cold a chill runs down my spine. Through gritted teeth he says, "You were going to kill me."

I shake my head, but we both know I'm lying. "They forced me. I didn't want to, but I didn't have a choice."

Krew points across the dune to where Thoa stands, his back to us. "Neither did he. So, he created one. He is the only one among you with honor."

His words sting, but more than that, they shock me. "The only one with honor? Do you know the other Raiders fear him? He's a killer. They call him the Bonecutter. I've heard horrible, terrible stories about the things he's done."

"I do not care what they call him. He is the one who saved me, the only one who didn't thirst for my blood," Krew says.

His eyes are not on me, and I turn just in time to see Thoa pass. Heat creeps through me as I wonder how long he was behind me. Did he hear my words? Would he care? Krew's eyes are on me again and he reads my expression with ease. He smirks, knowing the answer to my question but unwilling to tell me.

Without a word, Thoa takes up the skiff's ropes and starts walking, returning us to silence as we race through the night.

CHAPTER
FOUR

I t takes three days at Thoa's excruciating pace before we begin to see signs of the desert's end. Short, sparse grass interspersed with shrubs and succulents abruptly give way to denser grass and bushes. Storm clouds greet us as we pass into greener land and I can see sheets of gray coming down in the distance.

"Twenty minutes, if that," Rego says, nodding towards the approaching rain. "Looks to be a rough one."

"Nary a shelter in view," Thoa says, looking at the land around us.

I perk up as we climb over a rise and I realize where we are. Though the Raider camp had slowly traveled south since I brought Krew to them, our small band has returned to nearly the same place where I found him.

Far ahead are the mountain gods. Though I can't make out their giant faces carved into the land from this far out, especially with the rain clouds closing in, I can see them in my mind. The Raiders pass the sacred mountain every year as we travel north. We camp near the giant rock-gods to allow the worshippers among us time to honor them.

I do not worship the mountain gods, or any gods for that

matter. Though there are plenty to choose from, I've never felt a kinship with any one of them. Still, I respect the other Raiders and their dedication to whomever they pray to. Perhaps someday I will find a god of my own.

"There's a cottage a couple miles from here, a woman I trade with," I say, turning to the others. I came through these lands just two weeks ago when I trekked to the homesteader for supplies. "She'll give us a dry place to rest."

"Lead us, Little Star," Thoa growls.

We move with haste, leaving stealth behind as we try to reach the homesteader before the storm. I'm panting when we top the hill and see her cottage ahead, buried in a copse of trees. Rego leans heavy on his left leg to give his other a break. I point and say, "There she is."

A crack of thunder erupts overhead. The clouds, seeming to sense how close we are to refuge, open up above us. Fat drops of water pelt us, rolling down skin to soak us thoroughly. We run towards the cottage, sliding across slick grass and sending up splashes of muddy earth with each step.

I'm only a few feet away from Kavis' home when I hear something wild and reckless behind me, rumbling through my chest and digging into my bones. It fills me with something I have rarely felt, something I've longed for: joy.

I turn to see Thoa and Krew, laughing, throwing fistfuls of mud at one another in the fading evening light. They spin and duck, dodging the gobs flying at them as the warm water washes away their dirty efforts.

Thoa's dark curls and dripping wet, hanging limply about his face and shoulders. Streams of muddy water trickle down him now, coating his killing leathers from tip to toe. The glow of Krew's dark skin is dulled by the mud, but the smile on his face more than makes up for it. He is as bright as the sun will be after this storm. What a pair they make.

Rego and Nukiki move to stand beside me under the slight

cover of the trees. I glance at them as they watch the two men playing in the rain, surprised when they do not wear frowns or disappointed faces. Nukiki is open-mouthed in her own joy at seeing them, her eyes drinking in the sight. I can see that she wants to join them, that she longs to be free of whatever inhibitions hold her back. But her feet are rooted.

Rego smirks at them, shakes his head. From someone else it would be chastising, but Rego holds no malice in his eyes, no disdain on his lips. He looks as if he remembers something from long ago, something forgotten that this scene has brought forward. He looks as if his heart could take flight at any moment on the wings of that memory.

"What the piss on going on out here?" Kavis asks from the doorway. She's a slight thing, short and thin, but hard as mountains, fierce as flame. Her graying hair sits on her shoulders, but her fringe is knife-cut and jagged, framing her lined face in uneven strands.

"Hello, friend," I say. She speaks little Raider and none of the old tongue save for the handful of words she's learned from me. She has taught me some of her language as well, so we speak in a garbled version of all three, trying to make ourselves clear.

"Bon soir, Nova," she says.

Her language is lovely, soft and romantic in a way words have never been. I have spent hours in her cottage, listening to her stories, entranced by words I couldn't understand.

"I'm sorry to return so soon…" I begin.

"Absurdité," she says, waving us in. "Entrez."

Kavis walks to the corner of the room and pulls out thick woven cloth. She hands one to each of us and I press the cloth to my face, inhaling the sweet scent of smoke and citrus. Kavis raises a brow as Thoa and Krew step into the doorway, and both step back in response. Kavis points at a bucket by the door, then raises her finger towards the sky.

"Fill it and rinse off," I say.

"Dirty," Kavis says, wrinkling her nose.

Rego and Nukiki both laugh at this, but Thoa seems embarrassed. He dips his head low in reverence, wincing when he accidentally drips water onto her dirt-packed floor. He and Krew retreat into the rain, the door slipping closed behind them.

Kavis' cottage isn't big, a little larger than a mated tent, but it's spacious enough for us to all be comfortable as we stand inside her single room and dry off. There's a cooking fire going in the corner, the smoke snaking up through stones that lead outside. It's warm with the fire going, brushing away the chill from the rain.

I take in the familiar sights—flowers hung from the ceiling, bolts of cloth piled in the corner, a worn pink chair with sewing needles scattered about the feet. This is a refuge from the hunt, a welcoming place when I travel this path, and I'm always delighted to find my way to Kavis' hearth.

"Why are you here?" she asks in her tongue.

I explain the best I can with the words we share, switching in and out of languages with the words I don't know. Kavis nods at the parts she understands, asks me to mime out the parts she doesn't. She tells me the words I'm missing, a teacher to her bones.

She had a family once. This I know from visits past, from stories she's told. Three daughters, several grandchildren, but she's outlived them all. She didn't want to be near the things that reminded her of them, so she wandered into the woods and never looked back. She built this house and has accumulated the things that fill it from trading with the bands of Raiders who travel the lands.

Still, I see the way she looks at me sometimes, when she's trying to help me understand something. I imagine she looked at her daughters and grandchildren the same way when they were young. Though she's never said so, I think she likes teaching me her words because it means there's another person in the world that understands and can carry it on when she's gone, even if only in small pieces.

Thoa returns, rinsed cleaner than I've ever seen the big man. Krew follows him in and they dry themselves with the cloth Kavis gives them. She moves to her chair and picks up her needles. I know this signals a story and I move to sit on the floor in front of her. The others follow my lead, circling around her.

Kavis glances at Krew and says, "I met a star-man once."

I sit up straighter at this, and with a look to Krew I notice he does, too. "You understand her?"

He nods. "Oui."

Kavis lights up, a broad smile on her face. She speaks rapidly to him and I'm unable to catch her words, but he smiles in return. His eyes flick to me for a second before he says, "Elle est plutôt jolie."

She is...I don't follow the rest of his words, but I know he was talking about me. I look to Kavis and her sweet, dark eyes. Whatever he said, it was kind. Kavis wouldn't allow him to say otherwise.

She begins her tale in earnest, with Krew translating her words to the old tongue and me repeating in Raider. The story stretches long in this way, but it passes the time while we wait out the rain that spatters against the thatched roof, as the darkness spreads over the land around us.

"I was young," she says, "close to your age. I lived north by the edge of the world. My parents were merchants and we had all manner of folk who came through. One rainy night, much like tonight, a star-man came in. I'd never seen one before, for even then they were rare in this world. But I recognized him by his wrist."

Kavis points at Krew's bracelet with the glowing red light. He holds it up and all eyes turn to it as I translate the words to Raider. I ask, "What is that, anyway?"

Krew stares at his wrist so long, I don't think he's going to tell me. But then he whispers, "A way to keep track of our own."

Kavis says, "Yes, the star-man was trying to use it for just that. He was searching for a lost companion, another of the star-folk who'd come to visit, but who he couldn't find."

Krew asks her a question, but I don't understand the significance of the only two words I can make out: *wearing red?*

"Oui," she says. "He was handsome, this man, different from any I'd ever seen. Shiny black hair, eyes so different from mine." She traces the outside of her eye and I wonder what she's seeing in her mind. She continues, "I wanted to help him, gain favor with him, but I hadn't seen the companion he was seeking."

"Did he find him?" Thoa asks when Kavis stops speaking.

She shrugs, but there's a wistful look on her face as she continues. "I don't know. I didn't see him again. But the next night, there was a loud noise, a flash of purple light in the sky. It must've been my star-man."

Silence settles on us, easy and comfortable in the warm room, and a moment later a snore rises from the chair in front of us. Thoa asks if we should wake her, or if he should carry her to the bed, but I shake my head. I get a blanket from the trunk by the bed and put it on Kavis' lap.

"We should sleep here," I say. "Wait out the rain."

Thoa looks out the door into the night beyond. "I don't want to waste the time, but this storm holds. Perhaps it would be best to stay."

We stretch across the floor on the mishmash of rugs and furs that cover most of the area. Thoa and Krew whisper to one another long after the others have fallen asleep. I listen to their words, their laughter, but I am not part of the friendship developing between them.

When Thoa finally slumbers, Krew rolls over and faces me. I can see his surprise at my open eyes boring into his, thinking me already asleep. But he gives me an almost-smile. Being here has eased some of the tension between us.

"Thank you for helping with the story," I whisper.

He nods once. "I like Kavis. It was nice to share her words."

"How do you know her language? I've never heard anyone else speak it."

"I know several."

I bite my lip, unsure how many questions I can ask before I become a burden. "Your people speak many?"

"Yes. We keep as many alive as we can."

"Alive?"

"They're from before the world ended. Before the Cataclysm."

I watch his eyes droop, but I want to try one more question while his guard is down. "Who are your people, Krew? Why does everyone call you 'star-folk?'"

He doesn't speak and I hold my breath, waiting to see if he is pausing like before. But then his breath steadies, deepens, and I know whatever answers he has will not be given tonight.

TEETH SNAP AT ME.

I jerk up, covered in sweat, though I've managed not to scream this time. My eyes adjust to the light streaming in the small window as the snarling nightmares disappear. It takes a minute for me to realize where I am. But I see Krew beside me, his eyelids flickering with the movement of sleep, and I remember the stories and shared secrets from the night before.

Sneaking from the room, I find Kavis outside on a stool. She's mixing something in a large basin, though I can't tell what it is.

"He's a looker," she says, smiling up as I watch her work.

Heat creeps up my neck, but I can't help but smile. "Yes, he is."

"Now I understand why you wouldn't stay with me when I offered, why you had to return to the Raiders."

Her words make me queasy. Thrice she has offered for me to stay with her, to live as she does and make this place my home. Thrice I have refused, though it grows harder each time. If she asks again, I may not be able to say no. It is an enviable life.

"Krew isn't a Raider," I say.

Her brows furrow. "Krew? I was talking about the big one." She looks off dreamily and says, "Stars, those eyes."

"Thoa?" I ask, smiling at her expression. "I've never thought of him like that."

She raises her brows in surprise. "Good grief, child. What's wrong with you? He's lucky I'm not a few years younger."

I laugh at her words. She's easily triple his age, but knowing her fiery personality, I'm surprised age is even a consideration for her. I shrug and say, "I can help translate if you wish to woo him."

Kavis howls at my suggestion, but soon her face grows serious and she puts her gnarled fingers over mine. "Don't miss your chance, Nova. I would give anything to have someone look at me the way he looks at you. I don't know if I've ever seen a man more in love."

I shake my head to refute her, but my voice will not respond. Thoa asked me to be his mate, he kept me from killing Krew, he came on this journey. *Gods, maybe he does love me.*

But I don't have time to think about it more before I hear the others stirring in the cottage behind me. I push all thoughts of love from my mind. There will be time to sort it out, to figure out if I could love him, after we return from the City of Trials.

Kavis leaves her work and goes to the fire where breakfast is boiling. She shares with us a meal of lemongrass stew and dried fruit. We eat our fill at her behest, knowing we may not have warm food again for several days. The storm soaked through any wood we might find in the surrounding area, ending our chances of starting a fire.

Though we refuse every offer she makes, we still leave with more in our packs than we came with. When we try to temper her generosity, she ignores us and loads goods into our skiff on her own: more drying cloths, a needle and thread, a small bundle of dry kindling, and a blanket made with the waterproof grass her roof is thatched with in case we run into rain again.

She hugs each of us in turn, pulling Krew low so she can kiss each cheek and speak with him in that beautiful, melodic language. When she reaches me, she wraps her thin arms around my waist and holds tight while I rest my chin on her head.

"I'll stop to see you when we return."

She shakes her head against me. "You'll not return this way for a long time, child."

"Why do you say that?"

"I feel it," she says. She pulls back from me and taps her chest. "I know it."

The thought saddens me. "I will see you again, Kavis. I promise."

She nods, but there are tears gathering on her lashes. She rubs her hands along my arms one last time and whispers, "Au revoir, ma fille."

We walk through the meadow by Kavis' cottage. The grass is still damp, but the morning sun has dried it enough that it isn't slippery. Krew is at my side, a melancholy look on his face.

"What's wrong?" I ask.

He shakes his head. "I know this sounds weird, but I miss Kavis already."

"It doesn't sound weird," I say, a faint smile tugging at my lips. "She's a wonderful person."

"She loves you."

I nod. "And I, her."

"Do you know what she called you when we were leaving?"

I shake my head. She calls me the same thing each time I go, and though I can tell it is a sweet sentiment, I've never asked what it means.

"My daughter."

The word is like a vice around my heart. Each time I say goodbye to Kavis, I hurt, but somehow it is worse knowing that her affection for me is so deep. When you're out here, alone, the greatest gift someone can give is to become family. The Raiders gave me that gift when I was an orphaned child. My loyalty to them for doing such a thing is the only reason I didn't stay with Kavis when she offered.

As we walk, Krew hums a song that I've heard Kavis sing while she sewed. Something about it is inexorably sad and I find myself turning for one last look at Kavis. I stare down to her house, the copse of trees around it, but the woman is gone.

CHAPTER
FIVE

Hours pass in relative silence. Thoa and Krew's budding friendship seems to fizzle in the daylight, and though there's certainly no hostility between them, the silence seems to thicken to a point that it's impenetrable. Thoa's mood seems to sour as the time passes by, and even after stopping for a quick rest and bite to eat, he carries darkness on his brow.

Late in the afternoon we come to the road of the gods. Papa-du tells stories of this place. He says many flooded this path to visit the gods on the mountain. There were signs, he says, to lead people here and tell of the great deeds performed by the gods. I believe these stories; in fact, once while the Raiders were camped nearby, I saw a stone slab with the faintest hint of letters still carved into it. It didn't tell the full name of the Mountain of Ushmor, but I'm certain it did long ago.

They loom above us now, three faces smoothed by wind and rain and time. Some of the myths say there were once four gods who lived here. Sometimes when I look at them, I think I see where he may have been. Whoever he was is gone now, eaten away by time.

Thoa leads us down the cracked stone road. There are broken

pillars lining the remnants of the path, knee or sometimes waist high, covered in moss and ivy. I like to imagine they were once high columns, marking the path for worshippers to flock to the mountain. Whoever built this shrine to the mountain gods has been gone a long time, leaving only a trace of who they once were. Perhaps someday the gods themselves will leave.

As we near the sacred place, the road is cut off by the edge of a forest. We stop there, Rego and Nukiki refusing to go farther.

"We do not enter this forest, Little Star," Rego says. "We must find a way around."

Thoa sighs. "This is the fastest way."

"We cannot. None of us worship these gods. It would not be safe to pass through their lands without a worshipper to make an offering," Nukiki says.

"We have been this way many times. We are safe to enter."

Rego shakes his head. "It is not our path."

"You find another way, old man. I will go through." Thoa stalks away, headed for the trees.

I look to Rego, but he folds his arms across his chest and will not budge. Though I know his reason for refusing to go into these trees, I do not feel the same concern. But I recognize the face he wears now; he has made this decision and will not be changed. Instead, I jog after Thoa, catching him at the tree line.

"Thoa-gra," I say, catching him by the arm.

He pulls from me so violently that strands of his dark curls come loose from his braid, framing his face. "Careful," he growls. "You do not want to become just another bad story about me."

So, he did hear me talking to Krew. Three days in silence, letting my words turn through his head, and he remains angry. I am ashamed of my words, but I, too, am afraid of who the Bonecutter is. When I speak, my voice is frail. "Please."

He stops but doesn't look at me. He walks into the forest, slower now, allowing me to catch up. We walk side by side through trees grown full and thick, blotting out the sunlight with their leaves. I do not tell him now that we are here, these trees frighten me. I don't say anything for fear of breaking whatever is transpiring between us.

His voice is as soft as the rustling leaves when he says, "Do you know why they call me the Bonecutter?"

I open my mouth to answer before realizing I do not know. I shake my head, and though he doesn't look at me, he already seems to know my answer. "Like you, I was taken by the Raiders when I was a child. I have few memories of a life before."

I find myself hungry for his words, curious for the story I never thought to ask. He continues, saying, "I was adopted by a woman named Icara, to raise as her own. She was kind, and though she wasn't my true mother, after a time I loved her and thought of her as such."

He pauses, putting his hand against the bark of a nearby tree. I hold my breath, certain I do not want to hear what comes next. Thoa says, "Her husband killed her. He was angry that she turned her back to him at the solstice, though she did not take another."

Thoa turns to me, his eyes boring into mine, searching for something—I do not know what. Finally, he says, "I killed him for hurting her. When he was dead, I took the fingers from the hand that killed my mother and carved them into this." He moves his hair to show five white slivers pierced through his left ear. "I was ten."

He drops his hair and his gaze. I say, "Forgive me, Thoa-gra. I did not know." He doesn't look up, doesn't speak, and I step towards him, unable to stop myself. I place my palm against his cheek, drawing his attention back to me, and whisper, "I'm sorry that happened to you, sorry that it haunts you still."

He puts his hand over mine, closes his eyes, and leans into my touch. "Thirteen years, Little Star, since any Raider has laid a hand upon me."

I think back to every time I have seen Thoa. Alone. Avoided. I have lived among the Raiders for twelve years, and though I've been close to few, I have never been as utterly alone as he has. I close the gap between us and pull his head onto my shoulder. I am tall, but he is taller still, yet he hunches onto my shoulder and clings like a child to his mother. I hold him for a long moment, until his sobs subside.

We are different when I pull away. I am different. I have never held another, though Rego has comforted me with his arm on my shoulders. This was not the same. I'm not certain where to look and find myself staring off through the trees.

When Thoa begins to walk, it is back towards the others. I hasten to join him, but whatever transpired between us is over and his steps do not slow for me. Just before Thoa steps from the trees, he drops to a crouch. I mimic his motion, sidling through the underbrush to peek over his shoulder.

Krew, Rego, and Nukiki are on their knees while a dozen figures surround them. Rego's lips are moving, trying to talk them out of whatever is happening. One of the figures steps forward and smacks Rego across the face. Fire jolts through me and I begin to rise, but Thoa's hand grabs mine and pulls me back down.

"We can take them," I say.

"No," he says, but his hand twitches, aching to do something. "They have guns."

Guns. He uses the old tongue, for the Raiders have no word for such a vile thing. I see them now that I know to look. Metal tubes both short and long at hips and backs, colors of copper, silver, and gold.

I gasp and cover my mouth with my free hand. Rising behind them in the distance is a great beast like nothing I've ever seen. It flies though it has no wings. A bulbous red and black oval is at its top, with something akin to ropes dangling from it. As it approaches, my jaw drops at the massive skiff suspended below.

"An airship," Thoa breathes, more to himself than to me. His voice catches as he says, "I thought I'd never see another one."

"Who are they?" I ask.

"Sky Sailors."

The words mean nothing to me, but I don't say so. He's watching them with such intensity I don't want to interrupt. Instead I turn back to them and watch as they force Krew to his feet. One of the men is yelling, waving a short gun at Krew's head. Thoa squeezes my hand, but I ignore him, straining to hear their words.

The man throws Krew to the ground as Nukiki breaks free of her bonds and jumps to her feet. She spins, kicking the legs out from one of the captors. She grabs them and snaps their neck, almost faster than my eyes can see. She's running towards another, but my eyes find Rego. His lips are moving and I know he is begging—I don't hear him, but I can see it on his face. Even from this distance I know it is pointless.

A boom echoes through the air and Nukiki crumples to the ground before she reaches her next target.

A pause. Words are lost in this moment. But then his hand is on my shoulder, gentle, at war with the gruff voice that says, "Attack them."

His tone is certain. I face him, meeting his eyes. "You said not to," I sputter.

"That was before—"

"Before they killed Nukiki," I finish.

He nods. His eyes are darker than usual, like the sky before a storm. It brews inside him. He asks, "Do you trust me?"

I nod without hesitation. Yesterday my answer may have been different, but today I saw him, the core of why and who he is.

"Fight, but let them take you."

"What are you going to do?" I ask, fear coiling around my stomach.

He bites his lip, holding in whatever secret he's still keeping. He glances back to Rego and Krew as the sailors load them onto the airship. "They're leaving. You have to go." He places his hands on my cheeks, pulling my forehead against his. "I will come for you, Nova. Don't die."

I take a deep breath and let it out slowly, reveling in his closeness. It is strange to think that minutes ago he was still a stranger to me. I pull from his touch and stand. Without another word I bolt from our hiding spot towards the others.

I want to scream. My insides do. But outside I am quiet, the grass masking my steps as I dive for the first sailors. I hook my arm around his neck and use my momentum to spin around his body. My knife slices across his neck before he can scream. He falls to his knees trying to cover the wound with his hands while blood gurgles out onto his dirty clothes.

I have already moved to the next. I catch her from behind and slice through the tendons in the back of her knee. She screams as she stumbles to the ground. I admit that I'm impressed with how she scrambles for her gun, but her hand isn't quick enough. I stab her in the chest, deftly avoiding her sternum, and twist the blade as I rip it from her body. Blood arcs from my blade as my hand flies through the air. I take aim at the next sailor. Lightning cracks beside me—no, not lightning, a gunshot. My left shoulder is on fire. Pain flares along the skin. The bullet only grazed me, but the ache is sharp and throbbing as blood trickles out.

A bull-sized man tackles me to the ground. I struggle against him, unable to control the adrenaline pumping through me.

"Kill her!" someone shouts.

"No," a gruff voice says. "The Captain wants them alive."

At these words, I stop fighting him. After all, this is what I want. I curse myself as I lie there panting, trying to catch my breath. I could've killed at least two more if I hadn't been distracted by the gun.

The big man flips me over, shoving my face in the dirt as he takes my knife and ties my hands. He pats down my body, finding the blade strapped to my thigh and the one in the top of my boot.

He may have my knives, but I am far from defenseless. I am a Raider.

ON THE AIRSHIP, THEY FORCE ME ONTO MY KNEES NEXT TO REGO. His brows furrow, concerned. "Thoa?" he mouths. He heard the gunshot and thinks he is dead.

I give him a terse nod, hoping he understands: Thoa is fine. Thoa will come for us.

A whirring sound pulls my attention above. Flat metal blades spin in circles, pushing air into the oval. What I'd thought was the body of a beast now appears to be made of fabric, inflating as the metal spins. The deck beneath me shudders. We are flying!

A woman stands in front of me now. She has thick copper hair pulled over her shoulder into a braid, with gilded goggles perched on her head. She wears a plain white shirt, pristine compared to the crew around her, with pinstriped brown pants and heavy boots with an array of zippers and buckles. The only spot of color is the sea green suspenders that match her eyes.

My eyes, I think. They are the same color, same shape. I look at the spray of freckles across her nose and feel something itch inside my head. A memory, faint, taxing to think about. I push it away, like usual, but it persists like a bug bite on my brain. I know this woman.

But no. She was killed twelve years ago. This cannot be her.

"You killed two of my crew," she says, crossing her arms.

"They killed one of mine," I snarl back. "She was worth far more than those I killed."

The woman barks a laugh. She throws her hands in the air to draw the attention of the crew. "Do you hear that boys? This savage thing speaks our language." She steps closer to me, taking my chin in her hand. "Any other surprises, lass?"

She looks into my eyes and there's a spark of recognition there.

Like me, she knows it can't be true. I smile at her, relishing the moment of confusion. I say, "What's wrong, Aunt Rachel?"

Rachel drops my chin and steps back, her eyes going wide. She covers her mouth and speaks through her fingers asking, "Nova?"

I nod, but press my lips tight together. She falls to the deck in front of me and reaches towards my face, but I pull away. She held me, comforted me as a child, but she has not earned the right to do so as an adult. Hurt flashes across her face at my reaction, but I do not regret it. She is a stranger now.

"I thought you were dead," she warbles, her voice shaking with emotion.

"I would've been, had the Raiders not found me."

"Raiders," she spits their name like a curse.

I glare at her. "Do not speak ill of my family, Rachel."

Her jaw clenches and her eyes wander around the airship as she remembers where she is. She stands and straightens her back, slipping her hands into her back pockets. Her face clears in an instant, all signs of emotion gone, replaced with the detached grin she wore before. She calls out, "Back from the dead, my niece! Imagine my surprise to find the girl I raised has become one of the savages." She hangs her head, tsks. When she looks up, her eyes are only for me. She says, "We can turn her around though, can't we? We'll make a lady out of her yet."

"I'm good, thanks," I say, my lips curling into a sneer.

Rachel laughs. "So sassy. Just like your mother."

My breath catches at the mention of my mom. I only have one memory of her, so faint I'm not sure it's even real. She was tucking me under something, putting me in Rachel's arms, hiding us. Her eyes burned into me, then turning to Rachel she said, "Keep her safe." And then she was gone, and it was just me and Rachel.

I look into Rachel's eyes again. They're so much like my mother's. Rachel says, "Take the others below deck. I want her moved to my cabin."

A burly man wraps his arms around my waist and picks me up. I scream after her, "Rachel, please. Don't hurt them."

Our eyes meet, but I have no idea what she plans. There is darkness there, a storm cloud on a sunny day, and I am afraid. She is not the girl I know. Knew. This woman is a death dealer, and we belong to her now.

CHAPTER
SIX

The man carries me to a room and tosses me in. I hear the lock click into place as he leaves. The room is sparsely furnished: there's a bed in one corner with a threadbare blanket and a desk nailed to the middle of the floor. Papers are strewn about the desk, clothes piled on the floor.

There's a window behind the desk. I look at the ground speeding past. I don't know what Thoa's plan is, but I can't imagine how he can accomplish it when we're going so fast. My eyes track the blurred motion of the trees. We're over the forest Thoa tried to lead us through. What fools we were not to listen!

I press my forehead against the glass, relishing the coolness on my heated skin. Ropes dangle from the airship like tentacles reaching for the land. I watch them flap in the breeze. One is pulled tighter than the others. My eyes trace the line. I stand on tiptoes, pressing against the glass as hard as I can to see what trails beneath.

Thoa.

He hangs from the rope as the wind buffets him. Slowly, he climbs.

I hear the key turning in the lock and spin, putting my back to the window to shield my would-be rescuer. I cannot let him be seen.

Rachel enters. She does not wear the confident expression she wore for her crew, but she's also lost the confused joy she'd had when we first found each other again. I don't know what my face says to her—the squinted eyes, the clench of our shared angular jawline—we are the same, we are nothing alike.

I stare at her mouth, waiting to see if her teeth will snap at me like in my nightmares. But they don't. Her lips stay pressed together as she watches me.

She folds her arms and asks, "You're not even going to ask?"

"Ask what?"

She scoffs. "Don't be coy, Nova. It doesn't suit you."

I run my tongue over my teeth, letting the words build. I ask, "Fine, I'll bite. What happened to you? Where did you go?"

She presses her lips tight, fighting against the memory, but her eyes flash with pain. "When I went back for Lily, the Sailors grabbed me."

The name sparks in my mind, a candle's flame in a gale. "Who?"

"You don't remember," she whispers, unbelief clouding her face.

She walks to the desk, her eyes focused on me, and I move to the front of it, forcing her to follow me with her eyes. I can see Thoa behind her, his progress bringing him closer to her window. If she turned now she would see him.

Rachel closes the desk drawer and throws a dirty wad of cloth at me. I catch it, turning it over in my hands with a strange reverence. My doll. I'd left her behind when shadows chased us to the woods. So dark. We went in and crouched by a tree. I cried against Rachel as she tried to calm me. She promised she'd get her back for me. And she did.

She's watching me. Weighing me with her gaze.

"I can't believe you have this," I say, rubbing the grimy fabric between my fingers. Lily's face is rubbed off and her stuffing has gone flat, but she's still there, still mine. She's the only thing still connecting me to my life from before.

"Me either," she says, pursing her lips.

I meet her gaze, and a little of my hardness fades. "I'm sorry our reunion isn't what you'd hoped for."

She nods, swallowing hard. "My vision for us could never come true, because I never stopped thinking of you as a child. But you're not little anymore." Her voice breaks and she coughs to try to cover it. With a half-smile she asks, "How'd you get so damn tall?"

I am taller than her, but not by much. A few inches at best. I'd never considered where the height came from—thinking about the past is a sure way to have the nightmares—but surely someone in my family was tall. I venture, "Dad?"

Rachel's face is horror-struck and she's barely able to squeak out the words, "What of him?"

Her reaction has a dozen different questions parading through my head, but I shake them away, afraid to know too much. I ask, "Was he tall?"

She nods. "Do you remember anything about him?"

"No," I breathe. It feels like an admission of guilt.

She nods again. "I'm not surprised. You were so young when they came for him."

"When who came?" I ask, my pulse quickening at this small bit of information.

Rachel purses her lips, her eyes distant. "When I realized you were with the star-boy, I thought maybe you remembered, that you were trying to go there."

I don't know what she's talking about, but I don't want to give away too much information. She is my captor, after all. I hedge around the subject while trying to work things out. "I barely remember mom. Dad is more a shadow of a memory, a ghost."

"Better that way," she says. "Even ghosts have teeth."

Her words jolt me, remind me of the snap-snapping of my

dreams. I don't know why they always devolve as they do, lips snarling and teeth bared, but her statement makes me wonder if there's a reason for it.

She turns her back to me and faces the window. My breath stops, frozen in my lungs, and I'm unable to move, to speak. I expect her to react, to yell for her crew, but she's silent. She hasn't seen Thoa—not yet, anyway.

Rachel spins towards me and I jump. My breath rushes back in, tearing a cough from me. She pauses, her eyes narrowing. "Why are you so on edge?"

I try to keep a face of stone, but my top lip twitches. "Wouldn't you be, if things were reversed?"

"Fair point," she concedes. "But I would trust you to protect me, like I will protect you."

Her words sting, though it wasn't her intention. If the Raiders had her, I don't know if I *could* protect her. I couldn't protect Krew.

"And my friends?" I ask. "Will you protect them?"

She hooks her thumbs behind her waistband as she chews on her lip. "The Raider, maybe. But not the other. He's too valuable and my skydogs need to eat."

"What will you do with him?" I whisper, hating the way my voice betrays me.

"We aim for the Hole in the World. He'll fetch a pretty penny in the markets there."

I've never heard of such a place, but I nod anyway. Her plans don't matter. Thoa will save us long before we reach our destination.

She steps towards me and puts a hand on my shoulder. I wince, but fight the urge to squirm away from her touch. If her words are true, she didn't abandon me in those woods a dozen years ago. We were separated by a world gone mad.

"I'm happy you're here, Nova, even under these circumstances."

I give her a small smile. "And I'm thankful you're alive, Aunt Rachel."

She gives a puzzled look and I stiffen. My words are a high compliment among the Raiders, but she does not regard it as such. "What I mean to say—"

"It's fine," she says, cutting me off. "Our words are different, but the sentiment is the same."

I nod, grateful she understands. I don't trust her, and I plan to escape as soon as I get the chance, but that isn't her fault. She is a product of the Sky-Sailors, as I am of the Raiders. In our own, old way, we love each other; but the new way is who we are now, and love is not a factor.

She steps past me to the door. As she leaves she says, "Remain in my cabin. I'll be back when I can."

As soon as the lock clicks into place, I run for the window. I check the ropes, but Thoa is not there. Either he fell, or he's aboard the ship. All I can do is wait.

CHAPTER
SEVEN

My scream rips from my throat, tearing me from the world of snapping teeth and bringing me back to this living nightmare. Light cascades through the window behind the desk, shining on a raven-haired girl with golden skin and almond eyes. She nods her head at me and stands. She's close to my height, but lean where I am curved.

"Let's go," she says

I rise from the bed, my head still fuzzy with sleep. Her grip is firm when she takes my arm. I could probably get away, rip myself free of her, but there's nowhere to go aboard this ship. Without knowing where they've taken the others, it would do no good.

The girl leads me to the deck where Rachel stands. She doesn't look as we approach, but says, "Jessa, did she give you trouble?"

"No, Captain," Jessa says.

"I heard screaming."

Jessa nods. "She was dreaming."

Rachel looks at me then, but her words are still for Jessa. "Thank you. You're dismissed." When the girl is gone, Rachel says, "I have them too. The nightmares."

"It's nothing," I say.

She smirks, but doesn't contradict me. Instead she points across the land. My eyes search ahead until they find the spot on the horizon. It's a circle of white ringed in a crackling pink. There are trees along the bottom and storm clouds on the top, hissing against the pink ring but never entering it. I'm certain this thing is man-made as I watch it spit sparks of electric pink into the sky around it. Though I don't know what it is, I'm certain of what it's called: the Hole in the World.

Rachel says, "We'll be there by nightfall. I'll sell the star-boy, but you can decide what happens to you and the other Raider. Continue with us, or go separate ways."

She raises her hand and Jessa returns. "Take her back to my room and lock her in. She needs some time to think."

WHEN JESSA RETURNS FOR ME A FEW HOURS LATER, I KNOW SOMETHING is wrong. There hasn't been enough time to reach the Hole in the World. She steers me onto the deck where my heart sinks to my toes. Thoa's back is to me, his hands bound behind him as he kneels before Aunt Rachel. Her face is puckered, like she ate the yellow fruit Ukaru found last summer. *Lemon*, I think, remembering how we laughed at the faces we each made.

She glances at me as the girl shoves me to the ground beside Thoa.

"Nice rescue," I mutter.

Thoa's lips curl in an embarrassed smile. "Don't pretend you aren't impressed."

I laugh then, unable to help myself. There is no hope for us. With Thoa now captured, Nukiki dead, and the rest of us in chains, there is nothing else to do.

"Nova," Rachel says through gritted teeth, "this is no laughing matter."

"I agree," Thoa says, though his face is lit with a smile.

Rachel asks, "How do you know this man?"

I look to Thoa, catching his startling blue eyes. Still looking at him, I whisper, "I don't. He is a Raider, like me, but he is also *not* a Raider."

Rachel shifts, putting her hands on her hips. "What does that mean?"

I shake my head as I look up at her. "Apart. Separate. Like —like me."

"Captain," a voice calls. "Aeroport is in sight. They're requesting we dock."

"Requesting?" she asks.

"Demanding, Captain."

Rachel bites the corner of her mouth, then nods at the crewmember. "Do it."

"What's happening?" I ask.

Thoa smiles. "That's what she's trying to figure out."

"Dock in sixty seconds," someone calls.

Rachel spits out a curse and grabs the front of Thoa's shirt. Her face is an inch from his as she growls, "Tell me who you are."

"You'll find out soon. Free me and my party now and you will not be punished."

She pushes him away and he falls back onto the deck. Rachel runs a hand over her cheeks, tired eyes unfocused as she considers his words. After too long a moment, she shakes her head. She rakes her tongue over her teeth and says, "I may not know the rules to this game you're playing, but I'm a fast learner."

I watch her stomp away as the ship comes to a stop. The lean girl hefts me up as a thick-armed woman with a fine round belly hauls Thoa to his feet. I stare at her a moment, surprised she can lift him with such ease. Thoa is powerfully built, muscled from years of hunting, fighting, and working the anvil. The woman must be incredibly strong to handle him as she does.

She catches me staring at her, but I don't look away. She is lovely. Her dark hair is trimmed close to her head, accenting her angular face. She has eyes of honey and skin tanned from working in the sunlight, crisscrossed with silver scars both small and large. She is a woman unafraid, confident in her strength, and beautiful because of it.

I blush and turn away when she smiles at me. *Stop it*, I think. I can't afford to be distracted right now. By her, or anyone else.

I've traveled with the Raiders for years, moving our home with the change of the seasons. I've seen villages smaller than our traveling tent-town and cities so big I refuse to enter, for fear I won't find my way out. But never have I seen anything like the monstrosity we've docked against. Levels of windows and doors, snaking passageways and precarious bridges, are stacked to create a floating city larger than the largest I've ever seen.

And there's so much noise! Even near the bottom of the city, far below the markets and homes, there's a cacophony of sound. Metal clangs against metal, people shout and laugh and play, and underneath it all is the thrum of the city's propulsion—whatever that might be.

The women lead us onto a wood walkway lined with ship after ship. Some are like Aunt Rachel's, wooden vessels with balloons and ropes, but others are great hunks of metal that gleam in the light, propellers all around and smelling like the black rocks we burn when we travel the mountain path.

We turn away from the boats and cross a bridge made of metal and glass. I stare down past my feet at the ground below us, thankful I'm not afraid of heights. Thoa, on the other hand, is having a bit more trouble. He's leaning against the railing, his head tilted back so he doesn't see the drop. His guard stops holding him and starts pushing him across the walkway.

Rachel glides past us, eyeing me as she does. She's tidied her hair into a bun and changed into a tailored blue suit, though she still retains her scowl. I watch her climb into a glass tube at the end of the walkway, surprised when it rises through the air. She turns and leaves the strange contraption, but I can't see where she goes.

Part of me worries I will not see her for another dozen years, part of me thinks that might be best.

Relief floods Thoa's face when we reach the end of the bridge, but now mine is full of dread. I look up at the metal city, confident we will lose ourselves in this place.

The women lead us up switchback stairs. We are not important enough to use the glass tube and I am thankful for that. It is a strange thing I do not understand, nor do I wish to. After climbing more stairs than I could count, the women lead us through a copper archway. Each woman raps their knuckles against the metal as they pass through, and I wonder what it means.

We pass a dozen stalls full of wares for sale—leathers, rugs, candles, animals made of gears that jerk and move—and a dozen more full of sweetbreads and fruits and dried meats. Each smells better than the last, and the rumbling in my stomach gets worse.

On the other side of the market is a stone-paved circle with a pool of dark liquid in the center. Sunlight glints off the fluid, purple and blue and green swirling atop the black. *Oil.* The word from the old tongue comes to me automatically, though I don't know why I know it. The oil drips from a bronze statue in the middle of the pool; eight appendages attached to a mushroom-shaped head, with smaller circles lining the underside of the legs, create a strange image, a god from someone's imaginings.

A young man sits nearby, flicking burning matchsticks into the fountain. The oil catches the flame in small bits, but to my surprise, the liquid smothers the tiny blaze before it can grow larger. He smiles with each small fire, and I wonder what dark musings lie behind his charcoal eyes. Children run circles around the metal monster, chasing each other with raucous laughter. I watch them as we pass, envious of their freedom, their easy smiles. I do not remember a day in my life when I wasn't full of worry.

We walk through another archway, this one bronze. Each woman presses two fingers against her lips before touching this arch. Curiosity burns inside and I want to ask why they do this, but

I do not want to give them the satisfaction. So we continue forward in silence, moving into a dark chamber.

I can't see farther than Thoa, only a few feet away, inside this shadowed place. But I hear things: the scurry of rodents' feet, the scrape of metal as someone withdraws a sword from its scabbard, the click of fancy shoes on the stone, the distant trickle of liquid, like a waterfall in drought. The sounds form a strange picture in my head, incongruous with one another. This is a strange place indeed.

Flame sparks ahead of us in the room, accompanied by the woosh of a mighty wind. I watch as a row of golden orbs catch the fire, one after another. The sound of metal on metal fills my ears, a gear or pulley system in action, and the orbs begin to move throughout the room on some unseen contraption, lighting every part.

It is only me and Thoa now. I did not see the women leave us, but they are gone. We stand on a circle, a giant gear cut from the floor itself. On a platform raised around us is a semicircle of chairs. There are five people seated there, Aunt Rachel among them. Despite what I know about her, the fierceness bottled in her slender frame, she seems demure next to them.

The big man to the left of Rachel has thick braids pulled into a high ponytail that still manage to hang to his waist. His skin is as dark as the oil from the fountain, with a sheen that makes him glow. He leans hard on one arm of his chair, with one leg propped against the other. His casual nature is at odds with his formal dress —a forest-green velvet tux. He is the only one of the five smiling at us, and for that I do not trust him.

The mazulla person in the middle is lean and lanky. Their red-orange hair is short, just beginning to curl around their ears. They wear red; every scrap of cloth is a different hue, from their long crimson overcoat to their brick-red gauchos, their muddy garnet boots to their rose-colored glasses. Even their skin takes on a reddish hue, aside from the two white scars stretching temple to jaw. They stand, staring down on us with unfettered disdain.

"You contacted our city, demanding we acknowledge the Rite of Patrimony. So tell me, Raider, why are you here?" they ask. Their voice is clear, distinct, marking each syllable with importance.

The words surprise me. *He* contacted *them*?

Thoa straightens his back, though his hands remain bound. His voice booms through the cavernous space as he answers in the old tongue, "To seek my birthright."

"Your birthright?" the woman on the end asks. She is an old woman, short and squat with wrinkles crisscrossing her face. She has unruly white curls tempered by a leather cap, the strap dangling by her face as she leans forward in her seat. "What rights does a Raider have in our sky?"

"The same as you, Sage," Thoa says.

The old woman stands. "How do you know me?"

"I knew all of you, once," he says. He gestures with his head to the man beside Sage who has been silent thus far. Tattoos cover his bald head, neck, and the parts of his arms and hands that are exposed. "Bardlo Sutherland of *The Duchess*."

"*The Oracle*, now," the man says. He smiles, revealing teeth of gold, silver, and brass.

"A promotion, then. Congratulations," Thoa says. He looks to the old woman. "Sage Delaney. Owner of half a dozen ships, most famous being *Swift Vestige*."

"Wherever you got your intel, you should ask for a refund. Your information is outdated," Sage says.

Thoa continues, dipping his head to the person in red. "Lu L'Amour. Better known as the Sanguine Savior."

"Some things remain the same," they say.

"Captain Rachel MacGale is new to me, but as you've noticed, my information is dated. But you," Thoa says, smiling towards the man in the green tux, "Herol Hamrick, I would know that face anywhere. How've you been?"

Herol tips his head forward. "Good, dear boy. And you have fared well, I see."

"I have," Thoa says. "Sorry to disappoint."

Herol takes his leg off the arm of the chair and puts it firmly in front of himself, fixing Thoa with his dark gaze. "It was nothing personal, you know."

Thoa nods. "Piracy can be nasty work."

Bardlo laughs, the sound cutting through the room. "Holy smokes. You're Luca's kid, ain't ya?"

Thoa bows. When he straightens, he says, "Tabarus Horatio Ocassius Acconci, at your service."

Though I follow the conversation, I feel lost. Thoa told me he has few memories of his life before the Raiders, yet he speaks as though he belongs with these people. He recalls their names, their ships, their deeds with ease, as if he hadn't been living with the Raiders for more than a dozen years.

"Impossible," Sage hisses. "Acconci's boy was lost in the siege of Mont Beluch."

"I was thrown overboard after watching murderous dogs betray and kill my father," Thoa says.

Herol licks his lips. "Aye. It was mutiny. I threw the boy off the ship."

L'Amour spins towards him, red coat swishing with the movement. "You?"

Herol nodded. "It was bad enough he saw his father murdered. I couldn't let them kill the kid, too."

"Threw me into a lake," Thoa says. "Hurt like hell, and I almost drowned, but in the end he saved my life."

L'Amour turns back to Thoa and says, "But if you're Luca Acconci's boy, and you're calling on the Rite of Patrimony, that means—"

"It means this place belongs to me," Thoa interrupts. "I own this city, the treasures within, and the allegiance of the ships you captain. Oh, and you're sitting in my chair."

CHAPTER
EIGHT

I am in my own room, with my own bed, on one of the floors of Thoa's home. They say I am free to roam where I wish, but when I leave the room someone follows me. For my protection, they say, until things settle down.

Thoa's return has caused an uproar. The hierarchy of this metal city, Aeroport, as they call it, is fractured and the Council of Five (now Six, with his addition) is barely holding things together. Many familial properties were returned to Thoa, including the massive townhouse where I stay. Those forced to leave his homes are angry to have been displaced by a ghost.

I've been told that Rego and Krew are here as well, though it's been four days and I have yet to see either of them. Thoa is absent as well. He is a busy man, important, now that his identity is known. I thought he would talk to me, explain to me in private; instead he leaves when I enter a room, unable to meet my eyes. I think he feels guilt, or possibly shame, for keeping me here. I am a strange addition to his collection of fine things, reminding him of who he's been his entire adult life. Though he plays his new role well, he does not enjoy being Tabarus, the lost boy returned. I can see it on his face, even from a distance. He is Thoa, the Bonecutter, a Raider to his core.

I dress in the clothes I've been brought. They are not comfortable, not breathable like Raider clothes, and I feel hot every time I step outside the confines of Thoa's home. Inside though, it is cooled by some gadget that blows air through holes cut into the floor. I've asked the guards about it, but they don't seem to know *how* it works, only that it does.

I don't like it. The air is cool but not refreshing, unnatural. I want to be outside.

So I put on the slim-fitting white shirt and dark green trousers, tucking them into black boots that lace to my calves. I wander through the halls of Thoa's house and try to sneak to the first level, but two guards meet me as I'm going down the stairs.

"Going out, Mistrex?" the female guard asks.

I sigh. "Yes, I am."

"Mind if we tag along?" the mazulla guard asks.

"Do I have a choice?"

They both shake their heads and follow me out the door. I walk the cobblestone street in front of Thoa's home, down two flights of stairs, and towards the market in one of the lower districts. Here the road is narrower, with uneven chunks of rock and dirt beat into a path. I like the imperfection of it.

As we're passing through the arch that leads to the main part of the market, again I notice people touching their fingers to the metal. I ask my guards, "Why do they do that?"

"Superstition," she says with a shrug. "We're floating in a city made of metal. The least we can do is show respect to whoever keeps us in the air."

The market is loud. People push past one another, waving money to purchase the last of this or the best of that, arguing prices with vendors, shouting about which item is better. It is a cacophony of voices in various languages, though the old tongue seems to be the most prevalent. It's strange to think it was lost to me for so long while I was among the Raiders, when here it is common.

As I walk deeper into the throng of people, I notice a tall woman weaving through the crowd. She moves with graceful easy motions, doing her best to blend in, though I can't imagine anyone could overlook her. She is a ruby amidst pearls.

Each time she turns and I catch a glimpse of her face, my breath catches. She is the loveliest woman I've ever seen. Her hair is spun gold against flawless brown skin. Her eyes are green and gorgeous, brighter than fresh spring grass. With every stop she makes, every vendor she speaks with, she seems to leave a little of herself with them. They smile after her, enchanted as I am.

She turns from the market and walks into a tavern on the corner of the street. I desperately want to follow, but before I get a chance, one of the guards taps me on the shoulder.

"Mistrex, there's trouble ahead. Let's turn back."

I follow their eyes ahead to a group of men harassing a vendor. I watch for a moment as they turn over baskets in his stand, laughing as they damage his goods.

"We need to help him," I say.

"Not a good idea," the female guard says. "Those are some of Bardlo's men. It wouldn't do to interfere."

I grind my teeth in frustration. "A member of the council sends ruffians to hurt the citizens of this city?"

She says, "He has dealings that could be considered a bit unscrupulous. But again, it isn't our place to interfere."

I ignore her and push my way through the crowd gathered before the stand. Some of those watching seem concerned, others seem to be excited for the show. If that's what they're after, I'm happy to give them one.

"Hey, leave him alone."

Two of the men turn towards me, a third still content to knock things over. One of them says, "Mind your business or you're next."

I smirk. "I don't want to be next."

"That's what I figured," the man says.

"I want to be *now*."

I hop the counter to the man's stall with ease. A quick spin-kick and I've knocked one of the men on his ass. The second pulls a knife from his side. He thrusts at me, but I sidestep and slip behind him, then jab my fingers into his kidney.

He grunts in pain and turns to face me. "You little bitch."

I punch upward before he has a chance to strike, hitting him under his ribcage in his exposed liver. His body goes limp and he falls to the floor.

The first man I hit is up again, backing away from me. I step towards him and he hops over the stand. I grab for him, but he's fast enough to put some distance between us before I can hurt him like I did his friend.

"Look out!"

I spin at the words yelled from the crowd. The third man falls towards me but I dodge and let him hit the ground. I turn him over to see a pistol in his hand and a knife protruding from his jugular. He looks up at me from glassy eyes as his blood pours out his neck.

I look out over the crowd, or what's left of it. Most seem to be running for cover. I don't know who threw the knife. My guards grab me and haul me out of the stall. As they drag me back towards Thoa's house, I glance back and see that golden haired beauty. She winks, smiles, and disappears into the crowd.

———

LATE ON THE FIFTH DAY, I WAKE TO FIND A GOWN LAID ACROSS A CHAIR in the corner of the room. It is as blue as Thoa's eyes and just as lovely, the bodice shimmering with tiny sapphires. I trail my fingers along the dress. They itch with the need to hold it, to wear it. I've never *seen* so fine a thing, much less worn it.

Instead, I grab my dirty leathers and the rust-colored cloak that once belonged to Rego's husband. My leathers are snug against my skin, tighter than when we first arrived. The food has been kind to me.

I leave the bedroom and head towards the dining area. It is the only space where I sometimes see Thoa, and today I am determined to make him talk to me. As I come around the corner of the hallway, I stop. There are half a dozen people sitting at the table deep in conversation, and I know each of them.

Rego sees me first and stands, arms outstretched. I run to him, throwing myself in his arms. He is a comfort I didn't know I needed, and tears come unbidden to my eyes as I lean against him.

After a long moment, he pulls away to hold me at arm's length. His smile is broad as he struggles through the old tongue, saying, "I told you she wouldn't bite."

I look at him questioningly, but it is Rachel who answers. "And I told you we'll get her in that dress even if we have to do it at gunpoint."

I spin on her, ready to spit out a retort, but then I notice the way the others are dressed. Aunt Rachel and Sage Delaney have traded their pants for gowns like the one in my room. Sage's is a rich plum color and short, showing off sculpted calves, while Rachel's black floor-length piece has a thigh-high slit where I can just make out the strap for her pistol. The men are in fine suits: Rego in a brown that complements his tanned skin, Krew in emerald, Herol Hamrick in blue pinstripes with a top hat, and Thoa in charcoal gray with a tie and handkerchief to match my gown.

"Sit," Thoa says, all business.

I do, finding the empty chair between Sage and Krew. Thoa eyes me for a moment, the first time he's looked at me in days, and my heart hammers in my chest.

"We're leaving," he says, leaning his fists on the table. "Today."

I look between the others, but this is not news to them. These words are for me. I ask, "What's happened?"

Thoa shakes his head, but Rachel says, "They've given Tabarus most of his family's property and wealth, but the council is still in opposition to his return."

I look around, brows furrowed. "But three of you are here, so only two stand against. If you vote, the odds are yours."

Rachel sighs. "I cannot vote. Because of you."

"Me?" I ask. "What do I have to do with it?"

Thoa's neck and cheeks are flushed when I turn my attention to him. He struggles to hold my gaze. Finally he says, "They believe you are my wife. So your relative cannot vote in my favor, leaving the council tied."

I blink back at him, unsure what to say. The words trickle out, like pouring honey. "Why do they think that?"

"Because," he says, biting his lip, "that's what I told them."

Rego reaches across the table and takes my hand. "It was done to protect you."

Sage nods. "The Savior, L'Amour, has a son, an absolute bastard. They were sniffing up your tree the moment they saw you, hoping to marry you off to that little cretin."

"And Bardlo inquired about you as well. He has a collection of men and women he keeps on retainer. All well-paid, I assure you," Herol says.

I pull back, shocked by his words. I try to stammer a response, but Rego says, "Their ways are not our ways, but do not judge them."

"But I am not a possession, well-paid or not."

"I know," Thoa says. "I would never allow that. So I lied to them, hoping to avert their interests."

"Instead it bit us in the ass," Rachel grumbles. "And killing one of Bardlo's men didn't help anything."

"I didn't. I fought them, but someone else killed them," I say.

"You were the one the spectators identified," Rachel says. Her eyes tell me she doesn't believe I'm innocent.

"But we can turn the tides, if we move tonight," Herol says.

I'd forgotten the sound of his voice, the way it soaks into your brain like water in a sponge. He has a way about him, smooth and fluid, that makes him the perfect salesman for whatever plan they've cooked up. It also makes him the most dangerous person here.

"How?" I ask him, my voice barely a whisper.

"Tonight we join ports with Gearhaven. It's a smaller city, but they often have good trades and better wine. The mayor of Gearhaven has acted as a tiebreaker a time or two in the past. He is hosting a party in honor of Tabarus' return. We go, we woo him to our side, and Tabarus wins his life back."

I look to Thoa, searching his eyes. "Is that what you want?"

Krew says, "He doesn't have a choice. Now that they know he's alive, they'll kill him if he tries to leave."

"They'll kill him if he tries to stay," Sage says.

Rachel nods. "Winning the ruling buys us time. They can't openly revolt against him or they'll lose their positions in Aeroport."

"And if we can't convince the mayor to vote for us?" I ask.

"We run," Thoa says between clenched teeth. "We use the party as a distraction to escape."

I laugh, incredulous. "You fell from a boat once, Thoa. Are you eager to try again?"

"I'm eager to throw him again," Herol says as a smile turns up the corners of his full lips.

"I can get you out," Rachel says. "If things go south, we make for my ship."

The others nod in agreement. It seems I am the only one with reservations, so I hold my tongue. Rachel, Sage, and Herol move to the armchairs in the main living area, their heads bowed close as they finalize the plan. Thoa reaches his hand down to help me up. I take it, though I don't want to. The gesture feels strange, and I'm still uncertain how I feel about him saying I am his wife.

"Can we talk, Little Star?"

The words stop my breath. They are a reminder of who I am, of who he is, of our bond as Raiders. I nod and we leave the others behind, stepping onto the attached balcony that overlooks an oily river twisting through the city below. He stands behind me, close, and I can feel his warmth.

"I'm sorry," he whispers, his lips near my ear.

I don't turn, afraid to look at him in this moment. Instead I reply, "For ignoring me? For keeping me in the dark while you schemed?"

"I wanted to keep you safe. I don't trust these people."

"But I should trust you?" I ask, whirling to face him. "You hid who you are, you lied about your past and what you remembered, you lied to them about who I am."

His jaw clenches. "I shouldn't have said you are my wife. The choosing ceremony proved that is not something you want to be."

I open my mouth to respond, but no words come. I turned away from him then, and now I do the same.

He sighs and says, "You only have to play the part for one night. No matter which way the wind blows, tomorrow we'll be on our way to the City of Trials. I will deliver Krew there as promised. After that, you will never have to see me again."

My breath catches in my throat at his words. I am upset with him, I am angry that he locked me away without a clue as to what was happening, I am confused by the feelings in me about pretending to be his wife. But I do not wish to say goodbye to him. I hate the thought of not seeing him.

I turn to tell him so, but he is gone. I step through the open patio door, my eyes scanning the room. He is not here, either.

"They left," Krew says.

My eyes flick to him. He's leaned back in his chair watching me, a smirk playing at his lips. "Where?"

Krew shrugs. "They don't tell me much. A little more than you, I guess."

My teeth clench at his words, but he is right, and it isn't his fault. "When will they return?"

"Before the party, but that's all I know. Rachel said you'd better be dressed when they get back."

I turn down the hallway towards my bedroom, intending to leave him behind. My head is too full with Thoa's words and I do not wish to spar with Krew, verbally or otherwise. But he must be up for a bout, because he follows me.

When I reach my room, I turn to him, ready to let loose a flurry of words. He's leaning against the doorframe, and once again I am struck by his beauty. Even in this strange lighting that flickers and hums through the house on hidden wires, his dark skin is flawless. A small smile tugs at the corner of his lips, and though he isn't looking at me, I'm certain his smile is for my eyes only.

He stares past me to my dress. I follow his gaze. I say, "It's pretty."

"Yes, it is. It will look good on you."

The compliment takes me by surprise. I stammer, "Thank you."

Krew chuckles as he walks into the room. He plops onto my bed, leaning back onto his elbows. "So tell me, does Thoa know how you feel?"

I cough, caught off guard by the question. Sputtering I say, "I don't know what you're talking about."

"He told me about the ceremony," Krew continues. "Said he's wanted to choose you for a while. I can tell you care about him, so I can't figure out why you turned away from him."

You, I think. *I turned away because of you.*

But I can't say that. And it's only half true. The other half is more convoluted, unclear even to me. I turned because I was afraid, because I didn't know what to do, because I let my body react before my mind or heart. But I don't say these things either. Instead, I shrug.

I turn back to the dress in the corner. I pick it up, holding it against my body. When I look into the mirror, Krew is standing behind me. *So quiet*, I think. He moves like a Raider.

Our eyes meet in the mirror. I watch as his hand comes around to the front of the dress, running slender fingers over the neckline. He says, "I forgive you, you know. For capturing me." I nod, but he continues before I can speak. "I didn't know your customs until Rego explained things to me. I thought I was meant to be a slave."

I inhale sharply, bit by his words. "No, that is not our way."

"I know, now. You were making me part of your people. But why?"

"I wish to bring life to the Raiders," I say, the answer programmed into me.

"Rego said you've never brought someone back. That you'd killed the others you found."

I nod as I furrow my brows. "Not all. Some I sent away without death. But the ones who fought me, I killed."

"I fought you."

"Not well," I say, my lips curling in a smile.

Krew laughs. After a moment, his hand moves from the dress to my shoulder, pulling my hair away from my face and neck. He steps closer. "Why didn't you kill me, Nova?"

"Because," I whisper, unable to help myself, "I wanted to keep you. For myself."

The corner of his mouth lifts as he traces a dark finger against my neck. I shiver against his touch, my breath shallow and unsure. I watch his eyes, dark, drinking in the light of my skin. He stares at the spot where his fingers graze, biting his lip. I've seen this look before, though never about me. *Desire.*

I step away from his hand and face him. I hear myself ask, "What do you want?"

He smiles, tilting his head. "I thought you'd know by now. I came here for—" he pauses, searching my eyes as if they hold the right word, then says, "—adventure."

"And did you find it?"

We both turn to the voice in the doorway. Thoa stands there regarding us, hands on his hips. Krew turns his smile to Thoa and meanders towards him. As he passes him, he says, "You know, friend, I think I did. Or at least, the adventure found me."

With Krew gone, Thoa's gaze turns to me. I wonder how long he's been standing there, unseen. Did he see the way Krew touched me? Is he angry with me, like the night of the ceremony?

"Thoa," I begin, but he cuts me off.

His voice is soft, gentler than I've ever heard. "Get dressed, Little Star. The night is upon us, and with it, our freedom."

CHAPTER
NINE

W e take the glass tube to Rachel's ship, *The Disorderly Glory*. The motion of the thing Rachel calls an 'elevator' is gentler than I expected. I can see why the rich prefer it over the stairs; there's no way I could descend a dozen flights in this dress.

Thoa stands on the bow, letting the wind toss his dark hair. It shines in the last rays of the setting sun, hints of auburn now that it is cleaned and cut. The bones in his ear are gone, as are his long locks, trimmed to just above his collar. The ends curl around his ears, though he's slicked them back to try to tame them. I'm glad that part of him is still free from this place.

We circle Aeroport. Gearhaven is docked on the opposite side of the city from Rachel's port. The layout suits us though, as it gives us an excuse to take her ship, and a getaway option if we need it.

When the smaller city comes into view, I gasp. It is not the gray and brown of metal, like Aeroport, that I expect. Instead, it is a jewel floating through the sky. The city is an octagon, with tiers of sculpted terraces and a raised fortress on a hill surrounded by brightly colored buildings of every hue. The center of Gearhaven has tall walls of sky blue. Teal towers mark each corner, connected by cerulean walkways with cyan parapets. A lazuline kingdom sits behind the walls, small, but well-fortified.

Thoa steps beside me as we dock, offering his arm. He says, "From the moment we leave this ship, you must be my wife."

I nod as I take his arm. I take my cue from the others and plaster a wide grin on my face. Even Aunt Rachel wears her best smile, but it seems more predatory than the others. I wonder if mine is the same.

A woman greets us at the end of the dock. She is short and curvy, with curls tight against her head. She wears a knee-length scarlet dress with short sleeves allowing for easy movement, showing plenty of her warm umber skin and ample bosom.

Rachel reaches her first and pulls her against her, her lips greedily pressed against the woman's mouth. When they break apart, Rachel's cheeks are flushed, but her smile has turned genuine. The woman fans herself with her hand, making Rachel's blush deepen. Rachel takes the woman's hand and turns to face me.

"Nova, I'd like you to meet Permilla," she says.

"This is her?" Permilla asks, her eyes going wide. With her free hand she shakes mine, pulling me near. This close to her I can smell the sweet scent of flowers on her skin, lavender I think. Her hand is soft but her grip is firm, and I can't help but think this little woman packs a punch.

She releases me and her smile disappears, becoming all business. "I got the transport hidden in an alley ahead. Dino's watching it."

Rachel winces. "You brought him in on this?"

"Of course," Permilla says, pursing her lips. "He's a good kid. Just needs a little guidance."

"Or a babysitter," Rachel mutters.

Permilla leads us to an alley a few streets from the port. There's a chubby boy leaning against a stone wall, flipping an open knife in his hand. When he sees us, he misses his catch, nicking the side of his hand.

"Ow, that smarts," he says, picking up his knife.

"Dino," Rachel growls.

"Hiya Rachel," he says with a toothy grin.

"The transport?" she asks.

Dino chuckles. "Oh, right. This way."

He heads down the alley, scuffing his feet on the ground. I watch a look pass between Rachel and Permilla, but it passes quickly. Permilla seems to have a calming effect on Rachel, cooling her fiery temper enough to keep the rest of us from getting burned.

Dino stops in front of a copper globe atop a contraption with wheels and a stove on the back. There is a seat in front of the globe with a wooden helm like on Rachel's boat. Dino clambers onto the seat and takes hold of the steering wheel.

With a sigh, Rachel moves to the globe to try to fight open the door. When it doesn't open, a young woman with soot-covered skin hops down from the stove in the back to offer her a hand. As they pull together, I realize it is the same girl who hauled me around on Rachel's ship. The door squeaks open on rusted hinges and the girl grabs a tin can from inside the carriage to grease the mechanism.

"Dino, I told you to do this *before* you brought them back."

He shrugs, his smile never fading. "Sorry Jessa. I forgot."

Jessa shoots daggers with her eyes, but after glancing at Permilla she says nothing else. Jessa hauls herself back onto the rear of the carriage and shovels something into the stove as the rest of us climb inside. It's a tight fit with the six of us, and I'm glad Sage and Herol are meeting us there.

We sputter through the streets of Gearhaven, blue walls looming closer as black smoke billows behind. Permilla uses the ride to fix mine and Rachel's hair. She braids Rachel's long locks and pins the braid into a bun at the base of her neck, elegant but also out of the way. She takes more care with mine, brushing it with a comb she had tucked away in the folds of her dress.

"Her hair would be a bird's nest if I didn't force her to comb it," Permilla says, tipping her head towards Rachel.

Rachel smirks but doesn't comment. Her eyes are focused on Permilla's hands. She watches them with squinted eyes, as if she's jealous when Permilla touches anyone or anything other than her.

Permilla finishes my hair as the carriage comes to a stop. I strain to see out the window, but I can't see past Rego and Krew. An attendant opens the door for us, much easier than when we got in the first time, and my friends practically fall out of the transport. Thoa places a hand on my arm to keep me in place. Once the others have exited, he climbs out and reaches in for my hand.

It's all part of the act, I think, though I relish the feel of his warm hand on mine.

He leans over and whispers, "You look beautiful, Little Star."

His words startle me. Raiders do not say such things to one another. They speak of strength, prowess in battle, contributions to the community. But never has another Raider commented on my appearance. It feels so intimate.

And yet, when I first saw Krew, it was his beauty I saw. I turn to look at him as he walks beside Rego. He is still a boy, and will remain so forever. The Raiders refused him and will never turn him into a man. Perhaps it is better that way. He will never have to see life drain from the eyes of a person he killed.

Thoa leads us towards the house. The mayor of Gearhaven lives in the biggest home I've ever seen. It's bigger than Thoa's townhouse, bigger than all the Raider's tents combined.

There are people lining the walkway. They're not in fancy clothes like us, but in work clothes and simple dresses, with dirty faces and hands, trying to get a glimpse of the returned Sky-Prince. I imagine being one of them, watching us pass. I'd probably be more comfortable than in these strange shoes and this poofy dress.

There's a tug at my leg and I look down to see a blonde girl around six years old. She looks up at me with round eyes as green as the grasslands in spring. Her clothes are tattered, barely more than rags, but she smiles with ease.

I stoop to talk to her. Thoa must notice I've stopped, because he kneels with me, smiling at the little girl. He asks, "What's your name?"

"Tess," she says with a slight lisp.

"That's a beautiful name."

"Thank you, milord."

"Where are your parents, Tess?" I ask.

"Momma is sick and Papa is at work," she says.

"Are you hungry?" Thoa asks. She nods fervently and he asks, "Would you like to go inside and have a bite?"

Thoa holds out his hand and Tess takes it. I take hold of his free arm as we take the girl inside. I can feel myself beaming at Thoa. Without thought for what was going on around us, he made an effort to help the girl. I wish I had known this man when we were Raiders. We were in the same camp season after season, but I only saw the death dealer, Thoa-gra, the Bonecutter. He is so much more.

The rest of our group scatters to different parts of the house to carry out our plan. We linger, greeting several important-looking people by the front of the house. I catch sight of us in the mirror, side by side, arms linked. I like how we look together. I'd never considered it before, how I would look beside a person I love—or pretend to love, in this case. But Thoa is handsome, his ruggedness reformed since we came here, and Permilla has done wonders with me. My long copper hair is intricately braided, despite the short time she worked on it, and pinned on my head with sapphires and diamonds, giving the impression of a crown.

I can't stop my wide-eyed staring once we're inside the house. The chandelier inside the main entrance is bigger than I am. Strings of crystal loop and twist around the oiled bronze fixture, sending light dancing through the room beyond. I'm not the only one staring, though most of the eyes are on us instead of the splendor around. They whisper, but it takes a moment to realize it is because of Tess. She is dirt in human form, amidst a sparkling sea of cleanliness.

Inside the reception room, servants carry trays laden with food and drink to a wide array of guests milling about. A woman catches my eye and winks. Something about her seems familiar.

She is taller than me, with long purple hair shaved on one side. Her eyes are green like mine, but brighter, ringed by black and silver makeup that matches her outfit. The dress is skintight, almost as if it were painted on, accentuating an hourglass figure. The bottom falls to a few inches above her knees, where long legs are covered by thigh-high black boots. I watch her grab a leather jacket and toss it over her bare shoulders, hiding her glowing brown skin, as she moves through a doorway into a different part of the house.

I watch her walk away, certain I know her but unsure how. While I search my mind for her, a man walks by, his eyes roving up and down Thoa's muscled form. He must like what he sees, because his lips curl up at the corners and his eyebrows raise. Jealousy rises up like bile in my throat. I watch the man's golden eyes as he continues to stare; he is handsome, with thick black hair neatly trimmed and dark stubble over a chiseled jaw. The urge to move away from him surges through me. I should lead Thoa to the kitchen to find food for Tess, but the man is in our path. To my chagrin, Thoa heads straight towards him.

"It really is you," the man says when we reach him. "I'd recognize those eyes anywhere."

Thoa releases my arm, clasping his instead. "I thought I'd never see you again."

The men embrace, both laughing. When they pull away, Thoa turns to me and says, "Nova, I'd like you to meet an old friend of mine."

The man takes my hand as he bows, brushing his lips against it. "Nigel Weatherfield, Mayor of Gearhaven, at your service."

"Mayor?" Thoa asks, raising his brows. His mouth quirks up at the corners and I can see he is pleased with this news. Perhaps it makes our jobs easier tonight.

I smile at the Mayor and say, "Pleasure to meet you."

He smirks, as if reading the jealousy inside me through my eyes. He says, "The pleasure is mine. Any friend of Tab's…" he trails off. Tilting his head he asks, "And exactly how are you acquainted?"

Tab.

I force my smile as wide as possible. "I'm his wife."

His smirk deepens as he grabs my other hand and lifts it to eye level. "Oh, darling, really? Where is your ring?"

Thoa takes my hand from Nigel's, winding his warm fingers with mine. "Lost, I'm afraid. Our journey was not an easy one."

"I've heard bits and pieces," Nigel says. "I hoped all parts were not true."

"Probably more than I wish to recount," Thoa says, donning a sad smile. He continues, "But enough of that. I am here on an important errand."

"Please, Tab, tell me how I can help. Your every desire will be fulfilled with only a word."

Thoa reaches down and picks up Tess. "This young lady needs some food, some now for her and some packed for her entire family. And some clothes, if you have them available."

Nigel runs his hand over Tess's wispy blonde hair. "Consider it done, my sweet."

He snaps his fingers and a young woman in black and white comes running. Nigel instructs the woman who reaches to take Tess from Thoa. As soon as she tries to pull her away, the little girl starts crying.

"Don't worry, I'll see you again. This nice lady is going to get you food," Thoa says.

"No, please," Tess says. "I want to stay with you."

Thoa smiles and pulls her close. "But if you stay with me, your mom and dad will be sad."

The girl sobs. "I don't have a mom or a da'. I just, I was afraid you would hurt me. But you won't, will you? You're a nice man. Please don't send me back."

Thoa looks to me, but I don't know what to say. Nigel speaks up instead, saying, "Tell you what: let's have my friend take you for dinner and a big piece of cake. Then we can get you a bath and some new clothes. After that, we'll bring you back to Tab."

"Promise?" she asks, looking between the two men.

"Cross my heart," Nigel says as he traces his index finger over his chest.

Tess lets the woman take her, but she watches Thoa over the girl's shoulder as they leave the room. Something about the child niggles at my brain, like an itch I can't reach. Something is wrong.

"Well," Nigel says, clapping his hands together, "shall we adjourn to the upper drawing room?"

Thoa takes a step towards him, but I plant my feet and say, "I'll find my own amusements and leave you gentlemen to your business."

He draws close, whispering, "This isn't part of the plan."

I laugh, hoping to cover up his discomfort in front of the Mayor. "That's sweet, but I'll be fine. Go on without me, *Tab*."

Thoa purses his lips but gives a curt nod. He doesn't know what I'm doing, and maybe I don't either, but he trusts me. And I trust that Nigel's interest in Thoa can be better exploited without me clinging to his side.

"Be careful," he breathes against my hair.

I nod and say, "Have fun, boys."

Nigel licks his lips and says, "Oh, we will, darling."

He takes Thoa's hand in his and leads him up the stairs and out of sight. I turn to take in the room, the multitude of guests in their strange finery, and an undercurrent of *bad*. I can't place it, and perhaps I'm imagining it altogether, but one way or another I am going to find out what this place is, and who we're dealing with.

I take a deep breath, thinking over the plan we made before coming here. The others are busy with their parts, so like it or not, I'm on my own. *A hunt*, I think, my mind returning to the Raiders and all they taught me. I've spent days on my own, scouring the land for anything or anyone who could help my people. This is no different. Except I'm not supposed to kill anyone this time. We'll see.

CHAPTER
TEN

I wend my way through the crowd. Despite the vast amount of people, I get through easily. The Raiders taught me to be silent, to move with purpose, and I use that same training now. I want to be unremarkable, unnoticeable in the crowd, so I am.

I step into an adjacent room where smaller groups are gathered. It isn't as easy to get lost here, where everyone is sectioned off in twos and threes. Several people turn as I step into the room, their eyes stuck on me as I move towards the back door.

The purple-haired woman steps in front of me, blocking my exit. She extends her hand and says, "Don't believe we've met, doll. I'm Coco Wyverstone."

"Nova," I say, shaking hers.

She flips my hand over in hers, tracing the lines on my palm. "No last name, Nova?" Before I can stammer out an answer, she says, "Your love line is quite peculiar."

"Excuse me?"

"This one," she says, her keen eyes meeting mine as she continues to trace her finger along my hand. "It's short and straight, so you're not really interested in romance. Or at least, you're more passive. You need someone to take charge. And I must say, that's my specialty."

I pull my hand away as heat creeps up my neck. Something about this woman's presence jars me. She's as out of place as I am. In a rush of recognition I say, "You were blonde when I saw you last."

She smiles. "Wasn't sure you'd recognize me. We didn't get a proper introduction in the market. Do you make a habit of fighting armed men?"

"Do you make a habit of killing them?"

She presses a hand to her chest in mock surprise. "Me? Never."

"That's too bad. I still owe someone a thank you."

She smiles devilishly. "Well in that case…"

I consider backing away from her, but instead I call her bluff. I take a step closer so our bodies are almost touching. Leaning towards her I whisper, "You're a good flirt, but that's not why you're here. What are you after, Coco?"

Her eyes flash—surprise, maybe—but she recovers quickly, a sinful smile curling her red lips. She moves closer, eliminating the space between us, her curvy form against mine. "Let me show you."

She takes my hand and guides me from the room. Coco places her empty glass on a passing waiter's tray as she leads me to a dark-stained door at the end of a hall. There are no guests here, only shadows keeping us company, and I wonder if I misjudged her purpose. She grabs me and presses me against the wall, her hand trailing down my side. She laughs into my hair just as a man steps into the hallway. His eyes go wide and he mumbles an apology before turning back the way he came.

Coco pulls away as soon as he's gone, turning to the dark door. She whispers, "Keep watch," then pulls a pin from her hair and inserts it into the handle. With a few twists of the pin, the lock clicks and Coco opens the door. She slips inside, leaving me in the hall alone.

A second later her head peeks around the door and asks, "Coming?"

I follow her into the dark room. *Foolish,* I think to myself. I don't know this woman, why she's here, or what she wants. But still I follow.

Coco lights a lamp. The small flame sends long shadows across the room. We're in a study, with a desk near the curtained window and walls lined with books. She makes for the desk and I follow, unable to fight my curiosity.

She rifles though papers scattered across the desk, stuffed into books, and stacked on the floor while whispering, "It must be here."

I put a hand over hers, stilling her frantic search and meeting her gaze. "What are you looking for?"

"Records. Lists."

"Of what?"

She looks at me like I've sprouted a second head as she pulls from my grasp. "The children, of course."

Her words are like a punch in the gut, but I keep going. "What about them?"

"You really don't know?" she asks, tilting her head. "They said my contact used to be a Raider. And you brought the little girl. I thought she was bait."

Tess.

My stomach is being twisted by cold fingers clawing at my insides. "We met her outside and wanted to help her."

Coco stares at me, mouth ajar. After a moment she says, "Terrible way to help her."

"Please," I say, "what are you not saying?"

"They. Steal. Children."

I gasp. "But why?"

She shrugs. "Slaves, I think. I've been trying to track the kids from one town to the next, but Gearhaven is always the last stop. Or at least, the last I've been able to track."

Coco is looking through the papers again and I join her, looking for anything that might help. She says, "Names, traveling plans, receipt for goods exchanged. Hell, I don't know what I'm looking for."

I pick up a paper with a list of names scrawled in tight, looped print. Beside each name is there are two towns listed with an arrow pointing between them. "I think I found something."

Coco is at my shoulder before the words are out. She scans the paper in my hand, then takes it from me to read more thoroughly. She says, "He's not on here."

"Who?"

She looks up at me as if she forgot I was there. "Oh. Uh, no one."

"Who did they take from you?"

She presses her lips together in a thin line and I can see she's doing her best to fight her emotions. "My brother."

"I'm sorry," I say.

Coco swallows and turns away. "It's my fault. I should've been there to protect him, instead of caught up in whatever foolish relationship I was in at the time."

"You can't blame yourself," I say. "What they're doing is wrong and it's all on them."

She takes a deep breath and when she turns back towards me, her face is steel. "I'm going to find him."

I nod. "I believe you."

We finish searching the desk in silence. There are dozens of papers that look like they could be important. We need to take the records and study them closer, but we can't risk someone noticing their absence. Instead, we memorize as much as we can and hope it is enough.

Coco finishes reading the last paper and we turn to leave. I say, "Wait."

"What is it?" she asks.

I hear a noise, faint, scratching at the edge of my senses. I move around the room, prowling as I do on the plains, willing the sound to return. It does. It's coming from behind one of the bookcases.

"Here," I say, waving Coco to me.

She presses her ear to the books. After a moment, she shakes her head. "I don't hear anything."

With a sigh I say, "I know it was here."

"A hidden passage, maybe?" she asks as she pulls books from the shelf. Despite not hearing it herself, she's committed to helping me check.

I follow her lead, moving along the shelf as I search for anything unusual. Halfway to the corner my finger finds a groove in the wood, barely perceptible. "Bring the lamp."

She shines it on the spot, but my eyes can't see whatever my hand felt. I run my fingers over the shelf again, retracing my steps, and there it is; the indentation is barely the width of my index finger and goes straight back between two books. I slide my hand to the back of the bookcase and feel around until my fingers cross a cool circle, a button of some sort.

"Found it," I say, pushing the button.

The bookshelf swings on well-oiled hinges. Coco holds the light aloft. Stone steps lead down into darkness. Briefly I wonder if I'll be missed. My role was to be the wife—not a great use of my skill set, but necessary for our endeavors. Or at least we thought so, until learning that the Mayor happened to be carrying a torch for Thoa. Now that I've already deviated from the plan, it probably doesn't matter what I do next.

I glance to Coco for the briefest of seconds. She presses a smile, attempting reassurance, but I can see the nerve twitching in her cheek. I take her hand and squeeze it, hoping to infuse her with strength for whatever lies beyond, and we step concurrently down the stairs.

I trail my fingers against the cold walls. They are wet, moisture dripping down the rocks. We've only gone a few feet when we reach a hulking metal door. It is round, with a wheel in the center. I grab the wheel and try to turn, to no avail. Coco puts the lamp on the ground and toils with me, but it won't budge.

"There must be a way in," she says. She taps her fingers against her teeth as she looks around. "Ah. There."

Coco points to a series of levers on the wall. I ask, "Which one?"

She shrugs. "Maybe all of them."

"Or maybe you should mind your own business."

We spin towards the voice. A woman is there, a lamp in one hand and a gun in the other. She is a short woman with yellow-blonde hair delicately stacked on top of her head. I instantly recognize her plain white blouse and black skirt.

"Your Nigel's servant," I say.

She purses her lips. "*Servant* isn't the word I would use. More like *partner*."

"You run when he calls and you do what he says," I reply with a shrug. "Seems like a servant to me."

"You have a smart mouth, considering."

"Considering what?" I ask.

"Considering I'm the one with the gun."

Coco looks at me and says, "She has a good point."

I smile as wide as I can and say, "Right, but I know something she doesn't."

The woman sneers. "And what's that?"

"There's a Raider behind you."

REGO WIPES THE BLOOD FROM HIS BLADE ON A YELLOWED handkerchief. The knife slid in at the base of the girl's skull, cutting off her motor functions before he snapped her neck. It was a lovely kill. Surprising. Rego stopped hunting years ago, and I guess I thought it was because he couldn't do it, but now I can see his skill has not diminished.

Maybe he just didn't want to do it anymore. Not after his husband disappeared.

"Why?" he says, pointing his knife to the girl in the floor.

I know what he's asking me, but I'm unsure how to answer. I tip my head towards the door behind me. "Whatever is behind here."

Coco is standing in front of the levers. I step beside her and move them, playing with the combinations, until finally we hear a *click* as a lock releases. I turn the handle with ease and pull open the hatch. Coco enters, holding her lantern aloft, and throughout the room light glints as it catches in several pairs of eyes.

Fourteen children cower behind two large beds, their faces dirty and tear-streaked. A small blonde head peeks around the bed, her green eyes wide.

"Tess?" I ask, pushing past Coco to reach for the girl. She runs towards me and I scoop her up. She nuzzles her face against my neck and sobs against me, though she doesn't make a sound.

Coco puts her hand on my shoulder as she steps forward to address the others. "We're going to get you out of here. Gather your things."

A boy steps forward, wringing his hands. "We don' have nuffin, miss."

The others nod. A girl of around eleven, the oldest in the group, says, "Pipe down, Lemon. Put your shoes on—all of you—and line up for these nice ladies."

The kids shuffle around putting on shoes and grabbing extra clothes. They're in a line within a minute or two, and I'm thankful they listen to the young woman among them. I ask, "What's your name?"

She does a small curtsy and says, "Edith-Ann Roody, milady."

"Roody?" Rego asks, his eyes going wide.

"Yessir," she says as Rego approaches.

Though his eyes are fixed on her, his thoughts seem far away. I ask, "What is it, Rego?"

He shakes his head the tiniest bit and says, "Nothing, Little Star. Let's get going."

Coco takes the lead, but I'm close behind with Tess in tow. We climb the stairs and cross the study to the dark hallway. Instead of turning back towards the party, Coco takes a narrow servants' passage that leads to an exit on the back of the manor.

I stop at the door, hesitant. I lean back from Tess so I can look her in the eye. "You're going to go with Lady Coco and the other children, okay?"

Her tears start up again, but she nods her head. Coco hisses, "Where the hell are you going? We have to get these kids out of here."

I press my lips together. "I need to find my friends."

She grinds her teeth. "They can handle themselves. These kids can't."

"We can help," Permilla says as she rounds the corner. Rachel trails behind her, though she has her back to us as she scans for anyone following.

"Take the kids to the ship," I say.

Rachel swivels around, her eyes going wide. "This isn't part of the plan."

"The plan has to change," I say, gesturing towards the children. I whisper, "He had them locked in a secret room."

She scrubs a hand over her face. "Have we checked for other rooms?"

Coco and I lock eyes as I answer, "We were so caught up in saving them, we didn't think—"

"The kitchen," Rego cuts in. "If anyone else knows about the children, it will be those who prepare their food."

"Good thinking," Rachel says.

She steps as if she will go with him, but Rego puts two fingers against her arm. "Go with those we've found. I am an old man and will not draw much attention."

"You might need help," Rachel says, her lips pulled down at the corners.

"From what I've seen, he can take care of himself," Coco smirks. "Besides, he'll have Nova."

"Go," he says. "We're losing time."

To my surprise, Rachel heads outside without another word. Rego turns back towards the party and I follow. He moves like a shadow through the room of partygoers, imperceptible. I've never seen him like this and I am impressed. Just before he turns down the hall towards where the kitchens must be, he stops in his tracks.

I step beside him and whisper, "What's wrong?"

My eyes follow his gaze across the room to a handsome man early in his fifth decade. His olive skin is set against a tailored black suit as he talks with a group of people, laugh lines creasing the corners of his gray eyes, but his smile dies as soon as he sees Rego.

He steps through the crowd, pushing people out of his way as he approaches. He stops in front of Rego. His eyes drink in Rego's face with a thirst that doesn't end. I watch him, my mind trailing back through the years as I do. His hair was black when I last saw him kissing Rego goodbye, but now it is streaked with silver.

After too long he says, "What are you doing here?"

Rego's jaw clenches. "Minding my own business, Mr. Roody."

He turns to leave, but Jasper grabs his shoulder. Rego throws his hand away, but doesn't turn back to him. Jasper says, "Please. There is so much to say."

"I will not hear you," Rego says. Then he marches off towards the kitchens.

Rego's husband looks at me and I tap my fingers against my chest and say, "Nova."

He forces a smile, but there is too much heaviness on his face and it doesn't last. "I remember. You were still a child when I left."

"He waits for you," I say. I don't know if Rego would want me to tell him, but I can't stop the words tripping from my lips. "Every day. He sits on the dunes, or the rocks, or the grass--wherever we go, Rego waits."

"He didn't take another?" Jasper asks. I shake my head and he asks, "Why are you here?"

I watch his eyes dart around the room and remember Coco's words. She was here to meet a Raider who was going to help her find her brother. I ask, "Looking for someone?"

His eyes return to me. He tries to stammer a response but I hold up a hand. "She found them already and is on her way to safety."

Jasper's eyes go wide. "I don't know what you're talking about."

"Come with us. Rego will warm up when he knows why you're here."

"I—I can't," he says, shaking his head.

I nod. "I cannot decide for you. If you wish to see Rego, to explain these years to him, meet us at the dock in ten minutes."

I turn from him and head towards the kitchen, but Rego is already returning to the main room. He whispers, "There's another room on the other side of the house."

"Let's go," I say.

He shakes his head. "I will go. You find the others."

"You may need help," I whisper.

"Let me help," Jasper says, stepping beside me.

Rego's eyes narrow, but I touch his arm and say, "Let him."

Rego gives a slight nod and heads through the house, Jasper in his wake. I turn to the stairs to find the others. Before I can take a step, I hear a gun cock and find a barrel pointed at my eye.

CHAPTER
ELEVEN

"What are you doing here, Lady Acconci?"

Bardlo Sutherland has a revolver aimed at my forehead. He smiles at me, a lopsided grin made straight when he tilts his head. He is handsome in a way I can't explain. Frightening. Dark. Every bad thing in me tries to answer the questions in his eyes, his very presence pulling at the monster in me. I suppress a shudder.

I could take the gun from him. I'm certain of it. I'm fast, faster than he would ever expect. But I can't guarantee it won't go off when it moves from his hand to mine.

"You know why she's here. The party is to honor her husband's return." A smile colors the husky voice, feminine and masculine rolled into one. The Savior, Lu L'Amour, steps behind Bardlo. They tug on their gloved right fingers and slowly remove the length of black lace. As they move to the next glove they say, "Put the gun down, Bardlo. You're making a scene."

Bardlo squints at me as if I gave him the order. With a dramatic flourish he holsters the gun on his hip. Lu says, "Where is Tabarus? With the Mayor already?"

I nod.

Lu smirks and says, "At least you're smart enough to stay out of the way. I'd wager he could woo Nigel if given enough time."

"Who's to say he didn't already?" Nigel asks. He and Thoa are walking down the stairs towards us. My eyes are immediately drawn to Nigel's arm tucked into Thoa's, clinging to him like a dying man holding his last breath.

"Mayor Weatherfield," Lu says, bowing slightly, "so lovely to see you. I was hoping we might have a word."

"We might have many words, but I doubt you'll be as convincing as Lord Acconci."

Lu presses their lips together into a tight grin. Bardlo isn't as polite. He raises his pistol and says, "Listen here, you're gonna listen to us and do what we say or things are gonna go very, very bad for you."

I watch six men step from the edges of the wall, so quiet they could kill a chigerbeast if they desired. Part of me wants to congratulate them on their stealth, to offer them a place among the Raiders, but the thought passes as I'm consumed with the moment.

The men are aiming long chrome guns at Bardlo. Nigel smirks at him and says, "Nasty way to address a man in his own home. I think you should apologize."

Bardlo spits on Nigels' shoes.

Nigel rakes his tongue across his teeth, slow, calculated before he says, "Take him around back and show him some hospitality?"

Four of the men put their weapons in their shoulder-straps and grab Bardlo, but the other two keep their weapons on him. They drag him from the room and towards the rear door.

I inhale sharply, worried about what they might see when they get around back. If Rego and Jasper are taking children out that way...

I throw my hand on my forehead and, with an exaggerated sigh, I faint. Thoa catches me and hoists me into his arm with little effort. "Nova, are you alright?"

I glance to the men and see they've stopped their progression. It might only buy a moment of time, but maybe it will be enough. I flutter my eyes at him and say, "Forgive me, my love. I'm just overcome with all this excitement."

Nigel sneers, but the look passes so fast I'm almost uncertain I saw it. "Perhaps we should take your lovely wife somewhere to rest while we continue our discussions."

But Thoa knows me. He has seen me return from a hunt with gashes from beasts or covered in the blood of our enemies. He has seen me exhausted, but standing; he has seen the depth of my resolve and the strength of my spirit. Only a fool would see these things and still think I would be overwhelmed by the nothingness this encounter was. Thoa will know this was a distraction.

"Perhaps I should escort her home," he says, pulling me against his side. "It has been a trying night and her nerves are frayed."

I barely resist smirking at his words as Thoa steers me towards the door. Nigel is still attempting to persuade us to stay, but to his credit, Thoa is undeterred and I'm certain it is because he trusts me. Though I haven't seen Sage or Herol since we arrived, I'm certain they'll be fine on their own. Their roles this evening were cloaked in secrecy and even I don't know what they were supposed to do. But they're resourceful and our departure will not hinder their plans.

As we pass under the chandelier, Nigel takes my hand and brushes his lips against my knuckles. "Thank you for so graciously offering the company of your husband this evening. I can't express to you what a pleasure it was."

He turns to Thoa and gives a small bow. "Tab, darling, I do hope to share your time again. Soon."

He kisses Thoa on each cheek, lingering just a second too long for my comfort. But then we are moving towards the door again. We are just about to step outside when Thoa stops and turns back to Nigel. "Apologies, Mayor, but I nearly forgot our young companion. Would you have Tess brought to us?"

The color is leached from my body. Of course Thoa would ask after her; he has no idea what has happened.

"She's probably asleep by now, darling," I say. "Could you return for her tomorrow?"

Nigel seems grateful for my offer. He probably hoped we'd forget about the child. It takes everything within me not to kill him where he stands.

Thoa offers a puzzled expression, but again he trusts me and asks Nigel if he can return for Tess at tea-time on the morrow. Nigel seems thrilled at the prospect of seeing Thoa again so soon, and he relaxes considerably when he thinks he'll have time to retrieve Tess from wherever he was sending her.

Once we've said our goodbyes to Nigel and are nearing the transport, Thoa loosens his grip around my waist and his body feels rigid next to me.

"What is going on?" he asks.

"Not here," I whisper.

He presses his lips tight, saying nothing as we climb into the carriage. Dino and Jessa waste no time. She scoops the rocks into the furnace, sending a rattling vibration through the body of the beast, and Dino moves us in an arcing turn on the cobbled driveway.

We're nearly to the gate when I hear the yelling. Thoa turns to look out the back window, but I don't bother. Instead I yell to Dino, "Hurry!"

The carriage shudders as they push it faster. Ahead the gates are closing, but Dino isn't slowing. We're going to make it. Then I catch sight of the guards standing by the gates. Their weapons are aimed at the ground where Rego is kneeling in chains.

My breath catches in my throat and I cough on the words that aren't there. Thoa must see him right after I do, because he opens the carriage door and dives out, rolling into a heap just before we pass through the gates. They clang shut behind me.

I beat on the seats, yelling for Dino to stop, but he doesn't. He pushes through the winding street until we reach the port, only slowing when he drives right out onto the pier. Rachel rushes to the door and whips it open, dragging me out of the carriage. My legs are numb; with Jessa's help, Rachel hoists me up and drags me onto the ship.

Permilla yells to Dino, "Get rid of the carriage."

I hear a crash and turn to see Dino staring over the side of the pier. A plume of smoke rises from the ground. Dino joins us on *The Disorderly Glory*, his expression sad.

"I liked that thing."

"You know the rules," Permilla says.

I hear footsteps and whip my head back towards the pier. Herol is barreling towards us, Krew in tow. I hurry to the plank as they board, panting with exertion.

Herol waves his hand and between gasps he says, "Go. They're coming."

Rachel dashes for the helm. Permilla pushes Dino towards the steps and says, "Get below deck. I want you with the children in case something happens up here."

"But Auntie—"

"No 'buts' Dino. Go on."

I watch as he heads below and my mind seems to come out of a fog. "The kids are okay?"

Permilla nods. "Fourteen with us, eight with Jasper."

"Jasper?" I hiss.

He appears as if from nowhere at the sound of his name. "Yes?"

I dive for his throat, wrapping my hands around it and squeezing. Permilla pulls at me, trying to loosen my grip, but she is not strong, not a Raider. But Jasper is. *Was.* Slowly, his eyes never leaving mine, he pries my fingers away until he can take a ragged gasp of air.

We stand there, both panting, him from lack of oxygen and me from anger. "You abandoned him again."

"He told me to go," Jasper rasps. "To get the children away."

Of course he did. It's exactly what Rego would do. But it doesn't still my rage.

When Rachel's ship shudders beneath my feet, all thoughts of Jasper fall away. I run to her instead. "Our people are still down there."

She doesn't look at me when she says, "They'll be fine."

"Rachel, you can't know that."

She takes a deep breath and lets it out slowly. "They're strong, Nova. They'll make it."

"They need us."

"Not as much as those kids do. The moment you pulled us into this, you gave up the safety of our people for them. You know it's true."

I bite my lip. Her words are right, but I still hate them. "Where are we going?"

"Coco has a safe place to keep them until we figure this out."

Coco. I'd all but forgotten her and the mission she had to rescue the kids. At least one of us succeeded.

I put my hand on Rachel's shoulder for a second before I walk away, hoping she understands that I don't blame her for any of this. I move to stand by Jasper. His neck is still red where my hands were and I'm certain he will be bruised tomorrow.

"I'm sorry."

"Don't be," he says. "Your love for Rego is deep. I understand."

"Do you?" I ask.

We stare at Gearhaven as it grows small below us. Jasper clenches and unclenches his jaw until finally he says, "I love him, too. I never stopped."

"Then why didn't you come back for him?"

"That's none of your business."

I shrug. "Maybe not, but I'm asking anyway. I've watched Rego hurt for you, year after year. You don't seem to be hurting. Why is that?"

He turns to me and I think he is going to answer, but then his eyes slide past me and I watch his face melt into an expression I've never seen on anyone. He pushes past me and runs across the deck towards one of the children we rescued. He falls to his knees, sliding the last few feet and wrapping the girl in his arms.

When they finally break apart, Jasper stands and puts his arm around her as he wipes tears from his eyes. He walks towards me and says, "Nova, this is my daughter, Edith-Ann."

"She came to find us, Daddy," Edith-Ann says.

He nods. "I know, darling, and for that I am forever grateful."

"Edith-Ann," I say, holding out my hand to shake hers. "How old are you?"

Jasper nods. "You already know, Nova. She is the answer to your question."

I don't say anything. I do not wish to shame him in front of his child, but I wish to diminish him all the same. He left Rego and found another nearly in the same breath, while my friend spent a dozen years waiting for a man who wasn't worthy. I hope he sees the disgust in my eyes.

"It isn't as you think," he whispers.

"Then what is it?" I ask.

He sighs. "Someday I will tell Rego the whole story, because I owe him that, but I do not owe it to you."

I nod. His words are true. "I hope you get the chance to tell him."

I watch his lips press thin for a moment before he says, "Did you see him?"

"He was at the gate, surrounded by guards."

"And your husband?"

The word bites me. Jasper doesn't know the truth of us, only the lie Thoa told to keep me safe. "He saw Rego and dove from the carriage to save him."

"Did he?"

"I don't know," I confess. "The gate closed and I didn't see what happened."

Jasper nods. "Then they are safe."

"How can you say such nonsense?"

"I choose to believe they are safe until I see otherwise. It is the best way to honor them until we can do more."

I nod, though I'm not convinced. Jasper must see the doubt on my face because he puts a hand on my shoulder, much like I did with Rachel. With that small gesture, a strange conviction rises inside me. I will help get these children to safety, and then I will move land, sea, and sky to rescue Rego and Thoa.

All they must do is keep living.

CHAPTER
TWELVE

K rew joins me at the railing, watching the green land come closer as the ship descends. I've seen grasslands before, but not like this. The Raiders pass through fields of tall switchgrass and bluestem as we complete our cycle each year, but these grasses are different, bright green and short, easier to manage than what I've seen.

"Look at those mountains in the distance. They're massive. This whole land is beautiful," Krew says, his white teeth showing in the most genuine smile I've seen from him.

"It is," I agree. My heart pangs at the words. Guilt eats at me. I should not be here, safe, while Thoa and Rego are trapped in Gearhaven.

They're alive, I think. I remind myself throughout the day. The words are beginning to lose their comfort.

Beasts gallop towards where we've angled the ship to land. They seem small at first, brown spots dotting the green. As we get closer to the ground I can see they are large enough for a person to ride them, and ride them they do.

We land lightly on the grass with only the slightest thud. I don't know how Rachel manages to control this monstrous ship as she does, but even to me her skills are evident. She joins me at the railing as her crew lowers the plank.

"Be on guard." she says.

"I'm always on guard."

Krew smirks, but Rachel presses her lips into a thin line and says, "Still. I don't know these people. Not sure who we can trust."

"Coco trusts them," I say.

"But we don't know her, either. Not really."

I nod, chewing on her words. Over the last two days, I've spent most of my time with Coco. We've played games with the children after making sure they're fed. At night we've told them fantastical stories about Zappho Curiosity falling from the sky to save the world. We've laughed and whispered and once, she cried, as we huddled together on the deck, under the stars.

But I don't know her.

She is the first woman to show me affection in years, and I hunger for it. There are moments where I am confused by this desire to be with her. At first I imagine it is the love Chief Eija and Nukiki felt, but no, not exactly. I'm certain her lips would feel nice against mine, I'm certain I would enjoy her touch, but neither of us pursue that course. Instead we lie together in comfort, in camaraderie, in pain. We share our heartache so that we don't have to bear it alone.

I was given to a woman when I was a child after I was separated from Rachel. She was kind to me for a while, motherly even, until her mate chose another. She sent me away then, saying I was to blame for his departure, saying I was too much of a reminder of what had been, saying, saying, saying…

It was hard after that. I was a cursed thing and none of the women would risk my company. It was then that Rego began to look after me. Small kindnesses, gentle words. But when Jasper left and did not return, the other Raiders knew my curse was true.

Only Rego remained a friend to me and didn't blame me for Jasper's disappearance.

Now Coco is becoming my friend. She doesn't know of my curse, that I will drive away anyone she loves with my presence. Perhaps it is cruel that I cling to her each night, knowing that her brother will not return as long as I am near her. But I do it anyway; I am lonely, and I have been for a long time but I was too afraid to admit it. I'm so desperate for the tender embrace of a true friend that I'm almost willing to dismiss Rachel's warning.

I don't know Rachel either.

I consider reminding her of this, but I bite my tongue. There's no point rehashing the same hurts. Besides, I will need Rachel if I'm to have any hope of rescuing the others.

Coco walks down the ramp with Jasper on her heels. Rachel, Krew, and I follow behind them. Rachel's shoulders and arms are tight, coiled and ready to strike. I try to look like I'm at ease, relaxing my own shoulders as I let out a deep breath. But inside I am a ball of worms.

The lead rider climbs down from the beast and grasps arms with Coco, pulling her close until their foreheads rest against each other. When they separate, I immediately see the resemblance in his sharp green eyes and rich, honeyed skin.

"Uncle Vern," Coco says, "these are the people who helped me."

Vern shakes hands with us in turn, a crooked grin plastered on his weathered face. "Pleased ta meet ya'll. I'm thankful you helped my girl."

"She didn't need much help," I say.

Vern laughs. "Aye, she's a tough one, but I thank you still."

Coco puts a hand on my shoulder and says, "Nova is being modest. She's actually the one who found them."

"Them?" Vern asks, eyes going wide.

Coco presses her lips in a thin line and gives a small shake of her head. "Twenty-two children rescued, but Wolfie wasn't there."

"Damn," Vern says. The word somehow has a fouler meaning than any other time I've heard it.

"Wolfie?" Rachel asks.

"My little brother, Wolfrick," Coco says. "I've been searching for him for months."

"You didn't find him, but you saved the others, and that's a win in my book," Vern says.

As if on cue, Permilla and Dino lead the children down the plank to join us. They're still dirty, still scared, but there are a few more smiles among them than there were two days ago.

One of the younger boys runs ahead of the others towards the beast that Vern was riding. The animal dips its long face forward and the child rubs his hand along the muzzle.

"Is that safe?" I ask, surprised at the ease the others show around the creature.

"What? The horse?" Vern asks, a chuckle shaking his shoulders.

"They're domesticated," Rachel says.

The word is unfamiliar to me in the old tongue, and Jasper must see it on my face because he translates to Raider. I nod my thanks, but find myself biting back the bitterness that comes with Raider-speak. I miss my people.

———

THE CHILDREN ARE SETTLED BY MID-AFTERNOON. THE TOWN WHERE Vern lives is full of families willing to take on an extra mouth in exchange for extra hands to help around the farms. I worry that we are putting the children in a different form of slavery, but Coco assures me they have a network of people that will work to get the children back to their parents, if they have them. Those who don't have a home to return to, like Tess, can stay here and hopefully find some happiness with a new family.

I walk with Tess to her new home. It is an apartment on top of a general store in the middle of town. The young man who meets us outside isn't much older than me, late twenties at the most, with curly dark hair and olive skin. His hands tremble slightly when he kneels to introduce himself to Tess and he seems to be on the verge of tears.

"We've tried for years, but we've never been able to have a child of our own," he tells me as we climb the stairs to his apartment. "When Vern told us about the children, my wife begged him for a daughter we could keep."

A young woman comes from the kitchen, wiping her hands on an apron. She is petite, with black hair pulled back from her face, and a smudge of flour on her cheek. Her smile is so wide her eyes nearly scrunch closed as she says, "Hello. My name is Meen. I'm your new mother."

Huge tears form on Tess's lashes for a moment before cascading down her cheeks. "I want to stay with Thoa."

I bite my lip. "Thoa isn't here, Tess."

"But you're going to get him. I want to go with you."

"I'm sorry, but you can't go. It'll be safer for you here, with these nice people who want to take care of you."

She clutches at my leg, wrapping her tiny hands around it. "Will I ever see you again?"

I almost tell her the truth. The Raider in me wants to. Instead I say, "Of course you will. When we finish our quest, we'll come back to visit."

I am not a good liar and she can hear my false promise. Hurt is heavy on her face as she whispers, "Tell him goodbye for me."

I nod and pull myself from her grasp. I'm finding it hard to swallow. I rush down the stairs and out into the afternoon sun before I lose my resolve. After a few ragged breaths, I realize someone is behind me. I turn to see Krew watching me, his brow furrowed.

"What?" I ask, more harshly than I intended.

He shrugs and turns away, walking down the street. I follow him, unsure why I do so. He slips into a store and I do the same, a tiny bell jingling as we enter. The woman behind the counter eyes us for a moment, then gives a nod as if she's approving us to continue with whatever we're doing.

I corner Krew as he's collecting an armful of fruit. "What are you doing?"

He looks at the fruit and back at me, as if the answer is obvious. "Getting food I can stomach, instead of that stuff you try to feed me."

"We've had plenty of food since we got to Aeroport," I say, unsure what he means.

"You have," he says. "But I've been scrounging."

"I don't understand."

His mouth quirks up on one side. "I'm a vegetarian." When I don't respond he says, "It means I don't eat meat."

"I know what it means," I say, glaring at him, "but I don't understand why you didn't tell us. We could have made arrangements."

His brows rise and there's amusement on his face. "You think your Raider friends would've cared?"

I chew on the inside of my lip, unhappy in the knowledge that he's right. "But once we got to Thoa's--"

"Thoa is a good man, but he doesn't like me. He sees me as an obstacle to get to you."

I stand in stunned silence as he collects the last of his food and goes to the counter. Krew pays for the items and steps out of the shop, leaving me standing alone, the shopkeeper's eyes boring into me.

It takes me a moment to gather my wits. When I do, I smile awkwardly at the woman at the counter and hurry outside before she can say anything. Krew is leaning against a post with his back to me, the clothes Vern loaned him clinging to his frame. I walk past him without a word and he falls in line behind me, keeping pace while biting into a heartfruit.

Around a mouthful of the crispy flesh he asks, "Wanna bite?"

I glance back at him. I do want a bite, but I shake my head. Instead I increase my pace.

"C'mon, don't be like that."

Ignoring him, I press on. I'm jogging now, trying to put distance between us. I look over my shoulder and he's still right behind me. He smiles. The sight is infuriating.

I break into a run, fast as a chigerbeast. I zip around buildings, flying through the streets, until I've left town and started into the farmland. I hop over a fence and dart past a group of black and white animals grazing the meadow. There's a small stream ahead, followed by a copse of trees. I jump the stream, managing to only get my toes wet when I land a little short, and dash into the trees.

I slow once I've reached the trees and hunch over with my hands on my knees while I greedily gulp in air. My heart hammers in my chest and I hear the blood pounding through my ears. I'm more winded than I'd like, but the exertion still feels good. I haven't had much exercise since I found Krew three weeks ago.

I've been in the trees long enough for my heart to settle when I hear something crashing through the underbrush. I spin to see Krew emerge from behind a tree. He is winded, breathing heavy, but when he sees me watching he sports that frustrating grin again.

"You're quick," he pants. He leisurely walks towards me, swatting at a bug as he draws near.

"Why are you following me?" I ask.

"Why does it bother you so much?"

I ball my fists at my side. "What do you want?"

He straightens, shakes his head. "Isn't it obvious?"

"No," I growl. "I don't understand you."

He steps close, so close there's barely air between us. I look up into dark eyes that swallow me whole. I am absorbed by the midnight of his irises, as if they pull all color from the world, leaving everything lackluster after he's seen it.

"I hated you at first," he says, his voice softer than any I've ever heard. "You had no right to take me."

"I know," I choke out. I step back from him once, twice, but he closes the gap again.

"Your people were going to kill me, *you* were going to kill me."

I nod. I step back again and feel tree bark dig into the back of my arm. He steps close again and there is no escape. My mind races to the secret places I've stashed my knives and I prepare to defend myself.

"Despite that, I've seen who you really are," he says. "I didn't know your words, but looking back I can see how you tried to help me. When you came in the tent to loosen my bonds, when you stood in front of your people while they sided against you, when you killed those from the airship who tried to take us. You saved those children. You hurt saying goodbye to that little girl today."

I don't know what to say. He speaks of things I do not wish to think on. Those are soft spots, things that make me weak in the eyes of the Raiders. They are proof that I am not as strong as I should be, proof that I am not fit to be a hunter or a life-bringer.

But Krew does not sound cruel when he says these things. He does not mock me. I look into his eyes and the darkness seems to shine, offering up all the light and color they had stolen before.

He leans forward and presses his lips against mine. They are softer than I thought lips would feel. He only lingers for a second before pulling back and resting his forehead against mine.

"You are kind, and warm, and more than I thought. You are fierce, and strong, and ferocious for those you care about. I've never known anyone like you."

I have no words for him. I don't know the girl he speaks of, but she isn't me. He sees the woman I want to be. Still, when his hands slide over my waist and pull me close, when his lips crash against mine this time, I don't pull away.

WHEN I RETURN TO THE FARM, UNCLE VERN HAS SET UP A LONG TABLE laden with food. Coco, Vern and his wife, Abigail, and the three children they're housing are all seated on one side. I sit across from Coco, squeezing between Dino and Edith-Ann Roody.

There is polite conversation throughout much of our dinner, mostly centered on how delicious Abigail's cooking is. We eat bowls of bean soup flavored with onion and a pink meat called ham. There are fried potatoes and a crumbling yellow bread that she encourages us to mix into our soup, then she passes around a jar of pickled peppers that offer a medley of sweet and spice. When Krew joins us ten minutes after me, I watch him pick the meaty bits from his soup, though he seems delighted with the rest.

My eyes find his more than they should. Each time I steal a glance I find him looking at me. I avert my gaze, sliding over the soft smile tugging at his lips, and instead I turn towards the other end of the table where Rachel and Vern are discussing plans. My mind is buzzing with thoughts of Krew's lips, and it takes longer than it should for me to pick up tidbits of conversation that create a ball of burning rage within me.

They're making plans to go somewhere else—somewhere that doesn't lead back to Rego and Thoa.

"Coghelm?" I ask, drawing their eyes to me.

Vern nods. "Yeah, it's the last floater to check in the middle country. After that we'll need to head north."

"Where is it?" I ask.

Rachel takes a deep breath and puts down her spoon. "They're usually around the Augusta Ruins this time of year. It's only a few hours away."

"Coastal. The opposite direction of Gearhaven," Jasper says, understanding clear on his face. He presses his lips into a tight line and closes his eyes.

"Yes," Rachel says, still unable to look at me. "A report came in this afternoon indicating Coghelm has been selling children up and down the coast. We're going to go see what we can find."

"What about Rego and Thoa?" Krew asks.

My cheeks redden at the mention of Thoa and I dare not glance to Krew. I feel his eyes on me, searching for a reaction, but I hold steady and try not to respond.

Rachel finally turns to look at me. I don't need her to speak to know what she's saying. She thinks they're already dead.

Permilla pushes Dino aside and slides in beside me. She takes my hand and says, "Even if they're still alive baby, we can't help them. They'll be watching for Rachel's ship. And we don't know if they're even still there. Aeroport is big, slow, so we could probably find it if we wanted. But if Gearhaven has undocked they could be anywhere. Small towns move fast."

"But there's a chance they haven't left?" Coco asks.

I meet her gaze and see the steel resolve. I think she will go for them if I ask her. I don't know how we'll get there, but she does, I think. I can almost read it on her face. My heart swells, full of admiration for this woman, my friend.

Rachel says, "A chance, yeah. But it's a two day ride back for a maybe, when there's a much better chance we'll find Coghelm and, hopefully, Wolfie and the other children."

Coco winces at her brother's name before she nods. "Sounds like you've got it figured out."

"Just about," Vern says. "I expect you'll be ready by then, darlin'. We'll be leavin' at first light."

"This is wrong," I say, pounding my fists on the table. I can barely contain my anger, so when Rachel glares at me and urges with her eyes for me to keep quiet, I bare my teeth at her in frustration.

"I agree," Coco says. "I don't feel right about leaving Nova's friends."

Vern's spoon stops midway to his mouth. He asks, "You feel okay leavin' those kids where they are?"

His words break her. She mumbles, "No sir."

"And Wolfie? What if he's there? You need to be the one to find him if you want redemption."

She nods and sinks her elbows onto the table in defeat. As she deflates, so does my hope.

CHAPTER
THIRTEEN

After dinner Coco takes my hand and leads me onto the porch. Some of Rachel's crew is sitting around laughing, shooting dice, sharpening weapons—whatever they can do to fill the time when they're not on the ship. Coco smiles brightly and tells them dinner is ready for the second shift. I don't know if I've ever seen anyone move as fast as they do.

"How is your family paying for all this food?" I ask, awed when I realize how many people have been in and out of their house since yesterday.

"We're not," she says. "Rachel paid for her crew's food and gave Aunt Abby a good wage to cook it."

The revelation surprises me, but I'm not sure why. Rachel is good to her people. She puts them in danger, sure, but I suppose that's expected when you're a pirate.

Coco pulls me around the corner of the house towards the barn. Fat birds cluck and scatter as we pass them. We walk through the dark stables, the earthy smell of animals thicker as we go deeper inside. All at once a square of light catches me in the face and I blink against it. Coco has pushed open the back door to the barn and we're back outside, the last rays of the setting sun slanting towards us.

"Where are we going?"

She hushes me and continues pulling towards a green building in the distance. A few times she turns to check behind us, but sees no one. When we reach the hangar, she pulls a key from between her breasts and turns it in the rusted lock. We go in and she flips a switch. A loud buzzing begins above us and globes of light slowly come to life.

Coco says, "I can't go with you."

My eyes go wide. This is not what I expected her to say. I ask, "Why?" I can hear the hurt in my voice and there's no way I can hide it from her.

"I want to," she says, "really, I do. But if I go with you, Uncle Vern will come after us and it could ruin any chance you have of rescuing your friends."

"Are you sure he'd do that?"

She nods. "He let me go on a few missions alone, but only the ones he thought were safe, small. This one is neither. Coghelm is a bad place, Nova. They'll need all the help they can get. And if Wolfie is there..."

She trails off, but I understand. "You need to be there."

Coco goes to the side of the room and pulls a tarp off a large, rusty machine. "I can't go, but I can give you this."

"What is it?"

"A personal flying machine. Takes two people to run, but I figure Herol will want to go."

"Herol is gone." We both turn as Krew moves from the shadows to stand beside us. "He left before dinner, when he heard some of the crew talking about their next move. Said he wants to get back to Aeroport, back to the council, before he loses everything he's worked for."

"Damn," Coco mutters.

Krew looks at the flying machine and says, "Two bicycles

strapped together and attached to a turbine. Does this thing really work?"

Coco nods. "It'll work if we can get a second person to power it."

"Not a problem. I'll go," he says.

"You?" I ask.

Krew frowns. "Why not me?"

I flounder a moment before saying, "I'm just surprised."

He shrugs. "Thoa is a friend, of sorts. Besides, he saved my life. It's time to return the favor."

Coco nods. "It's settled then. Let me show you what to do and you can be off."

"Now?" he asks.

"The crew is distracted, getting dinner and making plans for tomorrow. And they'll expect Nova to mope off somewhere, so it shouldn't be a big surprise that she isn't around."

"And no one pays attention to me," Krew says with a smirk.

"They do," Coco says, "but not much. They seem afraid of you."

"Why is that?" I ask. I've wondered for so long, but never had the chance to ask. The way Ukaru and the other Raiders reacted to him...

"I'm not from around here," he says, almost apologetically.

"And?" I ask. "No one is. The Raiders are nomadic, the sky-people, too. It isn't as if you're the first stranger we've seen."

"Where are you from?" Coco asks.

I look between her and Krew as they stare at each other. Finally he raises his hand to show her the fine silver bracelet he wears. Her hand goes to her open mouth and her skin pales. I do not understand.

"What does it mean?" I ask.

"He is not one of us," Coco whispers.

"I'm not here to hurt anyone," Krew says. "I just wanted to see this place for myself, to understand it."

"And then you'll return home?" she asks.

He nods. "Soon. We were on our way when we got caught up in all this."

"The City of Trials," I say. "That's where we were going."

"Thoa understands. He's been trying to get me there."

I furrow my brows. "That's your home? You told me you were from the 'Station,' whatever that means. Do we pass through the City of Trials?"

"There's more than one way home," he says, avoiding my question. "I came through the grasslands but I'll return through the Trials."

Coco mutters, "Or you'll vanish when the tides turn against you."

"I haven't left yet."

"Why is that?" she asks.

He glances at me for the briefest second before planting his hands on his hips and turning his back to us. I press my fingers to the bridge of my nose. Krew's words are spinning through my head but they don't make sense. I've gleaned nothing from this conversation except a headache.

"You need to go," Coco says, cutting off my thoughts.

"No," I say, turning to Krew. "I want to know who you are. No more secrets. No more 'cursed one' business. Tell me the truth."

"I want to tell you. I *will* tell you. But I want to do it right and now isn't the time."

I huff. "And when will it be the right time? I've been patient with you so far, but—"

"He's right," Coco interrupts. "Leave now, while you can."

"And you can't tell me either?"

She shakes her head and mutters, "It's not my story. I wish I could, friend."

She and Krew move to steer the strange machine outside. It has two wheels at the front and back, with thin spokes that look like they're made from metal. I've seen something like it when I was younger, a bicycle, as Krew called it. But as he said, this is more like

CITY OF TRIALS   113

two of them joined side-by-side with a wide bench welded to the middle where the seats would be. Sticking straight up from the middle of the bench is a rod that connects to curved blades that sit several feet above the riders head.

"Stay on the ground until you get away from town," Coco says. "When the street turns into a dirt road, press this button."

"What will that do?"

Coco smiles. "It'll lift you into the air."

"How does it work?" Krew asks.

"No time to explain," she says. "Just don't stop pedaling."

"If we do?" I ask.

"You'll fall."

Krew mumbles, "No pressure."

Coco points us towards the road and gives instructions on how to find Gearhaven. She straps a machete to the back of the bench—for safekeeping—and hands me a small sack containing dried meat and a block of cheese wrapped tightly in a cloth. Before we go, she pulls me tight against her and whispers in my ear. "Be careful. Trust no one. Especially not *him*."

WE PEDAL NEXT TO EACH OTHER, THE BAR CONNECTED TO THE propeller between us. I push the button when we reach the beginning of the dirt road. Though she told us what to expect, I'm still surprised when we lift into the air. It happens slowly. We rise to the level of the fence that runs along one side of the road, then we're at the height of the town's houses that grow small behind us, then we're gliding above the trees.

We pedal at a steady pace, no faster than when we were on the ground, but I can tell we're gaining speed. After a few minutes, I see a light ahead of us weaving through the trees. Pointing, I ask, "What is that?"

Krew cranes his neck to see over the steering handles. "It's Herol."

He left more than an hour before us, but we've already caught up. "Should we pick him up?"

"Can't," Krew says. "Coco said not to stop pedaling."

"I'm sure it will be fine."

"What if we can't get started again?" he asks.

I look back down to Herol and, with a pang of concern, I realize he's running. My eyes follow the trail behind him and see a dark shape in pursuit, though I can't tell what it is. "We have to help him. Something is chasing him."

Krew takes a deep breath and pushes it out with puffed cheeks. Without a word, he swings his backpack around to his lap and rummages in it for a second before pulling out a coil of rope.

"Don't stop pedaling," he says.

The machine lurches and drops lower when Krew stops pedaling. He glances at me and I nod—I won't let us fall. He anchors the rope around the center bar of the machine and drops it down below us before yelling for Herol.

There is a rumble growing louder as we continue over the land. I'm certain Herol can't hear us because of it, but when we are nearly overhead he finally turns back and sees us. Even from this height I can see the surprise light up his face. His eyes dart back and I follow his gaze. A massive black beast is chasing him on all fours, gaining on him. The Raiders call them dangerclaws, but in the old tongue I whisper, "Bear."

"Dip lower," Krew says.

I angle the machine towards the ground. Herol is directly under us now but can't seem to reach the rope. The rumble has grown into a thunderous sound I can no longer ignore. It sounds as if the ground itself is breaking open to swallow us whole.

As we crest the next gathering of trees, the source becomes apparent. A huge waterfall blocks Herol's path—and ours if we don't pull up. I try to yell a warning, but Herol can't hear me. Even

Krew, sitting only a foot from me, can't make out my words as he stares at me. I point and his eyes grow wide when he sees the blockade of churning water.

We've passed Herol slightly. He will not be able to reach us in a moment, but I must not stop pedaling. The torture of it sits in my chest. Herol is going to die because I can't save him.

The last few feet of land are racing below us as we approach the falls. I tip the steering bars higher, knowing that we must rise to avoid the falls. Krew knows it, too. He is no longer slumped on the seat trying to reach Herol with the rope; now he sits straight, moisture resting on his lashes, as he begins to pedal again.

I spare one last look at Herol as we start over the water. The beast is nearly on him when he reaches the edge of the river and jumps.

CHAPTER
FOURTEEN

The flying machine plummets, pulled down by Herol's weight as he clings to the dangling rope. I push my legs as hard as I can and I'm certain Krew is doing the same. We're flying parallel to the face of the waterfall, so close that Krew could reach out his fingers and touch it. Rogue sprays of water pelt us and miniature rivulets roll down my shoulders, slipping between me and the clothes I borrowed from Rachel after fleeing Gearhaven. The water is cold and my teeth begin to chatter.

Just as we reach the shore, a squelching sound lands on the bench beside me. The sudden appearance of Herol shocks me and for a second I forget to pedal. The machine drops again but my legs start moving on their own.

The machine is tilting with Herol's added weight but there's nothing I can do. He's in no condition to take my place. I lean as close to the center as I can while still reaching the levers. We level off a bit, though we're still slanted enough to throw us off if we don't course correct. As if reading my thoughts, Krew withdraws a compass from his pocket, then turns the steering handle to adjust our direction.

After a few minutes of labored breathing, Herol finally sits up.

He turns his head and glares at me. A strangled voice chokes out, "You were going to let me die."

"Of course not," Krew says, forcing a chuckle.

I nod. "Yes, I was."

Herol purses his lips, gives a terse nod. He looks past me to Krew and growls, "Never lie to me."

"I was just trying—"

"I know what you were trying to do and I'm telling you that if I ever catch you in another lie, I'll break your neck with my bare hands."

He turns away from us both, leans back against the bench, and closes his eyes. Within a minute he is snoring.

HEROL SLEEPS THROUGH THE EVENING AND INTO THE NIGHT. KREW and I talk little, afraid to wake the hulking beast beside us.

When the lush mountains have grown small behind us and the land below is flat and yellow as far as we can see, Herol rouses. He nudges me to move aside and takes over pedaling. I try to do the same for Krew, but he will not let me. I know he is tired; though Krew is in good shape, he is not accustomed to the same level of exertion I am.

Instead of letting me pedal for him, he ties the rope around my waist and secures me to the machine so I won't fall out. "Sleep, Nova, and don't worry. I'm okay."

I nod and he puts his hand to my cheek, presses my head onto his shoulder. I allow myself to rest against him, though part of me fears this closeness and what it means. I want to think about this action, let the meaning roll around in my head until I've puzzled it out, but my body is desperate for rest and I give into the need for sleep before my mind has unpacked what is happening between me and Krew.

I wake up to the feel of the sun on my back and for a moment I forget all that has happened these last few weeks. Instead I am in my tent with the other unmated Raiders, heat beating through the canvas as we pile together. Then the flying machine jerks and my eyes pop open.

Krew's eyes are wide, red, and I can tell he was dozing only a moment ago. I sit up and stretch my arms wide, exaggerating the sweetness of my rest. I could sleep for the next day and still be tired, but if he knows that, he won't let me take over.

I elbow him and say, "Your turn."

He shakes his head. "I'm fine. You should try to go back to sleep."

"No," I say, letting my voice go firm. "You are going to rest now."

He nods, giving in without much hesitation. We trade places and he ties the rope around himself, falling asleep even faster than me.

We lift higher as Krew sleeps and the machine seems to take better to the air up here. We sail over a wide river that stretches long in either direction. I know this place from my travels with the Raiders. It is the last stop before we turn north for the hot season. Rego called it *Issippi*.

There are broken stone paths crisscrossing the land near the river, traces of cities eaten away by nature. Sometimes we see pieces of buildings taller than any dwelling has a right to be, though they are few and fragmented by vines and trees. Still, it makes me wonder what sorts of people roamed this land in the time before the Cataclysm.

A short time later, Herol points out a dark cloud in the distance. He grunts, "Gearhaven."

I jerk my head towards him. "You're sure?"

He nods. "I know the floaters as well as anyone. I've bounced around the cities longer than you've been alive."

"Floaters?" I ask. "I've never heard them called that."

The corner of his mouth droops into a half-frown. "You've never been in the belly, only the top tier where everyone and everything is clean and proper."

His voice has changed. It is no longer the lilt of the upper class, nor the sardonic instrument his tongue uses to cut his transgressors. It's heavy and accented in a way that drops letters off the end of his words. Propriety has left him.

This is a Herol I haven't seen before. Dark, brooding, and unpredictable.

"I'm not from the high houses, Herol," I say, trying to break this foul mood he's taken on. "I've lived among the Raiders most of my life."

Herol turns and spits off the side of the flying machine. "Raiders, bah."

I clench my jaw, biting back my initial response. When I can pry my mouth apart without cursing him, I say, "They were good to me. Took me in when I had nothing."

"They stole you, just like that bastard mayor stole those poor children. Hell, maybe it's the Raiders supplying Gearhaven."

I growl. Can't help it. He doesn't know the Raiders like I do, the honor and love among them. Through gritted teeth I say, "We. Would. *Never*..."

He must hear the truth of my words, because he doesn't press further. Instead he says, "Children are not property to buy and sell as you please. I'm going to kill Weatherfield for what he's done."

I nod. "Someone should."

"It won't matter though."

"Why do you say that?" I ask.

"Another will take his place. Another always does."

We don't talk much after that. His dark mood has brought me down as well, and I dare not give words to the thoughts slithering around in my mind.

KREW AWAKES AROUND MIDDAY WHEN TREES ARE STARTING TO DOT THE land again. I point out Gearhaven on the horizon, angry that it doesn't seem to get any closer. My frustration grows as my legs get weaker and I say, "We have to take a break."

Krew begins, "But Coco said—"

"I don't give a damn what Coco said. She's not here," I say. "I need to rest."

"And I've gotta drain the sea monster," Herol adds.

We set down in a narrow field. There's a stream on one side of us and a row of spindly trees on the other. Herol hops down and heads for the trees while Krew goes straight for the water. I ignore them both. I pull the machete off the bench and cut a path through the grass. We'll need some room to get the flying machine moving again, I tell myself, but the deep part of me knows this is only half of my reason for cutting the grass.

I was thirteen when I watched Malidesh go into the tall grass alive and return dead. He was a good boy, a bit younger than me, with sharp wit and the fire of a Raider. He dove into the grass chasing a jumprat, but he wasn't the only hunter out that day. A snake lunged for the jumprat but sunk its fangs into Malidesh instead, sending poison through his flesh.

I was nearby, stalking my own prey. When Desh didn't rise, I called for those doing washing in the lake. I brought them to his prone body and watched as they carried him from the grass, wailing for the loss. A man lost on a hunt did not receive such tears, for he was taken as a gift for Death, a payment that the Raiders would continue to flourish. But an innocent boy, too young to warrant Death's gaze...this boy was missed.

Even now the spark in his eyes burns brightly in my memories. That was the day I understood how dangerous our world was; that was the day I decided to become a hunter.

The path I've cleared should give us enough room to take off. At least, I hope. For now, it puts my mind at ease and I can rest without fear of what lurks beneath. I lie down and stretch my legs, my machete in reach just in case. The grass feels softer than I expected and cool beneath the exposed skin on my arms and shoulders.

I stare up into the sky. When I hear Krew stomping through the grass, somehow able to make a ruckus even in the soft field, I close my eyes and pretend to be sleeping. He's normally so quiet that I wonder if he was loud on purpose. I don't know if he believes I am asleep or if he is avoiding me also. Either way, he doesn't disturb me.

Herol returns after nearly an hour. He is running through the grass, yelling for us to get up. I grab the blade and bolt upright, hurtling towards the flying machine. Krew is slower, but not much, and we are both ready to go when Herol gets to us. He slides in beside me and pants, "Go, go, go," waving his hand forward.

The grass isn't as easy to maneuver as the road had been. We have trouble gaining speed, so when I push the button to take us into the air, the bicycles shudder and rise only a few inches. I pedal faster, hard as I can, and so does Krew. We're a few feet up now but starting to gain speed.

Herol's eyes are cast towards a far-off point, never wavering. I glance in the same direction, but see nothing. It isn't until we've passed out of eyesight of the meadow that he takes a deep breath and stops staring at the distant spot.

"What happened back there?" I ask.

He releases his breath and fixes me with a steady gaze. "I don't know exactly."

I furrow my brows, noticing for the first time that his hands are shaking. I place one hand over his and say, "You're safe, Herol. It's okay."

But he shakes his head. "We're not safe, not by a longshot." He eyes Krew for a moment, the expression on his face unreadable. "They're coming for you, star-boy."

Krew inhales sharply. "Who?"

I watch as Herol fights—and loses—to suppress a shiver. "A group in red, shaved heads."

"How many?" Krew asks, his voice rising.

"Four."

"Who are they?" I ask.

"The Chasseur," Krew whispers. "They're hunters from my homeland."

Krew pauses for a long moment, smacking at a pack of gnats that seem intent on his face. Finally, he looks at Herol and says, "Four? You're sure?"

"That's what I saw."

Krew nods. "Good. That means the leader hasn't arrived yet. Until that blue-eyed bastard finds me, there's still time."

"Time for what?" I ask. I hear the frustration coming through my voice. I've given him several chances to tell me these things on his own, but he hasn't. I'm tired of being left in the dark. I ask, "Where is home?"

Herol shakes his head, "Stop asking, kid. The less you know, the better."

"What do you know of it?" I ask him.

"Absolutely nothing," Herol says. Then he closes his eyes and leans back against the bench, refusing to say anything else.

BY LATE EVENING WE'VE HAD A STROKE OF GOOD FORTUNE. GEARHAVEN has grown large in the horizon and we'll reach it tonight. Herol thinks it has broken free from Aeroport and is heading for a rendezvous with another floater.

"Rookwood will come from that direction," Herol says, pointing south.

I follow his finger with my eyes, but there's nothing but the fading sky. "How do you know this?"

Herol shrugs. "Long before I made it to the council, I worked the cargo decks. Loading and unloading at first, but they saw I had a good mind and promoted me. After awhile, I took over routes, got familiar with the comings and goings of all the steam cities."

"So how did you end up running the place?" Krew asks.

Herol screws up his face and mumbles, "Just lucky I guess."

"It was the coup," I say, the realization coming to me all at once. "When Thoa's father was killed."

Herol gives one slight nod but doesn't speak. I don't need him to. I've already worked it out. He was rewarded for eliminating the heir. I ask, "Was it worth it?"

His jaw clenches and unclenches several times before he says, "I lost my way. Before that day, I was a good man, a moral man who wanted to do right by his family. And in my memories I think maybe I made the right choice when I threw the boy off that boat. I spent years wallowing around, wondering if he lived or died, drinking myself to numb the pain and dull the guilt. Seeing him alive makes it easier. And harder."

"Why harder?" I ask. "Doesn't it make you happy that he survived? I mean, you're helping him."

"Don't confuse my help for kindness. I do it because of the guilt for what I did to him."

I shake my head. "I don't believe that. You're not a bad man."

His eyes take on a hard glint as he says, "You don't know me, the things I've done. Trust me when I tell you I'm not a good man. I know what I'm about, girl."

I close my mouth and save my words. If he will not allow himself to be redeemed, that is his choice. Instead I focus on the floating city growing larger in my vision, the last rays of the setting sun gleaming upon the tops of colored buildings.

I remember thinking the place was beautiful before the sour secrets made their way from shadow to light. Has it really only been four nights since we went to Nigel's party? So little time to turn a magnificent city into a broken shell full of despicable souls in my mind's eye. I will never see it's beauty again.

Herol flies us higher into the clouds. He says the city has look-outs for approaching ships to help guide them into port and he doesn't want to be spotted. When the air is harder to breathe and the wind buffets us off course, I worry we're too high. But he straightens us out and presses on as if nothing is wrong. He knows the skies like I know the hunting grounds, so I keep my fears silent and let him direct us as he thinks best.

When the sky is black with dots of white and silver, Herol takes over pedaling for me and tells me to sit on the outside of the bench. He can't be sure where we will land when we make our descent, so I am ready to pounce on anyone who may attack. I cling to the machete as he angles us down.

We dip below the clouds and swoop towards the city like a bird diving for a mouse. The wind presses me back against the bench, but the men keep pedaling. Herol yells encouragement as we drop, but I can't make out his words over the air wooshing by my head and the strange pressure in my ears.

Nigel's house is in the center of town. Herol seems to be aiming for it, but as we approach he skirts to the side and levels out the flying machine so that we come to an easy landing in a garden.

I'm off the machine before we've fully stopped, crouched low as I spin around to check for attack. The thin trunks and blossoming branches offer little cover and I don't understand why Herol landed us here.

And then I see the guns.

Soldiers rise from the ground surrounding the garden. More pour in from the courtyard beyond. There must be two dozen of them, all with weapons aimed at my head. *My* head, not Herol's.

I turn to look at him and he gives me a shrug. "It's preservation, kid. No hard feelings."

"When? How?" I ask, unsure what I want to know more.

Krew answer for him. "In the woods, when he saw the Chasseur. He made a deal."

He gives Krew a smile as if to congratulate him on figuring it out. Without a word, Herol turns and walks towards the guards. They let him pass. I watch his back as he strolls through the garden, under the archway to the courtyard, past the fountain, and out of sight. He didn't even spare us a second glance.

A stout woman grabs my shoulder and spins me around, roping my hands together. I don't try to fight. I could take five or six of them hand-to-hand, maybe more if I was rested. But not this many, with all their weapons, after all this time cycling through the air. Easier to give in; at least I'll live to fight another day.

Krew struggles when they grab him. He tries to get to me. I don't know what he thinks will happen if he does. But he doesn't get the chance. One of the soldiers hits him with the butt of her gun, knocking him out. They drag him ahead of me along the trail that Herol took.

Though I follow without fighting, they still handle me roughly. A man with thinning hair and a bruised eye walks beside me, giving me a hard shove every few steps. My lips curl up as I ask, "Where'd you get that bruise?"

He glares at me, confirming my suspicion that it was Rego or Thoa. I chuckle. "Raiders are tough."

"You don't seem so bad," the woman says. She jerks my arms backward as the man gives me another shove. I don't mind their hostility until I hear her snicker. That's when I know I will kill her. Not tonight, but soon.

They take us downstairs. The man shoves me on the last step and I stumble, my face hitting the stone floor. The woman hoists me up by my wrists and my bones slide against one another as my shoulder dislocates. Blackness seeps in around the edges of my vision and I blink back the white flashes of pain. I will not cry out.

A trickle of blood is migrating down my forehead. From the slow procession I can tell the cut isn't severe, but the blood will reach my eye in a moment so I close it in preparation. Even if the cut is bad, my mind is too focused on blocking out the pain in my shoulder to process such a small injury.

I hear a *drip, drip* in the distance, but I can't figure out which direction it's coming from. My head feels like a dagger is being jabbed into it—probably from trying to distract myself from the way my arm hangs limp against my bonds. I can barely see in this windowless corridor, but I think it's better that way. The smells of feces and filth rise around me like floodwaters, fast and inescapable. It's better if I can't see the cause.

I hear the scrape of metal as they push me towards my cage. Shapes move just beyond the bars. One of the guards hisses something, but I can't make it out. Then I hear the patter of feet as the people in the cell fall back and the guards toss Krew in with them. The woman behind me shoves my bad shoulder and I fall in after him.

The clang of the door shutting is the loudest sound I've ever heard. It echoes from the walls, echoes off the ceiling, echoes through my mind. Warm hands try to lift me under my arms and I yelp in pain. They drop me, likely from the shock of my yell, and I'm left to find comfort on the stone floor, slick with who knows what.

I heave against the ground, my body rising and falling in shaky breaths. It takes a moment of fighting my body to realize I'm lying on my damaged shoulder. I roll onto my stomach just before the blackness consumes me.

CHAPTER
FIFTEEN

I wake up on a sofa that smells like lemon and dust. I hear voices nearby and try to peek open my eyes, but they're too heavy and will not budge. I strain my ears until I can make out the voices and that is when I know I am dreaming; one is Mayor Nigel Weatherfield, which doesn't seem so strange, and the other is my father.

I take a deep breath, relishing the sound of his voice. I haven't heard him in so long, I'm not sure how I know it is him. But I do know, with the confidence you have in dreams, and I am delighted with it. He barely fits in my memories—overpowered by Rachel, and then the Raiders—but there are snatches of him still there. The crisp part to his slick blond hair, the way he always smelled of tobacco smoke and leather, the timbre of his voice when he called my name…

I want to see him so badly, but I can't open my eyes no matter how hard I try. And then I'm falling, falling, until my face hits a wooden slab and I'm jolted awake.

My eyes are open now, my body turned to the side as I face the sweating stone wall. I grunt as I try to turn over but a hand on my back stops me.

"Don't move, Little Star," Rego whispers. "You're in bad shape."

I slur my words and my tongue feels heavy in my mouth. "Just my shoulder. It needs to be popped back into place."

"I know how," Krew says. "Let's get her up."

They steady me on the bench and put my back against the wall. Krew says, "Hold her arm straight out and keep it steady. Nova, put your other arm against your collarbone, like this."

He moves his own arm up to show me and I do as he says. Krew has Rego pull on my arm while he manipulates my shoulder blade. I fight myself, holding back the scream begging to fly from my throat. I grit my teeth so tight I think they might crack.

After a few agonizing seconds, the bones slip back into place. The relief is so sudden I almost cry.

Rego sits beside me and pulls me against his shoulder. "You're okay now, Nova-du."

His comfort redoubles my tears and I cry against him for a long moment. Finally I'm able to say, "I'm so glad you're okay."

"I'm alive, but that's hardly okay," he says, his voice soft.

I sit up at his words, my eyes roving his body as I take in his injuries. There are multiple cuts on his arms, though none look too deep, and his face and chest are covered in bruises both old and new. His bottom lip is cracked and swollen.

I turn to Krew. There is blood by his left ear, but otherwise he seems unharmed. It is only the three of us in the cell and panic rises in my chest as I ask, "Where is Thoa?"

Rego puts his hand on mine to calm me. "He's alive. Nigel takes him out sometimes."

"Takes him where?"

"I don't know. He doesn't say much when he comes back."

I grit my teeth together, worried about what Nigel may be doing to him, how he may be hurting him. My mind runs with the thoughts for a long time before I hear the scrape of metal and look up to see Thoa being shoved into the cell.

I'm on my feet and across the room before the door is closed. A hiss sounds between the bars and one of the guards—the woman

I'm going to kill—holds a metal stick that crackles on the tip. Thoa shields me with his body, putting himself between me and the woman. She's lucky my gaze cannot pierce her or she would be dead already.

When the guards are gone, Thoa rests his forehead against mine and says, "Nice rescue."

I laugh and say, "Don't pretend you aren't impressed."

After a moment we separate and move for the bench. I glance to Krew, but he is making a point of not looking at me. Shame burns my cheeks, my lips, everywhere Krew's lips touched; I am glad the cell is dim and no one can see.

We sit in silence for a few minutes before Thoa says, "So, what's the plan?"

Krew laughs and I hear madness there, reaching out for me. I try to ignore it and say, "Our plan fell apart as soon as we got here. Herol betrayed us to the Mayor to save his own skin."

Beside me Thoa sighs, but it is not his voice that returns through the darkness. "I warned you what kind of man I am, Nova. It's your own fault if you didn't believe me."

I'm on my feet, catapulted to the door before I can control myself. Herol is free, outside the bars thanks to his treachery, a wicked smirk on his full lips. His sweaty skin shines like an oil slick. I look into his dark brown eyes and spit at his face before saying, "You spineless piece of dung. You waste of air, weak-willed, mean-spirited dimwit. I hope your eyeballs wither and your manhood falls off."

At some point I hear Rego chuckling behind me and realize I've started yelling at him in Raider. I put my fists at my side and take a breath while I gather myself.

Herol says, "I don't know what you said, but I'm pretty sure I get the meaning. Though I'm not sure I deserve it."

"You...what?" The rage is burning so hot within me I can barely get the words out.

I reach through the bars and grab his jacket lapels. A guard yells from down the hall and I hear them moving towards us. Herol wraps his hands around mine and something jagged presses into my palm. He makes a show of shoving me away just as the guard arrives. The boy looks young, too young to be here, protecting a monster.

"I'm fine," Herol says. "I can handle the little bitch."

The guard raises his brows. "She's a Raider. I hear they're pretty tough."

Herol smirks. "Maybe if she could get out of this cell. But I'll be leaving in an hour, so there's not much time for her to catch up with me even if she did manage to escape."

The guard nods. "Nothing to worry about, sir. There are three guards stationed at each end of the hall, not to mention the dozen patrolling the grounds."

"That's about half of your force, isn't it?" Herol asks as they walk away.

"Yessir," the young man says. "The others are stationed to protect the Mayor."

Their voices fade as they move towards the stairs. I join the others on the bench, cupping the key that Herol slipped me. I count to fifty before I speak, just to make sure no one is within earshot.

When I tell them of the key, Rego says, "He said he was leaving in an hour."

"He's giving us time to escape and find him," Thoa says, puckering his lips in a frown. "Why?"

Krew says, "Because of her."

Thoa's smile is bright even in the dim light. "She has that effect, doesn't she?"

"What are you talking about?" I ask.

"You appeal to our better nature," Krew answers. "Even when we try to fight it."

I don't know how to respond. Rego saves me the trouble by taking the key from my hand and moving to the cell door. He slips it in and turns. I hear the door as it clicks open and in the quiet it is deafening. He retrieves the key and steps back from the door, turning to us.

"Nova, with me. Krew and Thoa, go left."

We follow him into the corridor without question. Rego is the elder among us and I do not doubt him. As we leave the cell, I spare a glance at the others, but I'm not sure which I'm hoping will turn and meet my eyes.

The guards do not hear our approach. I have snapped the neck of the first guard and pounced on a second when Rego signals me to stop. I look at the scared boy in my grasp. He was the young one who came to help Herol. I don't know what it matters. He will surely call for help if I don't kill him now.

Rego reaches out a shaking hand and points at the name scrawled on his uniform. *W. Wyverstone.* I say the name in my head three times before I realize who he is. I spin him around and ask, "Wolfie?"

His face pales. "How do you know my name?"

"Coco. She's a friend."

Tears threaten to drip from the corners of his eyes. "She doesn't have friends. She only has herself."

I shake my head. "Maybe before, but not now. Losing you…"

"*Losing* me?" he asks. "Is that what she told you? My sister sold me so she could party."

"No, that can't be right," I mumble, shaking my head.

"Trust me, it is. I've had six years to think on it."

"Six years? I thought you'd only been missing a few months," I say. I don't know why I think that. Coco never mentioned how long he'd been gone. I trace my mind over the things she has said about Wolfie. She did not lie to me, not outright, but she also did not tell me the truth.

"Doesn't matter," Rego says. "Let's go."

"You'll have to kill me," Wolfie says.

"So dramatic," Rego says in Raider.

He reaches forward and grabs the boy's jaw, squeezing and

pressing upwards. Wolfie tries to struggle, but I'm still holding him and he can't lose my grip. After a few seconds he stops struggling and his full weight presses against me.

I hear footsteps approaching behind us and drop Wolfie on the ground to attack. Thoa and Krew come through the door. Thoa is holding a bloody knife in his hands and there are spatters of it on his face. It is the blood on Krew that makes me stare. His eyes are wide, his hands trembling.

Thoa doesn't seem to notice as he pats him on the back and says, "He did well. We shall make a Raider of him yet."

I step forward and take Krew's hands. His eyes find mine, but I don't see him in there. I say, "Is this your first?"

He nods, his mouth open as blood trickles from where it was split.

"I'm sorry," I say. "I would take it from you if I could."

He nods again, this time saying, "I had to. It was me or him."

Rego is there now, his hand on Krew's cheek. "Doesn't make it easier. Doesn't make it right."

My brows furrow at Rego's words. I've known him most my life, but I never knew he felt this way about such things.

Thoa says, "We pulled their bodies inside and closed the door. We should do the same with these."

He reaches for Wolfie and I say, "Wait! He's not dead." Thoa moves to snap the boy's neck but I grab his hands. "Not this one. He's Coco's brother."

"Who is Coco?"

His question reminds me of the comfort I've had while he's been here. It's all I can do to mutter, "A friend. We need to save him."

I worry that Thoa will argue with me, that he'll tell me we must save ourselves, but I should know better. That's not who Thoa is. Instead, he helps me drag the other two bodies into the cells before hoisting the boy over his shoulder.

It is dusk as we scurry along the sides of buildings, looking for a sign of Herol. I'm certain it has been nearly an hour. Though I'm grateful we haven't yet been discovered, I'm nervous he grew impatient and left without us.

Then I hear the yelling.

We move towards it. Herol is standing a hundred yards from us, one hand holding Mayor Weatherfield by the hair while the other holds a small egg-shaped thing above his head. He yells, "If you shoot me, I will drop this. If I drop this, you'll be unemployed. And also he'll be dead."

There are a dozen guards at least surrounding him in the court-yard. They look between one another as if they aren't sure what to do. I hear Nigel say, "Don't shoot, you morons."

I spot the stout woman in the crowd, the one I promised myself I would kill. Before I know it, the Raider in me takes over. I swipe the dagger from Thoa's hand and dash towards her. I tackle her to the ground and try to pin her arms down, but she is stronger than I thought and manages to flip me off. She grabs my shoulder—the shoulder *she* dislocated—and wrenches as hard as she can. Pain shoots through me, my muscles still tender from the injury. I squirm from her grip and we circle each other, teeth bared like animals.

"Thought I put you in your cage," she growls.

"You should've killed me," I say.

"It wasn't up to me."

I swipe, releasing a stream of blood down her cheek. "Guess you need smarter bosses."

She swings and I grab her arm. I pull it behind her back and lift until I hear the shoulder dislocate. She screams in pain and I relish the sound. I pin her to the ground, pull her hair back, and put the blade to her neck.

"Nova!"

The voice holds me in place. I look up. He's right in front of me. Cornflower eyes. White-blond hair, parted to the side. A whiff of tobacco hits me, knocks me off balance.

"Daddy?"

"Stop this," he says, his voice sending a pang of shame through me. "I raised you better than this."

The words tumble around my mind until at last they shatter. I stare into his eyes as I pull back the stout woman's hair and slice her neck. "You didn't raise me. The Raiders did."

Blood spatters the bottom of his pale pants and I laugh, laugh, laugh.

CHAPTER
SIXTEEN

Rego and Krew drag me from the courtyard. I feel it happening, but I cannot help them. I cannot do anything but laugh and stare at the pale pants of the pale-featured man who was my father.

We're on a small boat flying away from the city before my fit stops. Without my laughter, the silence rings in my ears and threatens to rip my head apart. I search for a familiar face, but find none. They have their backs to me, and rather than draw their attention, I turn to the slender woman steering the ship.

Her eyes dart forward, then to me, again and again. She seems unable to stop. I watch her openly. I don't know her, but there's an uneasiness in me as if I should. Not like the recognition I felt when I saw Rachel again, or the kinship when I saw Coco; this girl is important to me somehow, and I don't know why.

When I stand, her eyes jerk away again. I study her as I approach. Her shoulders are tight, her posture stiff—she is guarding a secret, but not with ease like a practiced liar. She is younger than me by several years. Fifteen, I would guess, maybe sixteen. Freckles dot her cheeks and nose, sprinkle across the top of her forehead. Her hair is a strange color between red and blonde, her eyes the exact color as…

"You're his daughter," I say.

She nods, her cheeks coloring as she gives an awkward smile. "So are you."

Her voice is high and sweet as it rings in my mind like a bell. I can do nothing but stare in wonder at this girl, my sister. She seems so delicate, so fragile. But then I realize she is meant to be a distraction and it has worked.

I spin and drop into a defensive position, but it is only Rego who approaches. His arms are outstretched as if trying to calm a wild thing. "It's okay, Nova-du."

"Rego," I say, "it's *not* okay. Where are the others?"

He tries to embrace me, but I'm all hard edges and will not be comforted. Finally he sighs and says, "Everyone is fine. Krew is underdeck with Wolfie. Thoa and Herol are over there with Nigel and your father."

I follow the wave of his hand and without thought I march towards them. I reach for a weapon, but find none. No matter. I've killed with my hands before.

Herol steps between us but I shove him out of the way. I am free because of him, but there is no love between us. Thoa is next to try to stop me. He grabs my arms but I jerk from his grip and spin past him. He puts his arms around my waist and throws himself backwards. We topple across the deck.

I scrabble for purchase and try to claw myself away from him, but he holds tight. I kick at him and hear him groan, but he won't release me. He flips me over, straddles my body, and pins my arms down.

"Damn it, Nova, listen to me. For once in your life, stop being so stubborn," he growls.

I stare into eyes of blue polished stone. Thoa-gra has returned. He was gone, a gentleman in fine clothes had taken over his muscled form, but now I look upon a Raider again.

I grow still under his grip. "Say what you must. I can wait a moment to kill them."

"Them?" he asks, confused.

"Nigel and my father."

His eyes go wide. "I understand why you'd want to hurt Nigel. But your father saved us."

A cold ball forms in the pit of my stomach. "What are you talking about?"

He releases my hands but doesn't move off me. He points around and says, "This is his ship. He was trying to get the Mayor to let us go when Herol kidnapped him."

"Why?" I ask. "What is he doing here? He's supposed to be dead."

"I don't know the details, but maybe you could talk to him instead of attacking?"

I breathe through my teeth, seething. He won't let me go until I agree, so finally I nod and he climbs to his feet. He reaches a hand to help me up, but once I'm standing he doesn't let go. Part of me enjoys holding his hand like this, but most of me knows he does it in case I try to attack again.

When we stand with the others, I turn to Herol and ignore the others. "I thought you were going to kill him."

Herol's lips quirk up at the corners. "That's the plan."

"Then why is he here?"

"Because I can help you," Nigel says.

He straightens the cuffs of his jacket though his hands are tied with rope. I inspect the bonds, see that they are Rego's knots, and know the Mayor cannot escape them. As quick as a spring, I pull my arm back and suckerpunch him in the face. He stumbles as blood dribbles from his nose.

He sputters, "Are you going to let her treat me like this?"

Thoa shrugs, his shoulder brushing mine. "She didn't kill you. That's the most I can get from her."

"Neither did I," Herol says, "but I really want to. You'd better make yourself worth saving."

Nigel turns to each of us in turn, eyes widening as he sees the unbridled hatred on each of our faces. He says, "I can lead you to the children. I kept records."

"I've seen your records," I say. "They were senseless."

He shakes his head and says, "Not to me. I made them vague in case someone else saw them, but I know what they mean."

"And where are these records?" Herol asks.

"Still in your office? They won't do you much good there," I say.

He pales and tries to take a step back, but Herol grabs his arms and pulls him forward. "You've got three seconds to figure something out, Mayor, or I'm tossing you off the ship."

"He'll do it," Thoa says, raising a brow. "Trust me."

Herol pushes Nigel back a step. And a second. Nigel squeals, "Maps. I can draw maps to show you where they are."

Herol grabs the front of Nigel's shirt and for a moment I think he's going to drop him. But he doesn't. He pulls him back on the deck and shoves him towards the center. Herol jabs a finger in his face and says, "If I think you're lying or holding back from us, I will scatter your body parts from here to the coast."

I turn my attention to my father. "Why are you here?"

He smiles uncomfortably. "Sweetie, why don't we go to the cabin and talk about this privately?"

"You can speak freely here, Ledwin. These people are my friends, my family. Unlike you, I don't keep secrets from family."

He grits his teeth. After a moment he looks past me to the others and dips his head. "My name is Ledwin Kennedy. I am Nova's father."

I roll my eyes and say, "I think they've gathered that."

"All these years, I thought my daughter was dead," he continues, ignoring me. "I didn't discover the truth until recently. I came to find her as soon as I could, tracking her movements with slight complications. When I reached Gearhaven, I discovered she was a prisoner and I attempted to negotiate her release with Mayor Weatherfield. That's when you arrived," he says, waving a hand at Herol.

Herol says, "You were chummy with the Mayor, that's all I saw. Having drinks and smiling."

"Of course," Ledwin says, chuckling as if his actions were the most natural in the world. "Do you think he would just *give* her to me? No. I was buying my daughter's freedom. Or at least, I was trying to."

Rego says, "So you followed them outside? Why not take the opportunity to go find Nova and free her yourself?"

Ledwin frowns. "I'm not a fighter, good sir. I'm a businessman, a negotiator. I know where my strengths are. I was hoping to convince your man to release the Mayor and therefore win his favor."

"I heard you," I whisper. "This morning, when I first woke up."

Ledwin nods. "I had him bring you to us so I could make sure you were alright."

I bite the inside of my cheek. His words sound true, but I don't know for sure. This man is a stranger and as he said, his strengths are in convincing others. I say, "I will let you live, for now. At least until I know what you're really doing here."

He reaches over to stroke my cheek and I catch sight of a strange metal bracelet on his wrist. It's darker than Krew's silver one, but just as thin and with the same glowing bump on one side.

"I'm here for you, Nova. It's time I take you home."

―――――――

ECHOES OF LEDWIN'S WORDS WHIP THROUGH MY MIND AT THE MOST unexpected times: when I lean on Rego's shoulder like we did by the fire each night at the Raider's camp, when I watch the stars and listen to Krew name each one, when I steal glances at my new sister, Ivy, when jealousy rears up at her easy smile.

Home. What does the word even mean, to me, to him? Home isn't the house in my memories where Rachel and I hid under floorboards from...someone. It isn't the place where I lived with my parents, the place I can't see when I try to remember, the place tucked in the corner of my mind where the nightmares lurk, where the teeth gnash at my throat.

Home is a night on a bed of heather after catching my prey. Home is the crook of Rego's arm after a nightmare, the salty smell of his tanned skin, his dry hand on my cheek. Home is the roasting pit in the middle of our traveling tents, Raider song filling my mind, heart, and soul. The forest is home, and the lake is home, and the desert is home—though I may never see the same place twice.

This home he speaks of is not in my heart, for my heart is full and overflowing with Raiders and there's room for nothing else.

We take Wolfie to Vern's farm. Coco, Rachel, and most of the others are gone in search of Coghelm and the missing children, but there are a few faces I know. Dino is here, and Edith-Ann, alongside her father, Jasper. Rego tenses at the sight of him as we walk towards Vern and Abigail's farmhouse.

Aunt Abby is ecstatic to see Wolfie, fawning over him with slender fingers brushing against his dark hair, smiling when he pushes her hand away and storms out the farmhouse, her eyes drinking him in as she watches him walk away.

"He's been gone a long while," she says, dismissing the pity in our tones when we try to console her. "He'll come around."

She prepares a celebration dinner that has no rival. She has Thoa slaughter a fat pig and she prepares the meat half a dozen ways. There are cheeses and nuts, fruit, vegetables, creamed soups, and piping hot bread drenched in honey or dipped in fruit jams or coated in salt and seeds. My favorite is a stew with roasted tomatoes and onions and strange seasoning that makes me feel cozy and adventurous at the same time.

Wolfie sits at the end of the table in silence, his plate full and untouched.

After dinner I follow the fence posts away from the farm, away from my father and sister as they huddle together all smiles and comfort, away from Thoa and Krew as they smoke pipes on the front porch and fill the evening air with smoke and friendship, away from the candlelight in the upstairs window where Jasper tells Rego all the secrets meant just for him. I walk until the sun has settled behind mountains in the distance and the sky has purpled like a bruised cheek.

I sit against a fence post and pull my knees to my chest. The tears begin to fall before I realize that's what is happening. There is sadness in me, behind the anger and the fierceness the Raiders taught me. I am a girl, small and scared and alone, wondering why my family never looked for me. Rachel, and now my father, appear after all these years. They both thought I was dead, they say. Did they try to find me? Did they hurt like I hurt when I thought they were dead?

My mind runs wild with scenarios of what could've happened, how life might've been, if I'd stayed with them. I wouldn't have been the outcast, the bad luck charm, of the Raiders. I wouldn't have learned to fight, or hunt, or kill. I would've grown up with a sister—a sister!—and maybe my smiles would come as easily as hers.

I sob, open-mouthed and ugly, drooling against my legs, until there's nothing left but a hollow feeling and a stitch in my side. I wipe my hands over my face and take a few deep breaths, then stand and turn back towards the farm.

In the distance, beyond the jagged mountains barely visible against the black sky, there's a column of light. I didn't notice it when we were here before, or as we traveled back to bring Wolfie home, but now I can look at nothing else. It travels into the sky, shifting from crimson at its base to a barely-there pink at the top before it disappears into nothing.

The light disappears when I'm walking up the drive to the farmhouse. I have no idea what it is, but there's no one around to ask. The yard and porch are empty, and I don't feel like facing a bunch of questions inside, so instead I pass the house and go around back where my father's ship is parked. I climb aboard and find a place out of the way to watch the stars until dreams overtake me.

I KNOW I'M DREAMING WHEN I SEE HER FACE. GREEN EYES AND AUBURN hair to match my own, pale skin and freckles like Aunt Rachel, but her smile has no equal. My mother hums a lullaby as she tucks me under a lavender blanket. Faint traces of her perfume linger around me and I breathe them deep, trying to hold the bergamot and sandalwood inside me.

"You're so angry," she whispers, tracing slender fingers along my cheek.

I nod. "They abandoned me."

She sighs, shakes her head. "No, darling, not truly. Not in their hearts."

"How would you know?" I ask. "You're dead."

She takes on a strange expression, like I've just reminded her of something she forgot. Blood forms on her temple, matting into her hair and trickling down her face.

"Oh, Mom, I'm sorry," I say. But it's too late. She slumps onto the bed. Her eyes turn glassy as bright red blood clings to her perfect white teeth.

I WAKE WITH A START. NOT SCREAMING THIS TIME, NOT TERRIFIED. JUST sad. It isn't the dream that has terrorized my nights for years. This was different, almost hopeful in comparison. It's been a long time since I've seen her. I've stolen glances in my memories of her eyes, her hair falling around her face as she turns, the purse of her lips. She was beautiful.

I sit up and look towards the horizon. The world's edge is tinged pink, the night's darkness passing from black to purple, purple to blue. I turn to exit the ship only to find Thoa sleeping nearby. His lips are parted slightly and a whistle is barely sounding between his teeth. His recently shorn hair is fanned out behind him, a dark halo around his tanned face. I stare at him, relishing this unhindered look, unafraid he will catch me as I take in all the ways he is beautiful.

His muscled chest rises and falls, the tattoos upon it dancing a steady rhythm. My fingers itch with the need to trace the black swirls that color his body, but I refrain. Barely. Instead I look to the puckered scar along his side and wonder how he got it. Or the marred shoulder that looks like it was bit by a massive beast. Or the tiny row of scratches above his brow that shine silver when his skin darkens in the hot season.

I wonder if I love him.

I leave the ship and the man I might love and head to the farmhouse. There are people walking towards the barn and they smile and nod to me. I smile in return and wonder if perhaps their kindness has brought a bit of ease to me after all.

Abby has already filled the farmhouse with the smell of fried meat and eggs. She stands in the kitchen with her braids tied up and a smear of flour across her forehead. I watch her for a moment, the graceful way she moves through her domain as she serves those around her, and I wonder if anyone notices all the things she does. She is a woman who lives in the quiet places between words and deeds, magnificent in her simplicity.

She catches me staring and smiles, motions me to the table. I sit and eat, relishing the warm bread and melted butter on my tongue. After today, I may never have this luxury again.

The others join the table as they rise: Ledwin and Ivy, followed by Jasper, Edith-Ann, and Rego, who somehow looks ten years younger and smiles in a way I've never seen before. Krew and Wolfie enter, their voices low and fast, and I worry at the expression on Krew's face. Finally Herol joins us, dragging Nigel by the ropes he's tied around his wrists.

"Can't you untie him?" Abby asks, her kindness bleeding through. "At least to let him eat."

Herol scowls. "He's lucky I'm letting him sit here at all, instead of putting him out with the animals like he should be."

"He didn't hurt those kids," Wolfie snarls.

"You think you get a say in this, boy?" Herol asks.

"I think I'm the only one here who *was* a child Nigel rescued. So yeah, I get a say."

Herol scoffs, "Rescued? He's selling children!"

"So what if he makes a little profit when he finds a place for them?" Wolfie says. "He's giving them a life beyond what they would've had."

"Is that what you think he did for you?" Abby asks.

Everyone falls silent when they see the pained look on her face. Even Herol presses his lips together and has the decency to look embarrassed. Then Wolfie says, "It's what I know he did for me."

"How can you say that?" she asks. "Your father—"

"My father was a drunk, Abby. And after mom died, it just got worse. Coco was seventeen and dealing with things her own way. I blamed her for a long time, but now I just see what she did for what it was—a teenager rebelling the only way she knew how. Being taken from Grimwall was the best thing that could've happened to me."

Abby flees from the kitchen. None of us try to stop her. We know there is truth in Wolfie's words, even if they hurt, and she needs time to see that for herself.

Ivy says, "That wasn't very nice."

Wolfie shrugs indifferently, but I can see on his face that he regrets hurting Abby. He says, "Doesn't matter. I'm not staying here anyway."

"No?" I ask, surprise coloring my voice.

He shakes his head. "I'm going with you."

"No, you're not," I say. "We brought you home for your sister. You're not abandoning her before she even gets a chance to see you."

"She *sold* me. That makes it pretty clear that she doesn't want to see me."

And then it hits me. He feels the same abandonment as I do. My family didn't sell me, but in my head they gave up on me all the same. Maybe they're as sorry as Coco is. I say, "She was young and stupid. But she regrets it. She's been risking her life searching for you."

"Says you. How do I know you're not making it up?"

"It's true," Nigel says. His eyes flick to me for a second before fixing on Wolfie. "I've had several run-ins with your sister, though I don't believe she's aware that I know who she is. She's raided ships, factories, and even robbed people in my employ as they carried information between cities. I didn't know who she was looking for or I would've traded you for her silence long ago."

"Wolfie, you have a chance for a good life here with your family. Don't let it go because of your pride," I say.

I look up and meet my father's eyes. His eyes crinkle as he gives me the smallest of smiles. I nod to him before taking my leave from the table. The interaction is too close, too familiar, and I'm not fully ready to accept my own advice. Instead I make my way outside to wait for departure. I don't know where I'll end up, but I know it's time to go with him, to figure out this puzzle of my life, to leave this place as I've left all other places that tugged my heart and felt like home.

CHAPTER
SEVENTEEN

I watch Abby and Wolfie grow smaller as we rise into the air. She smiles and waves, he sneers with arms folded. I don't know what will become of them, but I hope for good things. Like me, Wolfie has been hurt by the absence of his family. Like me, he doesn't know how to find his way back to them.

Herol and Nigel stand off to the side of the house away from the others. I'm surprised Herol hasn't killed him yet. His desire for information, for a chance to save more children, seems to outweigh his desire for vengeance. I wonder if he lost a daughter or son to the scheming mayor, but I do not ask. Someday I will return to see what became of them, how many they saved, and perhaps then I will learn why this crusade weighs so heavy on his heart.

I try not to look at the others standing alongside them. My heart hurts even thinking of leaving Rego behind. But he chose to stay with Jasper and Edith-Ann.

"I don't understand. He abandoned you and you're going to forgive him and stay with him?" I asked him as we stood in the grass by the ship.

"You don't have to understand," he said, patting my shoulder.

"There are things you do not know, reasons shared between us. I understand, and that's what matters."

"But Rego—"

"No, Little Star. I know you care for me just as I care for you. You have been a daughter to me, a comfort when no one else could console me. You were at my side in my darkest days, bringing light to my world. And though I love you, you will not change my mind about this. Trust me and be happy for me."

I nodded. "As you wish."

He placed his hands on either side of my face and pressed his lips against my forehead. He whispered, "I will see you again. The Raider's heart binds us, and with it, our destinies intertwine."

I step away from the railing, unable to bear the thought of seeing him for the last time. Perhaps he is right and we will see each other again, but I worry that those words were meant to comfort me and nothing more.

We fly above mountains. They're carpeted in green, swathes of leaves reaching skyward. I like looking at the trees from this height. They don't appear to be the towering things they are from the ground. Instead, they are old men facing skyward, arms upturned in worship to the sun. They are children at play, warrior-women hunting. They are one thing and a hundred things and I can see each one.

The air is cool here. Ivy brings a blanket and we sit under it, side by side, sisters. We do not speak. I fear my savagery might frighten her away, so I do my best to sit still and silent, watching the land pass beneath us while I sneak glances at her face.

She has a lovely face. It is mine and not-mine at the same time. When I look—really look, not these stolen seconds—traces of my father and myself are evident. The slope of her nose, the jut of her chin, the spray of freckles across her cheeks.

I wonder what parts of her mother are here, lingering within my sight without me noticing. Maybe it's the way she tiptoes around like she's afraid her presence will break the world. I dare not think on that too long. Her mother is proof that my father loved someone else after my mother died, as if his world didn't fall apart like mine did. Thinking of her mother makes my stomach rise into my chest and jealousy course through my veins.

I do not want this to be the foundation of our relationship.

When Ivy departs from my side, she does it with a smile. She leaves the blanket with me and walks across the deck towards our father. He stands tall in the afternoon sun, his fair hair shimmering as the wind rakes through it. He is a handsome man, though his features are all sharp edges, rigid. His cheekbones look as if they would cut the hand that dared touch them.

Beyond them Thoa stands at the helm, staring off into the land ahead. I haven't spoken to him since this morning, since I stared at him sleeping and let my mind wander to a place I swore I would never go. Those I love have a tendency to disappear; though some have returned to me these last few weeks, more still are gone, never to return.

I swore to never love, to never lose myself to the whimsy of the heart. I didn't realize that's what my tears were swearing each night when I cried myself to sleep, but now I see it, now I know. It's why I've never considered choosing a mate at solstice. It's why I turned from Thoa when he chose me.

And yet…

Then there is the matter of Krew. In the woods, I did not try to stop him. I liked it. The feel of his fingertips trailing down my skin, the fevered pace his lips fell against me, as if he wanted to get as many kisses as possible before the moment passed. There was intensity, longing, and passion—things I never expected to find.

But we haven't discussed it. I don't know if it meant anything, if *I* mean anything to him, and part of me is afraid to ask. Some things are better left unanswered.

I shake my head to chase away the thought. I cannot dwell on maybes and what ifs. Our goal now is getting to the City of Trials, returning Krew to his home. Though honestly, I no longer

CITY OF TRIALS   149

remember our reasons. There was an urgency when we were with the Raiders, but it was more to save his life than anything else. Now that we're finally on the path again, my mind churns up questions.

Who is he? Where is he from? Why was he standing alone that night I first found him? Why is everyone afraid of him? And the newest question, the one that bothers me most of all: *Why does my father have the same bracelet?*

It isn't the sight of the city that stirs me from my slumber, it's the sound. I hear voices, more than I thought were in the world over, and they're chanting something. I rise from where I'd been sleeping and move to the front of the ship. Thoa is there, staring off into the night, and I step beside him while wiping sleep from my eyes.

"What's going on?" I ask.

He shakes his head. "Not sure."

I follow his eyes to the bright spot glowing against the dark sky. I can make out the profile of the city spanning out in the distance, but I can't see any details. A cheer breaks out and a burst of light illuminates the outline of a massive tower. From the top of the tower, a crimson column of light knifes through the sky.

"I've seen that before," I say. "Last night. What does it mean?"

"It means the players died."

Thoa and I both turn as Krew steps next to me. There's a hardness to his face that looks out of place. He stares ahead, not meeting my gaze, and I worry what his eyes are seeing when he looks at the city.

"What players?" Thoa asks.

"See the tower?" Krew asks, pointing at the shadow looming over the city. "There are eight levels, each more dangerous than the last. People compete through the levels to reach the top."

"What's at the top?" I ask.

"A treasure of some sort?" Thoa wonders as he rubs the stubble on his face.

Krew nods. "You could say that. It's certainly life-changing."

"Have you been through the tower?" I ask.

"No," he says, a look of amusement crossing his face. "The tower is for those far braver than I am. But I've watched the game many times."

"It's barbarism," Ivy says.

The sound of her voice makes me jump. I've heard it soft and sweet, I've heard it whispering kindnesses, but I have not heard her like this. She sounds...like me.

"How so?" Thoa asks.

She huffs, "Those poor people are forced to fight to the death for our entertainment. What do they get in return? Some scraps of food and a few gold pieces, if they're lucky."

"They get hope," Krew says. He folds his arms across his chest as if daring her to contradict him.

She does. "Hope is for fools."

"I wouldn't expect that view coming from you," Krew says. "Considering..."

"Considering what?" Ivy asks. She raises her brows, giving her own dare.

Krew purses his lips and looks from her to me, then back. "Considering who your father is."

"My father and I disagree about the games. He loves them."

Krew nods. "I know. Because they destroy hope as easily as they give it, and that's your father's deepest desire."

"You don't know him as well as you think," Ivy spits.

"How do you know him at all?" I cut in.

They look at each other and both press their lips tight. I say, "No, you're not doing this to me again. I've let you keep me in the dark all this time because there were other things to focus on. Not anymore."

Krew sighs and says, "It's probably best if you don't know."

"Best for who?" Ledwin says. He saunters towards us, sliding black gloves over pale hands. "Tell her the truth about why you're here."

"I could say the same to you," Krew growls.

"Or maybe you could both tell me," I say.

After a moment, my father says, "Do you remember the old stories your mother used to tell you about Zappho Curiosity?"

I nod. I don't remember my mother telling me, but I do remember Rachel whispering them to me after I'd had a nightmare. I say, "He came from the sky to save the world."

"Right," Ledwin says. "What if I told you those stories were true? Or at least they're based in truth."

I roll my eyes. "You want me to believe there are gods in the sky who watch us and bet for or against our little lives?"

He says, "Not gods, per se. They're just people, really."

My mouth opens to respond but no words come out. I look from him to Ivy, Ivy to Krew, and back to my father. None of them are laughing, or even smiling. "You're serious."

They all nod. Krew says, "That's where I'm from. I came down because I was curious about this world. I wanted to see what it was like."

"So you popped down for a stroll in the grasslands?"

He winces. "It was more than that, Nova. I've spent my life seeing the world through a screen, but never truly understanding it. Can you imagine never feeling the wind on your face, never breathing fresh air? This place is more than I ever imagined it could be. It's magic."

"But you're going back?"

Krew presses his lips into a thin line. "That's the plan."

"You let us bring you here, knowing we were sending you away from this world."

He nods. "There was never any doubt that I'd end up back on the station, even if I wanted to stay."

My gaze drops from his eyes, from the sadness there, and I find myself staring at the red light glowing against his skin. "And that bracelet you wear?"

"It's used to travel between the sky and the ground, and it can be used as a way for the people in the sky to keep track of me."

"Except after you took an illegal trip to the ground, you damaged your tracker so we couldn't bring you home," Ledwin says.

Krew nods. "I couldn't experience the world if you zapped me back up after a minute."

"A minute," Ivy scoffs. "I had your location pinpointed in eight seconds."

Krew sneers. "Well aren't you special? But it still takes at least sixty seconds for a transport to read a signal and complete a transfer. So you can find me as fast as you want and it still won't do any good if you can't get a lock."

"What the hell are you people talking about?" Thoa asks.

Ledwin flicks his hand in Krew's direction and says, "This asshole was my student. I taught him everything I know about tracking and retrieving anyone who takes unauthorized trips to the ground. He used the information against us and I had to come down here to chase after him."

"And you brought the Chasseur," Krew sneers.

"Of course," Ledwin says. "They must be included in security matters. It's not like you gave me much choice."

Krew rolls his eyes. "Led, you know me. Did you really think I would come down here to cause trouble? So much so that you included those hooligans?"

My father presses his lips together. His pale eyes take on a sadness when he says, "I didn't know what you were doing. All I knew was that you betrayed me."

"It wasn't my intention," Krew says. "I wasn't trying to hurt you. I just needed to see it for myself."

"You see it every day," Ivy says.

Krew waves his hands and says, "On screens. Through cameras. Following whoever is in favor with the Règle and her companions."

"What's wrong with the Règle's channel? She chooses fascinating characters to follow," Ivy says.

"Because it's wrong!" Krew yells. "The grounders are *people* with hopes and dreams and love. They shouldn't be treated like sitcoms of old."

They argue another moment, but their words are strange and I don't comprehend much of what they say. Finally I interrupt and say, "I don't understand your life in the stars, but it sounds as if you came here to study us." Anger gnashes within me and I bite out, "Are you satisfied with what you've learned?"

Krew looks at me as if I've wounded him, but I don't care. I am wounded by the knowledge of how his people think of us. How many years has he lived above our world and watched us in secret? How long have the star-people disregarded our plights? This revelation has made clear their lack of compassion and my anger will not be quelled.

"Answer me," I growl.

He straightens and says, "Yes. I have learned more in these few weeks than in a lifetime watching from above."

"And broken our laws in the process," my father says.

"I don't care about your laws," I spit.

"They're your laws, too. You are a citizen of Vaisseau."

I sneer at him. "I will never be part of that world."

Ledwin squints his eyes at me, confused. "Where do you think we are going?"

I jerk back as if slapped. "To take Krew to the City of Trials."

My father nods. "And for us to go home."

"No," I say, shaking my head.

"Nova," he says, "if you think I'm going to let you go after all these years, you're crazy. I just got you back."

"I am willing to travel with you, to get to know you. I am

willing to stay in the city longer to spend time with you. But then I will return to the Raiders."

"The Raiders?" he asks, his voice going high.

"They are my family."

"But they're killers, savages," Ivy says. "How can you want to go back after the way they've treated you--"

"Ivy," Ledwin scolds, cutting her off.

It takes a moment for me to realize what she said. I stare at her for a second as the words sink in and then I say, "How long have you known I was alive?"

Father sputters, "I just found out. I swear it."

I'm still looking at Ivy. She isn't the practiced liar my father is. She dares to glance up at me and red splotches creep up her neck. I ask, "Months? Years?"

She swallows hard at my question and my stomach drops. I was right. They really didn't come looking for me.

"You have to understand," Ledwin says, "we couldn't just pop down here to get you. There are laws about interfering. We had to be sure it was really you."

The words bubble up and tumble out before I can stop them. "How long did you watch me crying myself to sleep, or waking screaming because of nightmares? How many times did you see me scraping the ground looking for bugs to eat when the hunting grounds gave us no food? How long were you content to leave your daughter without a real family?"

"Three years," Krew says.

I spin to him. "What do you know of it?"

"I'm the one who found you," he says. "Work was slow, no unauthorized trips, so I took an extra gig scouting for a program director. I was tasked with finding people the general public might want to watch."

I run my hands over my head and sigh. "What does that mean?"

"There are cameras everywhere, Nova. They're disguised as

moths and bugs, usually. They fly around, follow people, record them. Then the directors take the footage and compile it into something the people up there want to watch."

"Like a play?" Thoa asks. He steps closer to me, separating us from them.

Krew nods. "But instead of actors and scripts, they use real people and whatever is happening to them. Anyone on this planet can be viewed at any time, anywhere."

"And you're okay with that?" I ask.

"No," he says. "At least, not anymore. I didn't understand, before. Some moments should be reserved for those involved and no one else."

Ledwin says, "None of this matters. The important part is that now that we're together, we don't have to be separated again. We can apply for immigration and you can live with me until we get you housing."

I blink at him momentarily before turning and walking below deck. He doesn't understand that I have no desire to go with him, and I can't understand why he is still trying to fix this. These years apart have made us different people. There is no amount of "fixing" that will bring us back together.

CHAPTER
EIGHTEEN

I sit on a crate and try to stop my head from spinning with everything I've learned. After a few minutes, Thoa comes down the steps. He stands at the edge of the space, his eyes flickering around as if he isn't sure he should be there.

"What is it, Thoa-gra?" I ask. I am not upset with him, but I hear the exasperation in my tone. He doesn't seem to notice as he steps towards me. His eyes still dance from surface to surface as if he's searching for something that isn't there.

When he's only inches from me he asks, "Do you trust me?"

I nod. "Of course. You're the only one I do trust right now."

He looks into my eyes and says, "I think you should go with them."

"What?" I ask. I jump from the crate and close the gap between us. "Why would I do that?"

He says, "It sounds like a great opportunity. You should take it and be grateful."

My hands start shaking at my sides, but then his eyes glance away from me again. In the corner of my vision there's a gnat buzzing around and I realize we are being watched. Or at least, we might be. Everything is in question, now that we know the truth. And if they are watching, Thoa is playing to the audience.

I take a deep breath and ask, "You really think so?"

His eyes dart back to me, gauging my words. I will myself to convey that I understand what he's doing, though all I have to give are false words and secret looks.

"It is for the best." He put his arms around me and pulls me close. "But I will miss you."

I can barely hear his whisper over the hammering in my heart at his closeness. "We will find a way to defeat them and end all of this."

He releases me and takes a step back, but I grab his arm and pull him back to me. I push myself onto my tiptoes and press my lips to his. At first I think I'm doing it for the cameras, to give them a show, someone to root for. We can play their star-crossed lovers until we find a way to end them.

But this is more than just playing a role for the people above. I want this for me, too.

His body goes rigid against me, but after a second he wraps his arms around me again and returns my kiss in earnest. He presses his mouth against me greedily; he is gentle in how he holds me to him, but there is hunger on his lips as he whispers my name into my hair, as he presses his hand against the small of my back. He tastes of salt and mint and hope.

This is what we could've had, if I had not turned my back on him all those nights ago. If I'd dared consider him for who he was, not for what the Raiders had made him into. But I didn't know, didn't want to see. I wasn't brave enough. But Thoa, he's always been brave enough for both of us. As I stand here pressed against him, I try to soak up some of that bravery for what's to come. If I am to go to the stars, I will have to say goodbye to him and everything that could have been.

Too soon he pries himself from my arms. Almost as if he knows my thoughts, he gives me a sad, doleful look with his strange blue eyes. He kisses my forehead and leaves without another word.

It is morning when I make my way above deck. Ledwin stands on one end of the ship, Krew on the other. I have no desire to speak with either of them, but I choose the one who has hurt me least.

Krew doesn't look at me when I step up beside him. We spend a quarter of an hour in silence, watching the lines of ships slowly make their way into the city. There are three lines of vessels on this side of the city waiting to enter the massive circles at the top of the city walls. I watch the ship ahead of us go through, amazed by the size of it all.

From a distance, the City of Trials didn't look any more impressive than the floating cities of Aeroport and Gearhaven. But next to it, I can see how enormous it really is. The boat ahead of us is easily twice the size of my father's cruiser, and as I glance around at others even larger. A brightly colored pleasure boat sails past our left, a steel-gray cargo vessel on our right. The entry port accommodates all.

We crawl to a stop at the edge of the entry. My eyes bulge at the thin man in a green jacket who rises into the air to meet us. He is standing on a flat disc with glowing lights along the bottom. His keen brown eyes meet mine and he says, "State your name and business in the city."

I flounder for a moment before my father steps alongside me. "I'm Ledwin Kennedy, the owner of this ship." He holds up his wrist to display his bracelet and says, "I'm returning home."

The man's eyes widen slowly as he jabs his finger along the rectangular panel in his hand. After a few seconds he nods and says, "Thank you Mr. Kennedy. Enjoy your time in the city and have a pleasant return home."

He lifts away from the ship on his disc and my father marches away from us. A moment later we lurch forward. I ask, "What was that about?"

Krew shrugs. "They keep an eye on who enters the city."

"Why?" I ask. "They don't want the wrong kind of people fighting to their deaths?"

Krew purses his lips. "How long do you plan to be mad at me over this?"

"I haven't decided yet."

He sighs. "What would you have done?"

I bite my lip, unsure of the answer, but unwilling to admit it.

"You know, I was here less than a day when you caught me? I was coming to look for you and instead you captured me, tied me up, and took me to the Raiders."

"Why were you looking for me?" I ask.

He hooks a thumb over his shoulder. "For Led. I thought it would make him happy."

I shake my head. "He knew I was alive for three years, Krew. He didn't care. He still doesn't."

"He does," Krew says. "He might not do a great job of showing it, but I know he cares."

"Why didn't you tell me any of this before?" I ask, changing the subject.

"Would you have believed me?" he shrugs.

"Maybe."

Krew laughs. "You know that's a lie. There was too much going on. The Raiders wanted me dead, then the pirates captured us, all the drama at Aeroport with Thoa and the kids—it was all too much to add this to your plate."

"There was time," I insist. "What about in the woods that day?"

A smile tips up the corners of his lips. When his eyes meet mine, a blush creeps up my neck. He says, "I had other things on my mind that day."

"Krew—"

"Nova," he interrupts. "By that point I was afraid to tell you. I'd started to develop feelings for you and I knew the truth would ruin things."

I stand there a moment, staring at his mouth because I can't meet his eyes. *Feelings*. What does that even mean?

After too long I say, "I'm sorry. I don't know what I'm feeling."

"Because of all this?" he asks, waving his hand around. "Or because of Thoa?"

It's a fair question, but the answer is more complicated than I know how to explain. I say, "Both."

He nods, as if he already knew. "He is a good man."

"So are you," I whisper.

He smiles, but it is not genuine. "I'm really not." He turns away from me, stares off into the city. "But when I'm with you, I think maybe I could be."

We drift into silence. It is neither comfortable nor awkward— it's just still. I distract myself from Krew's words by staring at the massive city spread out before us. The city itself is an oval made of stone, with gigantic arches along the top for ships to pass through and dock. Above the arches, colossal guns are set into the stone, swiveling back and forth as they search for an unknown threat. I wonder what other defenses this fortress might have.

The upper portion of the walls curve up and inward, but they are not made of the same stone as the rest. Instead we stare at sky through stained glass that paints the city a myriad of color. The tower in the center of the city is monumental, reaching up through the glass above and taking up at least a third of the ground below. People swirl around it like a rock parting a stream. Though I can't make out the details of what's happening all those floors below, I can see the river of people flowing through, their voices an accidental song as they yell and chatter and laugh.

From the opposite end of the cruiser, Ledwin curves us towards a harbor on our right. We dock above a faded red and blue carrier. Krew points to a green square on the wall with a number painted on it. "Remember the number and color, not what's around us. Ships are in and out, but the sign doesn't change."

"Why do I need to remember it?" I ask.

"In case you get lost."

Ivy steps up beside us. "She won't. We're going straight home."

"What?" I ask, my eyes going wide. "We're not going to explore the city?"

She makes a face like she just sucked on a lemon. "Why would we? There's much better stuff to see once we're off-world."

"If I'm going to leave the planet, can't I at least spend the last of my time enjoying this?" I ask. "Besides, aren't you at all curious about this place?"

Ivy bites her lip and I can see the war within her. She wants to explore, but she's afraid of Ledwin's wrath. She says, "Even if I was curious, which I'm not, there's too much to consider. We're not supposed to interfere on this world."

"Ivy, come on. It won't take long to walk through a few rows and check out some vendors. How much harm can we really do?"

She turns her head and stares at our father. She whispers, "He will be so mad."

"He doesn't need to know," I whisper back. "It'll be our first sister-secret."

She turns back to me and smiles. "I've always wanted a sister."

"Me too. I thought it was impossible."

She nods. "We'd need to be gone before dad finishes his business. As long as we're home when he gets there, that's all that matters."

I smile, but shush her when Ledwin approaches. There's a fury on his face I haven't seen before. He growls, "Where is he?"

"Who?" Krew asks as he puts himself between me and my father.

I'm surprised by this protective gesture. It's misplaced, as I could kill my father six ways right now without a weapon. Still, it's a small kindness.

"Don't play games with me," he says.

Ivy's eyebrows scrunch together and she asks, "Father, what are you talking about?"

"The Raider is gone."

"Thoa?" I ask.

Ledwin watches me for a moment, weighing my reaction. He must determine that I really am as surprised as he is, because he softens a bit before saying, "I went below deck to give him his options only to discover his absence."

"His options?" I ask.

Ledwin nods. "Normally I would sell him to the highest bidder, let him be a pawn in their bid for the tower, but I thought there might be more to him than that. Clearly I misjudged him."

I take a deep breath and force down my fury. I want to rail against this monster for the casual way he speaks of human life, of selling people for profit. He's as bad as the child-traders. But after my conversation with Thoa, I know that I need to go along with him. I ask, "Can't he just go with us?"

I look from Ledwin to Ivy, then to Krew, but none will meet my gaze.

Finally, Krew says, "The only way a grounder can get to Vaisseau is through the tower. He would have to win the trials to be allowed in."

"But he doesn't know that," I say.

Krew winces. "He does. I *may* have let it slip."

Ledwin rolls his eyes. "You sent him off to compete. Why? He would've been out of your way in a matter of hours without you doing that."

"I didn't know he'd run off to enter the trials. I was trying to be kind and give him a chance to say goodbye to Nova."

"Instead he's gone to enter the games," I say. "How are his chances? Do a lot of people win?"

"A hundred or so since the trials were invented," Krew says.

"When was that?" I ask.

He winces. "A couple hundred years ago."

My heart ricochets through my chest and pressure squeezes the air from my lungs. I know Thoa. He's looking for a way to go with me to Vaisseau and if the trials are the only way, that's where he'll be.

And if he went to the trials…

"He's going to die," I whisper.

Ledwin nods. "Pity, really. I thought he was smarter than that."

"Dad," Ivy chides. "He's in love."

Her words take a moment to sink in. He's risking his life for me. Because he loves me.

I take a deep breath and gather my thoughts. Thoa is brave. He is strong and resourceful. And he *is* smart. He will survive this. He has to.

Because there is no longer any doubt that I love him, too.

CHAPTER
NINETEEN

I expect a war with Ledwin when I tell him I want to find Thoa instead of going up to whatever world is waiting for me in space. But there's no fight from him. Instead, he agrees we should look for him while he finishes up whatever business he has. I find myself smiling at him, wondering if I've misjudged him, but then I see the guards, the Chasseur.

There are four of them standing side-by-side along the wall, tallest to shortest. Each has a shaved head and wears a tight red jumpsuit, just as Herol saw them in the field on our way back to Gearhaven. But Herol didn't mention the tattoos. They're stark against their scalps, strange swirls and patterns that stretch a couple inches above their ears. Patterns that seem familiar to me somehow.

Ivy greets a short mazulla guard with a peck on the cheek. They're cute, with dark, deep-set eyes, full lips, and dimples you could drive a boat into. They look to be about sixteen, and I wonder how they got mixed up with my father.

The female Chasseur beside them is watching Ivy from the corner of her eye. I doubt Ivy or her companion realizes the other girl is in love with Ivy. Probably not. But then Ivy leans over and kisses the other girl, too.

"Ivy," Ledwin scolds. "Leave them alone while they're working."

"Sorry," she says as she skips back to me.

Ledwin takes the two guards Ivy kissed and the other two follow us. Krew, Ivy, and I descend the steps and turn onto one of the market streets, the Chasseur falling in line behind us.

I elbow and whisper, "Who did you just kiss?"

"My loves," she says. "Timara and Jex."

"It is okay in your world to love both at once?" I ask.

"We do not restrict ourselves to one lover. I mean, you can if you choose to, or you can not take one at all." She looks at me with furrowed brows. "I thought the Raiders were more fluid in their perception of sexuality and gender?"

"We are. Raiders recognize all genders, all sexualities. But in practice, we only take new lovers on the solstice," I answer. "If we are mated we remain true to them until it is time to part."

Ivy nods. "So, short-term monogamy?"

"Not always short-term. Some stay mated for years, renewing their vows to one another at each solstice."

"What happens if you aren't mated?"

I shrug. "Most of the unmated are alone for a reason and do nothing to change that, though some still enact their basic needs with others who desire it."

"Does it bother you that we don't live like that?"

I watch my feet for a moment as we walk. I've never considered the ways of others in this regard, knowing only the ways the Raiders or my parents before that. After a moment of thought I say, "No, it doesn't. Love needn't be restricted if everyone is happy."

She smiles at me. "I'm glad you think so. You're so pretty, I bet you'll have a dozen people chasing after you when we get home."

Heat rushes to my face at her words. After all I've done to avoid love, after fighting against my own feelings for Thoa, the thought of these others she speaks of is exhausting. I tell her, "I don't think I want that."

"Maybe not yet," she says. "But you'll get over Thoa with time. And Krew," she says, rolling her eyes, "I doubt you'll be seeing much of him."

"Why not?" I ask.

"I'll be locked away for my crimes," he says.

My eyes jerk to his, meeting for only a second before he looks away. "For what? Coming here?"

He nods. "It's illegal."

"But you didn't *do* anything wrong," I say.

"Being here is wrong," Ivy says.

"You're here," I say. "And Ledwin and the Chasseur."

"Dad is in charge of on-world security. Our job is to track and return anyone who enters the world illegally."

"What about when *he* was here? Did he get in trouble for that?" I ask. "He had an entire family on-world."

Ivy furrows her brows again, looking like I've lost my mind. "You don't know what happened to him, do you?"

I shake my head. I don't remember much about him or my mother. Flashes of memory, sometimes a scent or sound, but they're mostly a piece of me that lurks in dark corners out of sight. I glance at Ivy, thinking she's going to tell me something about him, but her eyes are wide and she's staring at her steps.

"Ivy, what is it?" I ask.

She bites her lip. "I don't know if I should tell you. I mean, he might want to have this discussion himself."

My skin prickles at her words, wondering what secret she's keeping. "Ivy, come on. You have to tell me."

She winces, but Krew speaks up. "Your father came on-world as a contestant in an old game show."

"What's a game show?" I ask.

"A program we watch where people compete for prizes."

"So, like the trials?" I ask.

He nods. "Yeah, kinda. Off-worlders have devices that let them watch what's happening without needing to be there."

"Okay," I say with a nod. "I think I get it. But what did my father do on this game show?"

"It was set up to see how long our people could survive here. He came to the ground with nine other people. Most of them were gone within a few weeks, but he and a couple others lasted longer. A lot longer. Eventually he was the only one left, so he won the show."

"That's neat," I say.

Krew shakes his head. "By the time he won the show, he'd been here for years. He'd built a life here. He didn't return home after he'd won, instead choosing to stay with you and your mother."

I know the words he's going to say next. I want to stop him from saying them, to keep them out of my head so I can live in the dark a little longer, but I can't. His words tumble out as the scene unfolds in my head.

I was in the kitchen with my mother. We were baking cookies. Aunt Rachel ran in. She was still a kid, a little younger than Ivy is now. She said there were men outside and they'd taken hold of father. Mom grabbed each of us by the shoulder and steered us towards the cupboard. She picked up a board from the floor, revealing a crawlspace under the house. She pushed us inside, told Rachel to take care of me, told me to keep quiet. Then she closed the hiding spot and I never saw either of them again.

People in red passed over us, the floorboards creaking so loud it was like a thunderstorm in my head. I peeked over Rachel's shoulder as she held me, through a sliver between the boards, needing to see them though I prayed they wouldn't see me. They had creatures with them, dogs or wolves or something in between. Saliva dripped from snarling fangs, snapping at the floor above us. So many teeth—enough for dream, after dream, after dream.

"The Chasseur came for him," I whisper. "I remember."

Krew says, "They took your father home—"

"And killed my mother."

Silence settles around us, despite the chaos of the market. I don't know what to think or feel in this moment. I knew the space people were my enemies as soon as I heard about them watching us, but hearing why they murdered my mother infuriates me. I've killed before, many times, and I'm certain I will again. But never for something so frivolous as entertainment.

"So they took him home," I say, though my voice sounds thin, breakable. "Then what?"

Krew says, "He was a celebrity. He was given a big prize and everyone wanted to interview him. People wanted to be around him, to know the man who had survived so long on-world."

"I'm sure he loved that," I mutter.

"No," Krew says, shaking his head. "He saw his wife murdered, thought his daughter dead. They scrubbed the footage so he didn't know you made it out. After that happened, he was a broken man."

"Until he met my mother," Ivy says. I'm thankful she has the sense not to smile when she says this. "It was a few years after. He had healed some, but there was still pain there. My mom helped him return to the land of the living."

"How romantic," I say, bitterness seeping through my tone.

She frowns. "I'm sorry for what happened to your family, but that doesn't mean I'm not happy to have mine."

I sigh, nod. "I know it isn't your fault. It's not Ledwin's either. But that doesn't stop my anger."

"It shouldn't," Krew says. "You're allowed to be angry. Just make sure it doesn't take over. This stuff happened a long time ago. Don't let the past control your future."

I take a deep breath and let it out slowly. "So he was at home, had a new family, and decided to start working for the people who'd destroyed his old family?"

Krew lowers his voice. The market's sounds have finally filtered into my mind and I have trouble hearing when he says, "He didn't have a choice. The Règle specifically chose him to lead the Chasseur because he was so familiar with the planet. He doesn't like what he has to do. Or, at least, he didn't. But lately..."

He trails off. I'm not sure what to think of this revelation of my father. After everything I've learned, I don't know who he really is.

"Stars above," Ivy mutters.

She's staring over the railing into one of the lower rows of the market. I follow her gaze, immediately seeing what has caught her attention. Thoa is standing in the middle of an area that's been cleared of people. His chest is bare, but streaks of blood slash across his skin. Four fighters circle him, feinting forward as they try to wear him down.

Krew says, "We have to get down there."

"There's only four of them," I say. "He'll be fine."

"Four right now, but there's a line forming," Ivy says.

I find it now that she's pointed it out. Men, women, and mazulla are lining up on either side of him. "What are they doing?"

"He must be a frontrunner," Krew says. "They have to beat him to get into the trials."

I stare at him for a moment, dumbfounded. "That's how you get in?"

"If you don't have a sponsor," Ivy says. "There's a fee to enter. So contenders vie to get picked by a sponsor if they can't pay for it themselves. But he'll end up spending all day fighting until he's so tired he'll never make it through the tower."

"Or he could lose," I say. They both look doubtfully at me but I say, "I mean, it's not likely. But maybe we could help it along?"

"How?" Ivy asks.

"I could fight him and take him out of the running."

Krew says, "Are you crazy?"

"He won't hurt me."

"But one of the others might," he says.

I watch Thoa dispatch the fourth fighter just as another group moves up to face him. "I'm the only one who stands a chance against him."

Krew scrubs a hand over his face. "Yeah, I mean, I know you're strong—"

"Let's go," I say, moving away from the railing and cutting off any further arguments.

"Nova," Krew calls from behind me, "this is madness."

I look over my shoulder. The crowd has separated us, but I can still see him in the tide of people. I meet his eyes and smile.

CHAPTER
TWENTY

I push past the people in line and force myself into the fighting circle. There are voices yelling their complaints from the line, but I don't care. Let them fight me if they're unhappy.

Thoa spins to find me circling him. He growls, "What are you doing?"

"Same as you," I say as I swipe at him.

He dodges. "You're supposed to be above by now."

"Would be," I say, dodging a swing from another contestant, "if you hadn't left so early. Ledwin let me come look for you."

I spin, extending a brutal kick to a man's sternum. He stumbles back, gasping for air. A woman runs in to take his place, but I make quick work of her, too.

"I don't want to fight you, Little Star," Thoa says. He swings a meaty fist at a wiry man who approaches. The man ducks, but scurries backwards out of the circle to avoid another blow.

A mazulla fighter with thick arms and a soft belly bounds forward, a force of power radiating from them. I sidestep them, barely avoiding their charge. Thoa spins around and kicks them in the back but they seem to barely feel it. They spin around and charge at us again. Thoa catches my eye and I know what we must do.

I dive towards Thoa's outstretched arms. He grips my forearms and spins. My legs make contact with the mazulla fighter's chest and Thoa releases me to carry through with the momentum of his spin. Wind whistles through my ears as I whip towards our opponent. They go down hard, while I land on top of them.

Their eyes are rolled back into their head. I grab their wrist, putting my fingers over a small tattoo of a flower and sickle. I check their pulse and it is there, but faint. I yell for a healer, but within seconds the fighter is on their feet again, wobbling away from the circle of fighters. I can only spare a moment of worry for them as I watch them disappear into the crowd, then I return to Thoa and the others who try to give us pain.

A voice booms nearby, though I can't make out the words. The crowd parts as a squad of mercenaries-turned-guards marches towards the fighting circle. As they clear the area, forcing back those who were in line to attack us, I catch a glimpse of a woman in their midst. I step forward into the circle the guards have created and face her.

She is short, barely reaching my chest, but still she is commanding. Her face is deeply lined, her lips puckered. She watches me through narrowed eyes that seem to read my soul.

She turns her head as Thoa joins me, sending a multitude of white braids cascading down her back. She flicks her hand in the air, but says nothing.

One of her guards says, "Turn around."

"Why?" I ask.

"Because Hoshi said to," he growls.

"I don't belong to her," I sneer.

I watch the corners of her lips turn up. She speaks through a throat of rocks—hoarse and earthy and hard. "I'll take them."

"No," Thoa says, stepping forward. "Just me."

She folds her gnarled hands across her chest. "Both or neither."

He shakes his head. "Neither, then."

"Wait," I sputter, realizing what was happening. "We are yours. Just give me a moment to talk to him."

I grab Thoa's arm and turn him away. Before I can speak, he says, "You won't convince me."

"You'd rather spend all day fighting until you're too exhausted to make it through the trials?"

"Better than you going in there with me," he says. "You're supposed to be gone, safe from all this."

"But I'm not. I'm here, with you, and I'm not leaving until I know you're safe."

"You're so stubborn," he spits.

"And you're just now figuring that out?" I ask with a laugh.

He runs his hands through his dark curls. "Nova, I can do this. I can win. But it will be easier if I'm not worried about you the whole time."

"Then don't worry about me. I can handle myself."

"I know you can. You're tough. But when you care about some-one, you worry. No matter how strong they are."

I step closer to him and put my hand against his chest. "I'm sorry, but I don't plan to ever leave your side again."

I watch as his resolve melts. He brushes his knuckle against my cheek and says, "I'll hold you to that, Little Star."

With a smile, I say, "I hope so."

―――――

I CATCH GLIMPSES OF RED AT THE CORNERS OF MY VISION. I'M CERTAIN Ivy, Krew, and the Chasseur are following our procession, but the crowded levels make it impossible to catch us. The best they can do is follow at a distance.

Hoshi and her guards take us to the eighth tier. I don't see any vendors on this floor, but it is still crowded with people. We enter an apartment with lavish interior; the floors are covered in plush carpets, the walls decorated in gold and ivory. There's a chandelier in the middle of the room that stretches wider than I am tall.

Hoshi waves a hand and her guard says, "Make yourselves at home."

I wander to the window that takes up an entire wall. I can see the whole city below us, but the real view is of the tower in the center of the city. It glints in the sunlight and for the first time I notice the sparkle of gems decorating the sides.

I press closer to the window, trying to figure out what the tower is made of. From a distance it looked like stone, but now that I look more intently I can't imagine that's all it is. I turn to the room to ask, and find Hoshi mere inches from me.

"Lovely, isn't it?" she asks. Her voice is like the earth cracking under my feet.

"What is it?" I ask.

She shakes her head. "I've searched the world over and can find nothing like it here. It's from above. Win the trials and I'm sure they'll tell you."

I sigh. *Win the trials.* How did I get mixed up in all this?

But then my eyes find Thoa and I know I'm where I'm supposed to be. I look down at Hoshi and ask, "Do you think we can win?"

She's quiet so long I think she didn't hear me. When the words come, they are softer than I thought she could sound. "I always think my players will win. I always hope. But none ever do."

"Until now," I say, grazing her shoulder with my fingers. "We will win for you today."

She nods and smiles, turns back to the window. I leave her there and walk across the room to Thoa. He purses his lips and says, "I'm still not happy with you for this."

"Right. You'd prefer to be a martyr and do it alone."

He huffs. "I'd prefer knowing you were safe. I don't see how that makes me the bad guy."

"It doesn't," I say. I wrap my arms around his waist and look up at him. I've never held another person in this way, but it feels nice. He wraps his arms around me and I press my cheek against his chest.

He sighs. "We're in a mess, Little Star."

"I wouldn't have it any other way."

HOSHI GIVES US FOOD AND DRINK BEFORE MAKING US REST. SHE SAYS we will strategize before the trials, but her priority seems to be giving us comfort rather than advice.

After a glorious three hour nap in a bed that I'm certain is made from clouds, Hoshi's guard wakes us and leads us into the main room. She stands next to a table nearly as tall as she is, where figurines sit in metal circles.

As we take seats near the table and Hoshi says, "The tower has eight levels, each with a different objective. Some of the levels are simply about overpowering your enemy, while others are more like a puzzle. No matter what you face, you have to keep going. There is no way back. There is no way out. There is only up."

"Can you tell us what we're facing?" Thoa asks.

She shakes her head. "Not exactly. The tower changes every game." Hoshi pulls a small black box from her pocket and points it at the window. Pictures and diagrams now cover the glass. "This is what I've put together for level one."

A knock at the door makes me jump. I look to Hoshi, but she seems unconcerned. She tips her head and one of the guards goes to answer. As soon as the door opens, angry yelling can be heard from outside.

Hoshi says, "What's going on?"

Before the words have fully left her lips, Krew pushes his way into the room. He's panting, sweat beads on his forehead, but when his eyes catch mine he smiles.

"What the hell are you doing?" Hoshi demands.

"Entering the trials," Krew says.

Thoa and I both jump to our feet, but Thoa reaches him first. "Don't do this. We have trained to fight, we can protect ourselves. We won't be able to keep you safe."

Krew puts his hands on his hips. "I'm not the one who needs to be protected. I'm here to save you."

"Save us?" I ask, unable to stop the chuckle that comes with the question.

He smirks. "I know you're all strong and tough and all, but there's a lot more to the trials that you don't know. Trust me. I've watched them all my life. I know more about them than anyone."

Hoshi pushes past me and Thoa. "Tell me what you know."

"Give me a place in the game," he says.

She runs her tongue over her teeth. "That's a lot of money to pay for bad information."

Krew holds up his wrist, turning it so his bracelet catches the light. Hoshi's sharp intake of breath tells me all I need to know. She nods to her guard and says, "Register us for another."

Hoshi motions Krew to the table and puts up at the window. "The first level is used to weed out the weak. It's brute force. I've seen them fight; I'm not worried. But you…"

She trails off as she looks him over. Krew is not the bulky Raider that Thoa is. He is lean and tight, his lanky frame built for running, not fighting. Still, he smiles at her.

"I can handle myself," he says. "But you're right; the first level won't pose a challenge. The second will be an organized fight, the third a puzzle, the fourth some sort of team encounter."

Hoshi says, "I think you'll be fine at first, especially working together. But it gets tricky—"

Hoshi's guard bursts through the door. He runs to her side and says, "Mistrex Hoshi, there's a problem."

"What's wrong, Gim?"

"Star-guards at the game booth. They were checking everyone in line."

Krew jumps up and asks, "Did you get me in?"

Gim nods. "They got there as I was finishing. But something is up. There were a ton of them."

"Wait," Krew says, his brows furrowed. "It wasn't just the four in red?"

"No, at least a couple dozen," Gim says. "I overheard that they were staffed around the tower, too."

"Thank you for bringing this information to me," Hoshi says. She looks around at her guards and says, "Leave us for a while."

The one who spoke for Hoshi in the fighting circle speaks up now. "Mistrex, if they're looking for one of these—"

She waves a dismissive hand. "I appreciate your concern, Fergus, but we both know I can handle myself."

My brows raise in surprise at her words, but Fergus nods and leaves with the others as if there's no doubt in what she says. I've known small Raiders with more fire than others twice their size, but I did not expect to find such fierceness among the city's rich. Foolish, I suppose.

When the guards are gone she turns to us and says, "Wanna tell me why they're looking for you?"

At first I think she's talking to Krew, but then I find her eyes on me. I sputter, "What? Me?"

"I know why they're after him," she says, flinging a hand in Krew's direction. "But you're a mystery. Raider girl walking around with Chasseur guards? Doesn't add up."

"How did you—?"

She interrupts me, saying, "There's not a lot I don't see in this city, one way or another. I had my eye on you before your show on the ground. You just gave me a reason to get involved."

"Don't most people try to avoid getting involved with the Chasseur?" Krew asks.

Hoshi shrugs. "Most of them don't have the mind for intrigue or the stomach for danger. That's why they hire fighters to compete for them in the tower."

Thoa asks, "Why do you hire fighters?"

"Because I'm not stupid. I don't need the glory, I don't want the big prize," she says, pointing at the ceiling. "I'm after the money."

My stomach turns at her words. "How can you be so nonchalant about people dying so you can have a chance at some coin?"

She smirks at me. "Did I force you to come to my apartment? Did I sign you up for the games against your will? No. I paid your entry fee in exchange for your service. And you'd have agreed to those terms no matter who offered; I just got there first."

My cheeks burn red. She's not wrong. I was looking for any way to protect Thoa. She came along and provided that.

"What's wrong?" she asks. "Nothing to say when the truth smacks you in the face?"

"You're right, I guess. Doesn't make it less awful."

She nods. "I know. But there's nothing I can do about that. My mother won the games fifty years ago. Even in victory, it sucked."

"What happened to her?" I ask.

"She died an hour after she won. Internal bleeding couldn't be stopped."

I grimace, knowing the pain of losing a mother. "That's awful."

She shrugs. "It was a long time ago. The money she won from the games saved our family from a life of struggles. My sister was able to get out of the skin service, my brother opened a shop, and me, I invested. Sometimes in goods, sometimes in services, sometimes in people. After all these years, I recognize a wise investment."

"That's why you chose us?" Thoa asks.

"Partly," she says. "But there was something else I saw on your face in that grounder fight: desperation. You're running from something. But I don't know why. And since there's a platoon of starguards involved, I think I deserve to know."

"My father is head of the Chasseur," I say.

Her eyes dart to my wrist and back. There's a question there in the dark honey of her eyes. I shake my head and say, "I've never been up there. I was raised on-world."

"With the Raiders," she says, glancing at Thoa.

"Yes," I say. "Mostly. They took me in when my parents...when my *mother* died. I just found out my father is alive a few days ago. He wants to take me off-world."

A deep crease forms between her brows. "If he's taking you up, why the trials." Her eyes move from me to Thoa and she says, "Oh. But you," she points to Krew and then says, "Ooooh."

I bite my lip and look at the plum-colored rug. I can't imagine what she sees when she looks at us, but her gaze makes me want to put on another layer of clothing, as if it would keep her from seeing to my soul.

"Right then," Hoshi says. "What are we going to do about those guards?"

"If I turn myself over, I may be able to buy you some time," Krew says.

Hoshi shakes her head. "Screw that. I paid for three fighters in the games and I'm getting my money's worth. What else you got?"

"If they really are around the tower entrance, is there another way in?" Thoa asks.

"Ivy," I say. "She can help us."

Thoa's eyes find mine and he asks, "But will she?"

CHAPTER
TWENTY-ONE

I vy isn't difficult to find. She's on the topmost level where the crowds are minimal, surrounded by red suits. I approach with caution, hoping not to be recognized. Hoshi has given me a change of clothes—a fitted black jumpsuit that feels like a second skin— and I'm sure the Chasseur won't be looking for me in this. I've braided my hair back and coated it with oil that Hoshi had that turns it from copper to black. She painted my eyelids in black and silver, giving me the appearance of wearing a mask.

I stand near the railing facing away from Ivy and her guards, leaving myself room to run if they spot me. After a few minutes, I turn towards the wall where she stands. Her mazulla lover is next to her, close but not touching. Ledwin must be nearby. I scan the area but don't see him.

A large group of people are coming from the other end of the platform. I move into the trickle of people on this end of the corridor and aim to intersect with the large group. As I pass Ivy, I throw myself towards the wall, pretending that someone knocked me down.

As expected, Ivy reaches down to help me. "Are you okay?"

"Fine, thanks," I say, meeting her eyes.

She doesn't look at me, not really, as she helps me up. I slip a piece of paper into her hand and move away. The sharp intake of breath lets me know she read it, but thankfully she doesn't alert the guards. I disappear through the crowd and make my way back downstairs towards Hoshi's apartment. I won't know if Ivy is helping us until we try to enter the tower.

But I believe in her. I have to.

———

WE APPROACH THE TOWER. HALF A DOZEN PEOPLE ARE QUEUED TO enter, each more intimidating than the last. Some of these people make Thoa look slight, which is no small feat.

As Gim said, there are space-guards checking everyone before letting them pass into the tower. We fall in line behind the others. I try to scan the levels overlooking us to find Ivy, but I'm afraid to lift my head more than an inch or two. These guards may not recognize me through my disguise at first, but if any give more than a cursory glance, I'm busted.

I keep my eyes on Thoa's back. He's returned to wearing the tough leathers our people prefer, though his own killing clothes were left in his home in Aeroport. Hoshi forced him to wear a cloak to somewhat hide the leathers, insisting that he'd be too conspicuous without it. Now that other people are entering the tower, I'm certain she was right. They're all dressed like me in dark material that clings to them, highlighting every muscle twitching and eager for the fight.

Hoshi's guard shaved Thoa's head. It's strange seeing the stubbled scalp instead of dark curls. She took away some of his softness, the only indication of the gentle heart within the wall of muscle. I'm thankful he is on my side; I wouldn't want to face him.

There is only one person in front of Thoa now. My pulse is racing, my heart hammering so hard inside my chest I worry the guards might hear.

Krew leans forward and whispers, "Relax."

His voice is a rumble, but his breath on my ear as gentle as the flapping of a butterfly's wings. I close my eyes and take a deep breath, willing my body back under my control. Though Krew has helped to ground me, it is his presence that worries me the most. He is the one the guards are most likely to recognize. Some of them are his friends, his colleagues, his neighbors. He is both our weakness and our secret weapon.

Krew's disguise was the most difficult, because they know his face so well. We painted designs along his cheeks in white and red paint. Hoshi said it was an old practice from before the world was remade. It makes him look fierce. His hair is already short, so we used the white face paint to disguise the color. Like me, he wears the tight-fitting suit, but his has a white stripe on each side accenting the length of his body. She did not have to force him to take a cloak—he took it from her eagerly, drawing the hood up to shadow his face.

"Name?" a guard barks.

I look up, surprised. Thoa is no longer in front of me. I'd been so lost in thought I hadn't seen him move forward. The guard raises his eyes from the tablet in his hands. He squints at me and I can tell he's gone from bored to suspicious in the span of only a few seconds.

I hold out the token Hoshi gave me. It has the weight of a coin, but it's not a dirty copper or faded silver. The token is swirls of purple and gold with a stamp of two interlocked triangles in white. I say, "I fight for Mistrex Hoshi."

He stares at me, not bothering to glance at my token. I watch his jaw clench for a moment before he says, "I asked for your name."

I take a steadying breath and with the rough voice I practiced with Hoshi I say, "Alexis the Huntress." Her mother's name.

The guard lifts his wrist to his mouth and says, "Identity check needed at the tower. Alexis the Huntress."

He touches his ear as a reply comes back to him. I slowly lower my hand to the dagger at my side, only to remember it isn't there. No outside weapons allowed in the trials.

"Copy," he says. "Gamma Squad en route to your location. Keep eyes on the fugitive."

He turns to the guard down the line and calls, "She was spotted going in a shop on four. Alpha has the location surrounded."

"You sure it's her?" another guard asks as he approaches.

"Tall, red hair, and dressed like a Raider," the first guard shrugs. He radios his other men and as they gather he directs me to a man standing just within the tower's entrance. He's a round man with a thick red beard trailing down his stomach. "Give him your token. Good luck, kid."

He motions his arm towards the tiers and the other guards fall in line behind him. They quick-step towards a stairwell and out of sight. I step to the man and hand him my token. He eyes it for a moment, moving his hand up and down as if weighing it, then nods and lets me pass to the woman behind him. She pats me down to check for weapons and, finding none, lets me pass into the inner portion of the tower. Krew is quick to follow.

The light inside the tower is strange, cold. It travels in a circle around the inner tower on the center of the ceiling with blueish-white light. The people gathered underneath it are pale husks of the brawny fighters who waited outside.

We hover near the entrance looking around. We can only see half of the tower. Ahead of us is a metal tube that keeps us from seeing more. I reach back and take Krew's hand as we push through the crowd, afraid to lose him before we even begin.

When I spot Thoa, he's wearing a look of dread. As soon as he sees us approaching, it melts into a stupid grin. He glances at my fingers intertwined with Krew's, his smile faltering only for a second before his grin grows broader and relief settles in his eyes.

We're all wearing matching smiles, looking around at each other like this is the greatest day of our lives, elated that we've made it to the trials. Ivy came through for us, impersonating me to lead the guards away. Pride swells within at the thought of my sister. *My sister.* I'll have to remember to ask how she slipped the Chasseur.

A bell rings inside the tower and the chatter of the waiting players immediately ceases. My smile drops as reality sets in, mirrored on Thoa and Krew's faces as they lose the joy we just had. We are in the trials, the games that rarely have a winner, that may very well be our ends.

The lights go out and I hear a *woosh* of air. When they power back on, the metal tube is gone, replaced by a wall of weapons. The lights flash off again.

"We need to move!" Thoa shouts.

His hand grasps for mine and I take it, with my other still holding onto Krew. There is a mass of people between us and the weapons, each person trying to shoulder their way forward in the dark.

The bell rings again. When the lights flash this time, there is blood.

CHAPTER
TWENTY-TWO

Thoa grabs my waist and whirls me out of the way as a burly woman slices her sword through the air where I was standing. She spins towards Thoa and bares her teeth, a menacing growl low in her throat.

"Go get weapons," Thoa tells me. "I'll handle this one."

He squares off against the sword-wielding warrior. I don't have time to wish him well, nor do I have time to worry. I have to get us weapons if we're going to survive. I push forward. I may be tall, but these people are giants in comparison. I use my smaller stature to slip under and through their barriers.

I reach the wall and grasp for a sword that's tethered there. Another woman grabs for it just as I release it from the wall. Still holding the blade, I twist around and punch her in the nose. I hear the crack of bone and blood dribbles over her lips. I pull the blade from the wall and reach for another. I make my way down the wall, getting the sword, two daggers, a hatchet, and a whip.

I turn to pass a weapon to Krew and for the first time I realize he isn't behind me. My eyes dart over the crowd. People are everywhere, fighting with anything they can. There are bodies on the floor, some injured, some dead. But I do not see Krew among them.

As I make my way around the circle, my eyes finally light on the white-painted hair. He's on the ground, another body on top of him. I slide over the bloody floor to him and kneel to check his pulse. He turns his head to me and I breathe a sigh of relief. He's alive.

His dark eyes go wide. Before he can say a word I spin and jab upwards with the sword. Guilt flashes through me for an instant, but disappears just as fast. There is necessity in my kill, though I find no pleasure in it.

It's the mazulla fighter I'd kicked in the chest earlier in the fighting circle. Blood seeps from the wound as they fall to the floor beside me. I withdraw my sword from their belly and turn back to Krew.

"Can you move?"

"Yeah," he says. "I was just afraid to. I thought I'd stay out of trouble if they thought I was dead already."

The corner of my lip curls up. "Smart. But we need to move. Have you seen Thoa?"

He shakes his head as he rolls the body off himself. That's when I see the blood. Even against the black of his suit I can see that his midsection is covered in sticky red. I press his shoulder to urge him back down.

"Where are you hurt?"

"I'm not," he says, pointing to the other body.

I look from the other body to his hands. They're slick with it. I meet his eyes, but say nothing about his kill. Instead I squeeze his shoulder and turn back to the mazulla fighter, relieving them of their weapons. I offer Krew the second sword, but he declines, showing me his dagger. I hand him a second dagger, leaving me with just one in my boot, while I dual-hand the swords.

We move around the circle, noticing the area has cleared out except for a few stragglers, Thoa among them. As we move to his side, the remaining fighters still standing make their way through the mysterious doorway that has opened in the wall, leaving the three of us alone.

Thoa's head is spattered with blood, but he is well. He pulls me against his chest, puts a hand on Krew's shoulder and gives him a nod.

I offer him a sword, but instead he takes the whip at my side and pulls a blade from a body nearby. "You keep both. They suit you."

"What now?" I ask.

"The door to the next level is open," he says. "Not sure what triggered it, but I counted sixteen going up."

"Sixteen?" I ask, surprised by the number. But as I look around at the bloodied floor and the bodies around us, I realize there must be at least that many dead.

Thoa says, "Let's hurry, but keep your guard up."

"The second tier is usually an organized bloodbath, probably a versus match. It won't be," he pauses, looks around at the carnage and says, "like this."

"Still," Thoa says with a shrug.

Krew nods. "Yeah, I guess. Nothing is set. They could change the game simply because I'm here."

"What are you talking about?" I ask.

"There are cameras watching our every move, listening to everything we say. By now they know we're here, and I'm sure they're playing on my presence in the broadcasts. In the history of the trials, I don't think an off-worlder has competed. Since I know the games better than anyone else in here, I wouldn't be surprised if they change things up."

"Of course," I say as we start up the steps.

Thoa leads us, his blood-slicked blade poised to strike. We pass one body on the steps. Krew whispers, "Fifteen up."

We enter a circular room lit by the same bluish lights as below. This area is open and we can see the other people scattered through the space. There are two small groups at either side of the room, but most of the fighters stand alone.

As soon as we enter, a barrier slides down, blocking the stairs. The bell rings as before, but rather than the lights turning off, a warm, cheerful voice radiates through the room. *"Welcome to the trials. Congratulations on completing the first level."*

We players look around at each other, all unsure what to make of the voice. Krew has a faraway look on his face, one of sadness, regret maybe.

I raise my eyebrows in question and he points up, saying, "It's Baz. The voice. I know him." He turns his face up to stare at the person he can't see and mutters, "Sorry."

"We know you're expecting a standard versus fight on this level," Baz says with the hint of a smile in his voice, *"but we're playing things a little differently this time around. We want you to split into teams of six. Choose wisely."* When none of us moves, Baz says, *"Go ahead, we'll wait."*

Thoa is the first to act. He points to a woman against the wall—the one whose nose I broke—and says, "You. With us."

After his choice, everyone else scurries to group up. Thoa also pulls two people who were standing together into our group. He introduces me, Krew, and himself to the newcomers. The woman with the bloodied face is Borah. She smiles when she looks my way and I can see she is a seasoned fighter. She doesn't place guilt on an opponent simply for doing what they must.

The first man from the couple, Heinrich, is almost as broad as Thoa. His head is shaved as well, though not as short, and the lights gleam against his blond hair. His face is blotchy, red, and when he opens his mouth there's blood where several of his teeth should be. His partner, Morian, is built more like me, but his shoulders are slightly broader. His eyes are the most unusual shade I've ever seen—a striking violet with a gold ring on the outside of the iris. I'm sure they'd be absolutely beautiful if one of his eyes weren't in the process of swelling shut.

"*Great*," Baz chimes in after we're split into groups. "*Now, as a team, decide which one of your group members you're going to kill.*"

There is complete silence in the room as the words sink in. After a moment, I hear someone in another group say, "This can't be real."

"*I assure you, it is*," Baz says, sickeningly cheery.

It takes a moment for any of us to look up, to make eye contact with a person we're going to murder. When I do look up, my eyes go straight to Borah. I don't want to kill her, but it makes the most sense. She's alone, easiest to overwhelm.

I am not the only one who has thought of this. She looks at each of us in turn, but she will find no help among us.

"Aw feck," she says. "Ain't this some shite."

"It's nothing personal," Heinrich whispers.

She huffs. "Nothin' personal? Is that the best ye've got? Yer about to murder me!"

Morian clears his throat. "It isn't her. She's not our pick."

"Shut up, Mor," Heinrich says.

Morian shakes his head. "I have to, babe. It's the right thing to do."

"What are you talking about?" I ask.

Morian moves his arm away from his side, revealing a long gash in his suit. Blood oozes from the cut like a slow-moving stream, a miniature river.

Heinrich drapes an arm over Morian's shoulder. "You can get through this. We can make it as long as we stick together."

Morian's mouth turns up at the corner. "You know, I think we could've. But now I'm going to die." He turns to look at Heinrich and says, "Even if we keep going, I won't make it to the top. At least if I die now, I can save someone else. Maybe one of you will win the trials today. Maybe you, my love."

Heinrich catches Morian as he starts to slump. Now that he's made his decision, he fades fast. I help Heinrich move him to the wall, then step away to give them a moment of privacy. I look around as the other groups argue with one another. Our group is silent. I'd like to believe it is in honor of Morian's sacrifice, in respect of Heinrich's loss. But I know it is also the shame we feel for turning on Borah, the guilt we feel for not having the courage to make the sacrifice that Morian did.

Baz's voice comes through the speakers again, saying, *"You have one minute to complete your task. Any team that has not finished this trial at the end of sixty seconds will be disqualified and removed from the game."*

I kneel by Heinrich's side and look to Morian. He won't last much longer, but we can't risk missing the deadline. While I'm trying to figure out how to say this, Morian says, "Make it quick."

I ready my sword to slide into his heart. Heinrich puts his hand over mine and says, "Please, let me."

"I can make it painless," I offer.

Heinrich says, "Thank you, but I want to have as many seconds with him as I can. Don't worry; we'll make the deadline."

I nod and hand him my sword, turn my back to the sight. Though ready to do what was needed, I'm thankful I don't have to. I hear Heinrich whisper to Morian, who laughs in response. Less than a minute later Heinrich is standing beside me, handing over my sword. His broad shoulders are slumped, his pale green eyes are red-rimmed and tears cling to his lashes as he swallows back the pain.

As I take the sword, I put a hand on his arm and say, "I'm sorry."

He nods, but says nothing.

The five of us line up and face the center of the room. One of the other groups is fighting to hold the person they've chosen. The other group is still arguing with one another. Baz's even tone cuts through the air, counting down.

"Five."

The screams from the second group get louder.

"Four."

The victim in the first group gets an arm free and swings wildly. *"Three."*

They've recaptured their target and the man with the scimitar slices into his gut.

"Two."

Group one's sacrifice falls to the floor, color draining from his face as his blood covers the ground at their feet. Group two continues to yell and hasn't made a choice.

"One."

At the last second, the smallest among their group spins around, flicks a dagger from her waist into her hand, and plunges it into the neck of the person closest to her. The victim, a mountain of a man and easily twice her size, grabs his neck in surprise as blood spurts from the vein she's hit. When he hits his knees, he reaches out for her, sliding his bloody hand down the front of her jumpsuit, leaving a trail of condemnation.

The whole thing happens in that one second, but it feels like it took ages to play out. I hear Baz's voice over the speakers again, but it sounds so far away I can't make out the words. Instead, I hear the squelch of the knife being pulled from the man's neck. I hear the other group members clap her on the back. I watch her face, certain I can hear her blink, hear the scratch of stubble as she runs a blood-wet hand over her short brown hair.

She turns to me, smiling. Our eyes lock. In that moment I am certain she is my one true enemy in the games. The others will do what they must to win, but this girl, she enjoys the killing.

She points a finger at me and puckers her lips. *You're next,* she says with this gesture.

I look at the three bodies on the floor and wonder if she's right.

CHAPTER
TWENTY-THREE

At the third level we are met with a black wall. There are hexagons carved into it, but in the dim light I can't see anything more. The twelve of us stand by the wall, too close together to be comfortable. Comfort isn't in the cards for us anyway, not after what we've done already and what we're willing to do to continue.

The blood on our hands grows with each level, but what choice do we have? Now that we're in the tower, the only way out is death or victory. Even if we could get out and go home, I don't think any of us could be happy knowing what we are to the star-people. They've stacked us in this tower for hundreds of years to entertain them. What else are they willing to do?

The door slides closed again, sealing us in. When Baz's voice sounds this time, his tone suggests boredom, but his words are almost scolding. *"I hoped you've learned your lesson with the last activity. You'll stay in groups for level three as well."*

A groan travels through the group. Beside me Borah's tanned cheeks go pale.

"Don't get an attitude with me," Baz says. *"I can always throw out the rulebook and just make you start stabbing each other."*

My brows shoot up and I glance to Krew. He shrugs and says, "We're in uncharted territory."

"*Begin by choosing one member of your group for the first part of the task.*"

We look at each other, but no one says anything for several moments. Finally Borah says, "Hold on, ya bastards. Yer really gunna make me go, after what just happened downstairs?"

"It could be any of us," I say. "We don't know what's going to happen. Could be a reward."

"Or death," she says.

"I'll go," Thoa says.

"No," I rush out. Shame washes over me as my eyes catch Borah's and my lie is exposed. It was never going to be anyone but her.

She folds her arms over chest and says no more.

"*All right you three, choose a door and go through for further instructions.*"

Borah enters the middle door. I try to see into the room beyond, but I can't make out anything. The door closes and the four of us stand staring at our feet, waiting. I look around at the other two groups. The one who struggled with their sacrifice in the last challenge is subdued, like us. There are two men, one woman, and a mazulla person in their group. I do not remember who their fifth is.

The other group is more relaxed. The weight of the last challenge doesn't seem to affect them. *Makes sense*, I think. *They aren't the ones carrying the guilt of that man's death.*

I look to the girl with the short brown hair. She leans against the wall using a knife to dig blood from underneath her fingernails. Her eyes face down, or at least I think so at first. But I quickly realize her practiced nonchalance is a disguise for her real motive. She uses her disinterest to keep herself small, to appear harmless, all while studying those around her.

She catches me watching her and I don't try to hide it. Instead I walk towards her. She smiles and nods a greeting, saying, "Princess."

"Princess?" I ask.

She shrugs. "You buy an entry for you and your bodyguards to piss off daddy?"

"I don't know who you think I am—"

"I don't know who *you* think you are," she says, cutting me off. She pushes off the wall, knife still in hand. "But this isn't your day, girlie."

Rage runs wild through me and I realize my hands are shaking, itching for the steel at my side. But I don't know what the star-people would think of a fight here, now. The rules haven't been clear and I can't risk failing because of my temper.

Instead I tip my head to her knife and say, "I like your blade. Reminds me of my first knife, when I was nine. Outgrew it pretty quick though." I put my hands on the swords resting on each side of my hips.

Her grin broadens. "I bet we could've had some fun if we'd met before."

"Outside the trials?" I ask.

She shakes her head. "Nah. Level one. I would've loved to see the look on that pretty face as I slipped my knife in your heart."

"I look forward to slicing your throat," I say with a chuckle.

I turn my back to her and go back to my group. I can't help but breathe a sigh of relief when I reach them without a dagger in my back.

After several more minutes, Baz says, "*Okay groupies, time to complete the level. Your task is simple: walk through the door and listen to your teammate as they steer you through the darkness. Inside the room are multiple things that can kill you. You will not be able to see anything and if I were you, I wouldn't try to touch anything either.*" He laughs and says, "*Hope you picked someone you trust.*"

"This isn't good," I mutter.

Under normal circumstances, Borah might be the most trustworthy person this side of the Issippi, but we've nominated her for death, or potential death, twice. If I were her, I'm not sure I would let all of us pass.

I meet eyes with Krew and see by his expression that he is thinking the same thing. But Thoa puts a hand on each of our shoulders and says, "We're going to trust Borah. We're going to do everything she says. She will lead us to safety. Right, Heinrich?"

Heinrich looks up as if he hadn't heard anything that was said. He looks around at each of us, but I can see that he is far away. His grief is overwhelming him.

"I said we're going to trust Borah and do what she says. Can you do that?" Thoa asks.

Heinrich nods. "Yeah. Yeah, I can."

Baz says, *"When the door opens, one person from each team may enter. Do not attempt to enter while another player is in the room or your whole team is disqualified. Good luck, players."*

The doors open. Krew says, "I'll go first."

Before anyone can object, he enters the room and the door slides shut behind him.

———

I'M FIDGETING. I CAN'T STOP THE TWITCH OF MY FINGERS AS THEY TAP against my arms, my swords, my teeth. Thoa is in the room. Krew...he may be dead or alive. There's no way of knowing until I get to the other side.

Something about this whole thing niggles at my brain. It doesn't feel *complete*. Maybe because I don't know what they've told Borah. I don't know what the catch is.

The door opens. I look at Heinrich and wordlessly exchange a question. He says, "I'll go."

I nod and he steps through the door. A second later the black door closes and I'm left staring at the wall. I hear the hiss of another group's door lifting. I look around and realize there are only three of us left. It suddenly strikes me that this could be a race in addition to whatever else it is. If that's the case, we're neck-and-neck.

The man next to me looks nervous. I catch his eye and ask, "You okay?"

He shakes his head, barely perceptible. "We're going to die."

"You're just now figuring that out?" the girl against the wall chuckles. "I thought one of the requirements to get in here was a death wish."

The man frowns. "I don't want to die. I'm doing this for my family, my daughters, to give them a better life."

"A life without their idiot father," the girl says. "It'll probably be good for them in the long run."

I put my hand on the man's shoulder and say, "Don't listen to her. You're already at the end of level three. They're going to be proud of you."

He nods as the door in front of him opens. With a half-hearted smile, he walks through the door.

As soon as his door closes I spin towards the girl. "What is wrong with you? He was already terrified."

She bolts from the wall to get in my face. "He should be. This is the place where everyone dies. To abandon his family and come here was a fool's mission."

"He's trying to make their lives better."

"He's an asshole," she spits. "And he's going to die."

"Maybe not," I say, though I don't believe my own words.

Neither does she. "In the end there's only one winner, if that. And we both know that man isn't strong enough."

My mind is stuck on her words, but not about the man. I ask, "What do you mean 'one winner?'"

Her pursed lips tug into a smile, then a full-on grin. She stares at me with such delight, my stomach drops to my feet.

Her door opens and she walks to the entrance with a skip in her step. I grab her arm before she can go in and ask, "Why do you hate me so much? Who are you?"

She jerks from my grasp. "Don't touch me, *aciagla*."

I flinch at the word. It was a curse among the Raiders, one often directed at me. A verbal reminder that I was bad luck incarnate.

Her smile spreads so wide her face can barely contain it. "We've never met, so don't mistake my hatred as a grudge."

"How did you know they called me that?"

She steps into the door and says, "Lucky guess," just before the door slides shut.

WHEN MY DOOR OPENS, I SLIP INSIDE AND TRY TO LET MY EYES ADJUST to the darkness. But they don't. There isn't the slightest glimmer in the distance to give me a point of reference.

Instinctively I reach my hand forward to feel for anything to ground me. A voice crackles to life around me, yelling, "No!"

I jerk my hand back as the sound of metal sliding against metal rings in the air. The hair on the back of my neck stands on end. I ask, "Borah?"

"I'm here," she says. She sounds tense. "I'm not gunna let ya get hurt."

"What was that?"

"Prolly better if ya dinnae know," she says. "Just listen to my voice and I'll have ya across in no time."

I take three breaths before my heart has slowed enough to answer her. "I trust you, Borah. Tell me what to do."

She chuckles. "Ya trust me? Well, it's true that I've not been the one tryin' ta kill ya at every turn."

I wince. "You're right. We haven't been good to you."

There's silence for several minutes. Then she says, "Take one big step to yer left." After I move she says, "Good. Now three forward."

"Big steps or regular?" I ask.

"Ah shite," she says. "Glad ya asked. Regular. And keep yer arms tucked."

I take three steps forward. A gust of heat travels up my right side. I want to flinch away but I don't. I can't. I have to trust Borah, and whatever that heat is from is part of it.

"Right, this is where it gets weird. Turn and face that heat but dinnae move from the spot where ya are."

I take a deep breath and say, "Okay, I understand."

I turn my body to face the heat, making sure not to move out of my spot. Heat flares again, sweat appearing on my forehead as it does. The worst of the blast only lasts about two seconds before it fades.

"Yer gunna think my head's full o' mince for this next bit," she says. "After the heat comes again, hop until ya hit the wall."

"Hop?" I ask.

"Aye. There's stuff on the floor an' hoppin' seems to do the trick."

Hop, I think. She could be messing with me. I punched her on the first level, I was going to let her die on the second, and put her in this position on this one. I deserve whatever happens here.

Her voice crackles again, saying, "Get ready, Little Star."

I can't stop the smile that spreads across my face. Thoa's message is loud and clear, even through Borah's voice. This is the way through.

The heat smacks me in the face, causing me to instantly perspire. As soon as it passes, I hop. I understand why on the third bounce; the floor is so hot I can feel it through my boots, I can smell the burning as it melts my soles.

I hit the wall after six or seven hops and let out the breath I've been holding. Borah says, "Good work. A few more passes to get to the end."

I nod and say, "I'm ready."

"Reach up and you'll find some handholds. Yer gunna climb up and out across the ceiling."

I find the grooves in the wall in front of me and start climbing. I think I'm about eight feet up when the ceiling curves to the side and I have to turn my body around to find the grips that lead across the room. I've gone a few feet when Borah says, "Stop. Ya wanna turn and come forward. Dinnae let yer feet dangle."

I do as she says, but the muscles in my arms are starting to burn. I've done a lot of exercise with the Raiders to get strong, but nothing like this. I cringe at the pull of my weight on my joints, on the shoulder injured by the guard at Gearhaven. I try to use my other arm to make up for it, but I don't know how long I can keep this up.

As I go, the heat blazes under me. I tuck my legs close to my body. They aren't near the heat, I don't think, but it sends nervous droplets of sweat down my legs just the same.

"Okay, drop down," she says at last.

I drop to the floor and rub my sore shoulder. As I stand up, heat licks at my back, far hotter than before. The smell of burning hair fills my nostrils and I take a slight step forward, afraid to move too much.

"Sorry," she says. "Gotcha a little too close. We'll call it an accident, aye?"

"It's okay," I say, running a hand over my braid. The end is fried and my body is sweaty, but other than that I'm okay. I've dealt with heat before, roaming the desert with the Raiders, hiding in tents to avoid the heat. I wipe away the drops on my upper lip, dab at the perspiration between my breasts. This will not break me.

"Last thing, but it's a doozy," Borah says.

I force a smile. "I trust you. I know you could kill me in here if you wanted to, but you haven't."

"Ya keep sayin' that, but ya really shouldn't. No one is worthy of trust in a place like this. And don't mistake me not killing you for me not *wanting* to kill you."

I bite my lip, knowing she's right. But Thoa's words ring

through me, telling us to trust her, having her call me by my Raider nickname. I don't think she's going to hurt me, even if she wants to.

"There's a pit in front of ye."

"And I need to cross it?"

"Right y'are," she says, "but it's not that easy. Now don't panic, but it's full o' vipers. There's a beam above it to get across."

A shallow breath shakes out, then another. I hate snakes. They're one of the only things that truly scare me. But the game makers know that, of course. If they've been watching me all this time without me knowing, even if I've never been the object of their entertainment, they'd still have knowledge of my entire life.

"I can't," I say, barely able to get the words across my lips. Panic rises inside me and I know this is the end of my journey. After everything I've been through, this is the one thing I cannot do.

"Oh, dinnae be a wuss. You can make it. Just a wee pit ta cross, really."

I shake my head. "Borah, I can't do it."

"There's a handsome lad here who says ya can. Thinks you can do anything, seems. Be a shame to prove him wrong."

"I'm sorry," I whisper.

"He says he cannae do it alone. An' now he's tryin' ta get back in the room with ye. Get us all in trouble if he does. So I'm gunna need ya to take a step forward, find the beam, and walk across. Run across if ya need. Either way, get movin'."

I can picture Thoa pounding against the door, looking for a way in to try to help me. The thought gives me comfort, knowing that he's just on the other side of the door, waiting for me. "Okay, okay, tell him to stop. I'll do it."

I stand there trying to regain my calm. I think to my years of training, my life with the Raiders, my friend, Rego. He has always been light-footed, quiet, nimble. Even as he aged, he moved like a ghost. And now so must I.

I take a step forward and move my foot along the floor in front of me. The pit has a raised lip and above that is the beam. As my foot rubs against the wood, it moves. The beam isn't secured.

But it doesn't matter.

I take one last breath while picturing Rego in my mind. As soon as I release it, I jump onto the beam and bolt across it. The beam rolls under my feet. It's about to fall. There's no telling how much is left of the pit. I have no choice. I jump.

My feet seem to hang in the air for longer than they should. Time seems to stand still. My right foot lands on the ground but my left slips down into the pit. I lurch forward, dragging my leg up.

The door opens and light streams in. Snakes cling to my boot and I shake them, trying to get them off. One still attached rears back to strike my leg. In my mind I watch it happen, see it's fangs sink through the fabric of my pants and into my skin, see the poison course through my body.

But a dagger sails through the air, slicing the serpent's neck. I jump through the door and against the man who threw the blade. I look up and ask, "Krew?"

He wraps his arms around me and pulls me away from the door, saying, "You're okay."

It was Krew at the door, trying to get to me. Krew, *not Thoa.*

"The knife was you?" I ask, still surprised.

He looks down at me and smiles. "Don't be so surprised. I'm fantastic at darts."

"What are darts?"

He shakes his head. "I'll teach you when we get upstairs."

Thoa, Heinrich, and Borah come through the doorway ahead of us. All three join us in a massive embrace and I can't help but laugh at the situation. Enemies, friends, competitors—doesn't matter. We're all people, and surviving is a victory we can all celebrate. Even if that victory is short-lived.

CHAPTER
TWENTY-FOUR

As we stand together, the floor below us begins to rise. The ceiling opens and we slide up into a glass cylinder. On either side of us are identical tubes filled with the other teams. The stabby-girl has all of her team members alongside her, but the other team only has four in their tube. The father, the one I tried to comfort, he isn't with them.

"*Congrats on your victory,*" Baz says, his voice muffled by the enclosures. "*We are thrilled to see the ten of you moving on.*"

"Ten?" I ask. "There are fourteen of us."

Baz says, "*As some of you have already realized, there are more than ten of you left. However, as the last event was a team event—meaning your entire team had to survive to move on—one team is out of the running. We'll give you a few seconds to wave goodbye.*"

All eyes turn to the team with the missing player. They look around at each other, at us, at the tall gray wall stretching high in front of us. None seem to notice the pale pink smoke pouring in from the top of their tube. I want to warn them, to beat on the glass until it shatters and run to help them, but I know there is no use. And maybe it is better that they don't see their death coming.

One by one they fall as the smoke reaches them. Once the

bodies rest in a pile, the smoky cylinder and our competitors are lowered back into the floor, disappearing from view. The cylinders surrounding us and the remaining team are lifted up and vanish into the ceiling while we still cluster together on the ground—gripped by fear, camaraderie, or something else.

Baz's voice jerks me back to the moment. *"Esteemed guests, it is now time for your fourth challenge. Ahead of you is a maze. Simply find your way to the other side. You can use teams, pairs, or work as individuals. Just remember, we only have room for eight of you in the next challenge. First eight here, or last eight alive—whatever gets you crazy kids to the right number is fine."*

I put my hand on Borah's shoulder and say, "You kept us safe through the last level. Let us do the same for you. I promise I'll get you to the other side."

"I dunno," she mumbles.

Thoa says, "I understand if you don't want to work with us. We haven't been fair to you."

She bites her lip, but before she can answer Krew says, "We'll be safer as a group. There's no way this is just a maze. They've got something planned."

Borah nods, "I'm with ye."

I look around and realize the other group is already gone. "Where'd they go?"

"Damn it," Krew says. He runs to the wall and starts pressing his hands against it.

Heinrich starts walking towards the other end of the maze and says, "If we didn't see them go in, the entrance is probably down there."

We follow Heinrich to the end of the maze. He runs his hands along the surface for a moment, then says, "Here. There's a lever."

He flicks it and the entrance slides open. We crowd around him, trying to peer into the darkness beyond.

Borah asks, "Another sensory deprivation?"

"I don't think so," Heinrich says. "I think it's just dim. Maybe there's something in there to light it up."

"Unless the other team already controls the light," Krew says.

"Only one way to know," Thoa says.

He steps in front of Heinrich and starts off through the maze. Heinrich and Borah follow behind, leaving me and Krew at the entrance. He says, "You first."

"No way," I shake my head. "I'll take the rear in case something comes up behind us. I'm a better fighter than you."

"Unless it's against a snake." His smile lights up his face. It's a sweet reward after the last three levels.

Krew steps into the maze and I enter behind him. After a minute or so my eyes adjust to the darkness and I can see fairly well. The walls stretch a good twelve, maybe fifteen, feet in the air. I can't see exactly where the walls end and the ceiling begins, but it looks like there may be a little space between them. I assume there are cameras somewhere up there, but knowing what I do about them, I'm sure they're hidden through the maze or following along in miniature form as we go.

If I can forget about the cameras, it's like being on a hunt at night with only stars to light the prey. It was a night like that when I found Krew. For a moment I wonder what might've happened if I hadn't found him that night, or if he'd escaped me.

I shake my head to dismiss the thoughts. It does no good to dwell on such things. The girl who found him is gone, replaced by the one who stalks through this maze. Such a short time to feel like a different person.

"I have a question for you," I say.

Krew slows to match my pace and says, "Sure."

"The girl from the other team said there can only be one winner."

He doesn't say anything for a minute as we trudge along. Finally he says, "What's your question?"

My mouth parts, but the words aren't there. He didn't deny it, didn't try to hide it. But that doesn't mean it's a fact. "I mean, is it, you know...is it true?"

Krew sighs. "It isn't something you need to worry about."

"How can you say that? You and Thoa are here with me, part of my team. Of course I need to worry about it."

"Just remember, if anything unexpected happens, you're a citizen of Vaisseau even though you've never been there. They'll honor that. Plus, I have a plan. And Thoa knows..." he trails off. Krew stops so quick it takes a minute before I realize he's not with me. I turn back to him and he asks, "Where did they go?"

I look to where the others were only a moment before. They were in front of us a few paces, but now they're gone. I whisper, "I don't know."

"Should we try to follow them?"

"Of course," I say. "They could be in trouble."

We press forward, slowly, trying to avoid whatever has befallen the rest of our team. We're near the place where they were when they disappeared when I notice the air shimmering in front of us. It's so slight that at first I'm not sure I saw it. I grab the back of Krew's shirt and hold him still while I watch it.

When I'm sure of what I've seen I say, "There's something wrong with the air in front of us."

He stands perfectly still, staring ahead. After a moment he says, "I don't see anything."

"Trust me, it's there. It's sort of like looking into a pool of water. Even if it isn't moving, it still has a certain quality to it. Fluid."

He tilts his head, stares again, then reaches his hand forward. His fingers disappear into the shimmering air. He screams and jerks his hand back.

I grab for him, pull his hand to me. I turn his fingers over in mine and ask, "What happened?"

"Nothing," he says with a laugh. "It's a privacy field. At least, that's what we use them for on the ship. They block sight and sound."

"Why would you need something like that?" I ask.

Krew raises a brow and smirks. "Some people cohabitate and don't want their bunkmates watching them have sex."

Heat creeps up my neck and I say, "Yeah, probably should've worked that out on my own."

I look up at him and see the grin still plastered on his face. He traces a circle on my palm and I realize I'm still holding his hand. I let go of him and turn to face the privacy field. "So you think we should just go on through?"

"Yeah, it's nothing."

He steps through the field and I follow behind. On the other side we find Thoa, Borah, and Heinrich in a heap on the floor. Krew and I drop to our knees to check on them. A shadow looms over us. I turn just as the hilt of stabby girl's blade collides with my temple.

MY HEAD IS THROBBING WHEN I OPEN MY EYES. I'M LINED UP WITH Thoa and Krew, but there's no sign of Borah and Heinrich. Each of us are gagged and tied at hands and feet. I struggle against my bonds, but Thoa shakes his head and holds up his bloodied wrists. He's already tried.

I try to look around, but realize there's a privacy field on the other side of us as well. We're hidden between them, though I can't imagine what purpose it serves.

After a few minutes of angry silence, stabby girl enters through one of the privacy fields. She smiles brightly and says, "Hello, friends."

I start cursing her in Raider, unable to control my tongue. She *tsks* at me. "Don't wear yourself out on my account. We've got a lot to do and you're going to need your strength." She points at Thoa and says, "I'm thinking you're the patient one--the strong, silent type. I'm going to take off your gag so we can talk."

As soon as Thoa's gag is removed, he lets out a string of vibrant curses. Once he's finished, he says, "What the hell do you want with us?"

She shakes her head. "I want to survive, dimwit. You know, I'm really disappointed. I thought you'd be smarter."

"This is your way of surviving?" he asks.

She nods. "You see, this could go one of two ways. The first is that I kill you and leave you here. You're some of my strongest competition, so that would make sense."

"And the second way?" Thoa asks.

"We team up until the end. Truce for the next four levels. Then I'll kill you on eight."

"What's in it for us?"

She laughs. "Well, I won't kill you right now. That should be motivation."

"How can we trust you?"

"Oh you definitely can't. I am not trustworthy. At all."

I wriggle around until I catch her attention. She says, "I'll remove your gag, but I swear, if you start screaming or some other nonsense I'll just knock you out again. You got me?"

I nod. When she removes my gag I ask, "Why now? Seems like you were okay with your other team."

She rolls her eyes. "They're a bunch of morons. Did you see how hard it was just to kill one person on level two? I mean, why do they think we're here?"

"But if they're weak, wouldn't you want to face them on level eight?" I ask.

"Yeah, but if I'm relying on them, I won't make it that far."

I weigh her words, unsure what to make of them. She's already said she can't be trusted, so I don't know which way her words are trying to push us. She could just be weaving a lie. Then again, she had the chance to kill us and she didn't.

"I'm in," I say.

She leans back, her eyes widening. "I thought you'd be the one I had trouble convincing."

I shrug. "Not much of a choice. Kill us now or kill us later. At least later we'll have a chance to kill you first."

She grins at me. In another place, at another time, a smile like that would send butterflies through my stomach. The girl *is* beautiful. Her skin is dark amber, a sheen of sweat making her glow. Her eyes are the brown of tree bark, under dark lashes that stretch for miles. She has high cheekbones, a fine nose, and pouty red lips.

On a second glance, I think her lips may just be covered in blood.

She pulls her dagger and slices the bonds holding me, Thoa, and Krew. As I get to my feet I stretch out a hand and say, "Nova."

"Rekka," she says. She shakes my hand, then Thoa's, and turns to Krew.

"One question," Krew says, folding his arms across his chest instead of shaking her hand. "Where did you get the privacy fields?"

"My mother," she says.

"These are space station tech. They're forbidden on-world."

She shrugs. "My mother was something of a rebel."

Krew eyes her. "Who was she?"

"Sima Louvier."

Krew gasps. "She disappeared years ago. We assumed she was dead."

"She is," Rekka says. "I'm going to the space station to finish what she started."

"Maybe not a good idea to broadcast that to the cameras," Krew says.

"This is a privacy field. You do know how they work, right?"

Krews purses his lips. "Of course I do."

Rekka raises her brows and says, "Then you know it covers all angles and disables cameras within range. There's no way those off-world assholes heard me. Besides, I'm sure they're expecting me at some point, since the Règle murdered my mom."

"No, no way. She was a rebel leader. They would've wanted to make a show of her trial," Krew says.

"She was a *revolutionary*," Rekka hisses. "She was trying to free the people trapped on that damn ship."

"She blew a hole in the side of it!"

"Calm down," Thoa says, pushing his way between them. "We don't have time for this."

Rekka huffs and turns away, straightening her gear. She points to the corner of our little box and says, "Your weapons are over there. Gear up and let's go."

As we're grabbing our stuff, I realize Borah and Heinrich aren't included in this arrangement. I turn back to Rekka and ask, "What about the rest of our group?"

She shrugs. "What about them?"

"I told Borah we would protect her."

"Lies happen," Rekka says.

"Did you kill them?"

"No," she says, almost managing to look offended that I would ask. "I pushed them out of the privacy field and told them to run."

"So they left us?" Thoa asks. The tone of his voice makes it clear he doesn't believe her.

"I told them I'd slice them up if they tried to help you."

Thoa nods. "Makes sense. We're partners by happenstance. Loyalty has no place here."

"I still want them to make it to the next level," I say. "I understand if I can't help them after this, but I want to keep my word."

Rekka says, "Whatever. There's room for eight."

"Hey guys, have you noticed the water?" Krew asks.

I feel it as soon as he says it. My eyes dart to the floor where a few inches of cold water are splashing around my feet. It isn't enough to worry about—yet—but I'm sure they're going to do more with this than create a small nuisance.

"It's a flush," Krew says. "We've been gone too long and audiences are losing interest. They're trying to force us out into the open."

Rekka smiles. "Let's give 'em a show."

She squeezes a button at her collar and the privacy fields drop. Blade in hand, she charges into the adjoining hallway with a violent yell. A man from her team is there, frozen in place as she charges for him.

"Move!" I yell.

But it's too late. His instincts kick in only a second before her knife slices his throat. His mouth drops open as he grabs for his neck, trying to hold the blood in. He crashes to his knees and his eyes find me in his final moment.

"I'm sorry," I mutter.

"Thanks for looking out," Rekka says as she wipes her blade off on his sleeve. He falls at our feet, the water around him becoming a red cloud. I can't seem to take my eyes off him.

"Come on," Thoa says, wrapping a hand around my bicep and pulling me forward.

When we reach Rekka I stop and say, "You didn't have to do that."

She puts her hands on her hips and tilts her head at me as if confused. "You do know we're in the trials, right? These people don't give a damn about you. We kill them or they kill us; either way, somebody's dying."

"I know where we are and what this is," I say. "Doesn't mean I have to lose my humanity along the way."

She chuckles. "I'd always heard Raiders were tough. The truth is underwhelming."

I stomp past her, splashing my feet in the bloody water as I go. A second later I realize the splashes were more than they should've been. I look around at the water. It's past my ankles now.

"The water's rising," I say.

"Obviously," Rekka says.

She pushes into the lead, not stopping until we come to an intersection. She calls back, "Which way, star-boy?"

"How would I know?" Krew asks.

"Don't you plan these things or whatever?" she asks.

He shakes his head. "No. Not even close."

"Then why do you need to live?" she asks, her hand sliding to her blade.

"Because he knows other things," I say. "He doesn't plan the games, but he's watched them his entire life."

She looks at Krew, the corners of her lips turned up. "Then you know how this ends?"

He nods once but says nothing.

"And you're still here. You're willing to die for her?"

"What are you talking about? Why would you need to die?" I ask.

Krew doesn't look at me, won't look at me. His eyes stay on Rekka for silent seconds before he tips his head to the right and says, "It's this way."

"How do you know?" she asks.

He shrugs. "Sometimes you just know."

CHAPTER
TWENTY-FIVE

W e splash through the corridors, following Krew at each turn. I don't know if he really knows where he's going, but none of us do either, so we don't fight him for the lead. The water is nearing my knees, thigh-high on Rekka's small frame, when we reach the ladder. The corridors lead off in three different directions, but right in the middle of the intersection the ladder reaches into the darkness above us.

Krew stops in front of it. As we pile behind him, Rekka asks, "What's up? Why are we stopping?"

"I've never seen a ladder in the maze before," he says.

"And?" she asks.

He shakes his head. "It's strange. I don't know if it's a trap or a gift."

"Let's hope it's a gift," Thoa says, "but be ready for a trap."

"With the way this water is rising, up may be the only way we can go," I say.

Rekka pushes past Krew and put her foot on the first rung. As she climbs, water falls off her like rain. As she nears the top she looks back down and calls, "Nothing bad yet."

"Don't jinx it," Krew mutters.

I watch as Rekka waves her arm at something I can't see. A moment later I hear splashing at my right and turn to see Borah and Heinrich approaching, blades drawn. I put my hand on my sword hilt, unsure what to make of their arrival.

Borah sheaths her sword as a smile cracks across her face. "I thought ya were dead. We were comin' to take revenge."

Heinrich shrugs. "Thought it was weird that she waved us over."

"I'm glad you two are okay," I say.

I want to spill everything with them and tell them about our arrangement with Rekka, but it wouldn't help anyone. They wouldn't trust us, so we couldn't protect them from her. Honestly, it may already be too late for that anyway.

Rekka splashes down from the ladder, tearing me from my thoughts. She points in a direction the corridors don't go and says, "Exit is that way."

She takes off in the direction Borah and Heinrich just came from. Heinrich says, "We tried every passage over here."

"No you didn't," she says.

"We did," Borah says. She stops and folds her arms. "You're lying."

I look between them, unsure who to believe. Rekka seems sure of herself, and she's asked us to team up with her, but I trust Borah far more than the stabby girl.

"I'll double-check," I say, starting up the ladder.

"You're wasting time," Rekka says. "They just didn't look hard enough. If they had, they'd be out of this place already."

There's a few feet of space between me and the ceiling, letting me survey the area and look in the direction Rekka indicated. The exit hatch is in the distance, so I know Rekka is trying to lead us out. I trace a line through the maze, but can only see a clear path through a few corridors over. Maybe she sees something I don't, but I can't quite make out the whole path. Still, I think she's telling the truth. Or at least she's trying to.

"I can see the exit," I say, pointing the way Rekka said to go.

As I climb down, Borah glares at me like she isn't sure whether to believe me or not. I say, "I told you I'd get you out of here, and that's what I mean to do. You helped me through the last level when you could've let me die. But I trusted you. Now you're going to have to trust me."

Rekka starts off again and I follow. After a minute I hear the slosh of water as Borah and Heinrich catch up to us. With the six of us together, there's no chance the remaining three will risk an attack. We're as safe as we can be in this place. Somehow the thought doesn't provide any comfort.

We wade through the maze for fifteen minutes in pursuit of the exit Rekka spied. The water laps against my hips now, and though my jumpsuit has managed to keep it out, my teeth still chatter from the cold pressing against me and sloshing in my boots.

It has to be worse for Rekka, but she doesn't show it. It's nearly to her chest and sometimes the water's movement throws her off balance. But she presses on without complaint. It would impress me if I didn't hate her so much.

The act of hating her is more taxing than I expected. I'm spending too much time in my thoughts, thinking about who I wish she was, who I want her to be. But we can't be friends, despite how similar we are.

And we are similar.

Perhaps that's what I hate the most. We are fighters, we take lives, we've lost parts of ourselves to the star-people, to whoever the Règle is, and in the end we both want revenge on them. Watching the way Rekka dismisses the lives of those around her makes a sharp stab of guilt pulse through me. I've done that, as recently as Gearhaven, maybe even here, but never felt the pain from it until I watched her in action. She kills without discretion. That's not who I want to be.

She stops at a dead end and turns to face us. "Something's wrong. It should be here."

Thoa nods. "Remember how I stopped a couple turns ago? I thought I felt the maze moving. I didn't want to alarm anyone in case I was wrong, but I'm pretty sure they're adjusting the maze as we go."

"Of course," Rekka says. "I should've noticed."

Thoa shakes his head. "We weren't meant to. It's very subtle. I probably wouldn't have except I've been keeping track of a landmark."

"What one?" I ask.

Thoa presses his lips into a thin line. "I'm afraid if I tell you, they'll remove it."

"Don't tell us," Krew says. "They'll definitely remove it. Right now it's all we've got."

"Not all. We know we're close. Rekka saw the exit, so even if they're turning us around and messing with the corridors, it has to be nearby," I say.

"Stand on my shoulders," Thoa says. "Maybe you can see the exit again."

Rekka shakes her head. "I'm too short. Nova needs to do it."

Thoa stands against a wall and Heinrich boosts me onto Thoa's broad shoulders. He and Heinrich clamp hands around my ankles as I try to steady myself. Even this high up, I can't see over the walls. There's an overhang a couple feet above me, but can't make out anything else.

"I'm not high enough," I say. "I'm going to jump to try to reach the ledge."

Thoa says, "We jump together, on three. One, two, three."

Thoa's jump propels me upwards and my fingers scrape by the shelf. One of my hands manages to find a grip, barely, and I dangle from the overhang as my heart rattles around in my chest.

"You okay?" Rekka calls.

I take a few seconds to calm down before saying, "I'm good. Climbing up."

I put my other hand on the ledge as well and try to feel around for anything to give me a stronger hold. My hand grazes something cold, firm. I explore what I think is a metal rung of some sort, like the ones on the ladder that Rekka climbed. I wrap both hands around the metal and use it to pull myself on top of the wall.

Once my body is in place, I reach up until I find the ceiling. It's about three feet above where I sit, giving me room to crouch but not stand. I look around and spot the exit within seconds.

I look down at the others and feel a smile spread across my face. "I have an idea."

IT DOESN'T TAKE MUCH CONVINCING TO GET REKKA THROWN UP HERE with me. Catching her was easy with Thoa's expert toss. The water would overwhelm her soon anyway. It climbs against the others' chests now.

Rekka and I have crawled across the tops of the maze for the last several minutes. Because we can only see a few corridors ahead, we'll need to be in different places to direct everyone through. She's moving to the next section now, while I turn back to guide the others. From this vantage point, we can direct them as the maze turns to make sure they get where we need them to.

I guide the group through the maze until they're two corridors past me. Rekka will take over and get them out. All I have to do now is get myself to the exit.

Even as I think those words, my world shifts. It's much easier to notice the way the maze moves when you're on top of it. My eyes follow the trail of the section I'm on and I can't help but laugh, though there's nothing enjoyable about what's happened. Our sections no longer connect and there's no way to get across to her from up here.

My eyes find Rekka's. There's surprise on her face. I yell, "I'm fine. I'll have to jump down and head your way on the ground."

"It's a big jump," she says.

"Mostly water now. I'll be okay."

She nods. "I'll watch for you."

I look around until I figure out where the sections connect. I move a few feet down the wall until I can jump into the right section of corridor to get to them, though it will take longer than I'd like. I move to the edge and push myself off the ledge.

As I fall, I catch sight of three figures pushing their way through the water. I try to call out a warning, but I crash into the water before I can. The cold leeches all the heat from my body as I kick upwards to bring my head above the surface. I scrape my feet against the ground, but it's no use; the water is too high for me to stand, so I must swim. My teeth chatter so hard I'm afraid they'll crack.

I let my mind linger only a few seconds on the swimming lessons Rego gave me. We spent far more time in the desert than near water, but he wanted to make sure I could survive no matter what I encountered. I choke back the sob as I realize for the first time that Rego was the father I needed when I thought all was lost. Rego saved me.

I press down the sudden swell of emotion. I have to finish the games and figure out how to stop the star-people from using us before I'll be able to see Rego again. But I know I will see him.

I swim through the hall, pleasantly surprised at my progress. I might not be a great swimmer, but even my poor attempt is moving me through the corridor faster than if I tried to walk. And I need to hurry if I'm going to beat them. The other three competitors were making good progress towards the exit.

When I turn the corner, I run into a wall. I float there for a moment, stunned. I didn't notice it from above. But of course, that could've changed in the short time I've been down here. As I linger there, trying to figure out what to do next, something brushes against my leg. My blood runs cold as it slithers past.

"Bastards," I mutter.

They're taking advantage of my fear. And of course they are. It makes for good entertainment.

I survey the walls, looking for any way up. But there's nothing. I'll have to go back the other way to get out of here, swimming with whatever is down below. Another creature slithers against my leg and I suppress a shiver. I don't know if I can do this.

"Nova!"

I jump at the voice, turn to see Borah on the wall above me. Even with her help, I won't make it. She's too high up for me to reach her outstretched hand. I shake my head and say, "Go on without me. Get out while you can."

"I dinnae come all the way back to lose ya now. Climb the damn wall."

"I can't," I say. "There's nothing to grip. And with the water, I can't get enough speed built up to scale it with momentum."

"Yer tough as nails, lass. Ya can do it."

I move to the corner where the walls meet and place my back against it. I adjust myself in the water so my legs are under me, one on each wall. I place my hands against the wall on either side of my body and tip forward just enough to give myself balance. Moving my right foot up the wall, then my left, alternatingly pushing up with each foot, I manage to push myself up a little from the water.

"See?" Borah says. "Just a wee bit to go."

She's several feet above me, far more than a "wee bit," but her encouragement still urges me on. I creep up the wall until I'm almost within her grasp. My legs are tired, but I'm closing the gap and I know we don't have much time.

When I think I'm close enough," I say, "I'm going to jump for you."

"I'll catch ye."

I count to three and jump, my hands grasping for Borah. I miss, feel her arm brush against mine. I know I'm going to fall. But then she's got me. One hand grasps my wrist. Her other hand is reaching for me and we clasp forearms. She hauls me onto the top of the wall and we lay there panting and laughing.

After only a moment, she sits up and says, "We cannae delay. The other group was closin' in."

We look over the walls towards the exit. We aren't far, and there's a clear path if we stay up top and crawl. We move towards it as fast as we can on hands and knees. It doesn't take long for us to get there.

We have to get off the walls to get to the exit. I jump in the water below and swim to the ladder. It leads up to a round hatch in the wall with red lights surrounding it. I start climbing as Borah hits the water. I reach the circular doorway and climb inside, Borah on my heels. I spin around and reach out my hand to pull her inside. The door grazes the tips of my fingers as it slams shut.

Borah is on the other side.

CHAPTER
TWENTY-SIX

I slam my fists against the door. My breath is ragged. I don't realize I'm screaming until warm hands pull me away from the door. Thoa holds me against him, whispering in my ear as he tries to calm me down.

"I promised her," I say.

"I know," he says, smoothing my hair. "I'm sorry we couldn't keep that promise."

I look around the room for someone to blame. My eyes land on Rekka, but this isn't her fault. Then I catch sight of the other three members of her team and my mind clicks the pieces into place. This *is* her doing.

"You made a deal with them, didn't you?" I ask her.

She nods. "Yep."

"You killed Borah so they could get here."

"Technically *I* didn't kill her. She did that herself when she insisted on going back for you. But I killed one of theirs, too, so it's even."

I clench my fists at my sides. For one delusional moment I thought there was a chance that I understood her, that I could rely on her. I shake my head at my own foolishness. Rekka is only here for herself. She proves it with every action.

"*Well that was fun, right players?*" Baz asks, his voice so cheery I want to reach through the speaker and squeeze his throat. "*Since you're all a little damp and cranky after your swims, we're going to let you get cleaned up before this more* civilized *level.*"

"What does that mean?" I ask, spinning to Krew.

He winces. "It's been awhile since they've done one of these. Instead of measuring how well you fight or think, they measure your societal skills."

"What does that mean?" I ask.

"It means you need to watch your language and your attitude for this level. And you can't kill or hurt anyone. It's about fitting in with a civilized society with rules and laws."

"A society who gets amusement from stalking other people?"

Krew presses his lips together. "I know you aren't going to like this, but you're going to need to focus if you want to pass."

The ceiling opens and eight tubes lower into the room. They are mirrored on the outside and each has a name written on the side in fancy looped letters.

"*Please find your station. You have ten minutes to complete this task. Oh, and leave your weapons behind.*"

I glance to Thoa who shrugs and gives my shoulders a squeeze. "Whatever it is, we'll get through it together."

I nod, then move to the one with my name on it. There's a door in the side and I enter. The inside is not what I expected. There's a table with a basin full of water, a bar of soap, and crisp white towels. Beside the basin is a small rack of clothes with several outfits upon it. They all appear to be dresses.

Beside the clothes is a chair that looks too extravagant for a Raider to use. I immediately sit down. Part of me feels like it's from spite, dirtying up their furniture, but really I just need to get out of my boots. I pull them off and toss them on the floor. Water runs out onto the carpet. I take off my socks to see wrinkled toes. I grab one of the dresses and dry my feet on it, unable to keep myself from smiling about it.

I look around the tube for any sign of a camera, but it seems they've given us some real privacy. Probably an intermission for the home viewers to take a quick break. Whatever is in store for us next might not be deadly, but I'm certain it will be painful.

I strip off my clothes and use the items on the basin to clean my body. I can see my reflection in the mirrored walls and most of the oil on my hair has worn off, leaving it shining copper in the lights.

After I'm moderately clean, I flip through the clothing they've given me. I don't know if there will be a chance to change out of this after whatever they're putting us through, so I aim to select something that will allow movement if I need to fight. Two of the dresses I can rule out immediately for their bulkiness and long skirts. But the third is a slimmer fit and comes to just below my knees. I could cut it shorter if I need to.

I put on the clean underclothes they've provided and the navy-blue dress. It hugs against me and makes me feel exposed, unprotected compared with the clothes Hoshi gave me, and I worry what may be in store for the other levels. Perhaps that's part of the plan—remove our protection before making us fight to the death.

Baz gives a two minutes warning and I decide last minute to take my hair down. The red waves across my shoulders feel nice, but I grab a hair tie from the basin and put it around my wrist in case I need it out of my way in a hurry.

When I step out of the tube, it's a different world. The room has a dining area on one side and a flat square on the other. The whole room is ringed in massive pink and white bouquets of flowers I've never seen before.

"Nova," Krew says, drawing my attention, "where's your shoes?"

I turn back to my chamber but the door closes before I can get to it. All the cylinders ascend into the ceiling. Queasiness hits my gut. How could I be so reckless in this dangerous place?

"I'm sure it's fine," Thoa says.

I turn and give him a tight smile. We both know it's not fine, I needed those shoes, but I appreciate that he tries to make me feel better. He looks strange and sexy in the clothes he's chosen. He wears a tartan kilt with a black button up vest and a jacket over it. His thick socks cover his legs nearly to his knees, but the ensemble shoes off the fullness of his calves, the power often overlooked in his lower body.

Krew wears a navy suit that looks dull against his dark complexion. Where his skin seems to glow, the suit seems flat. His eyes twinkle with mischief as he meets mine and smiles. He touches a button on his jacket. The plain suit comes to life, shifting lights and patterns across it in a multitude of hues.

Heinrich and the other man from Rekka's team both look uncomfortable in similar zip-up jumpsuits that come to their thighs, one yellow, the other pink. The material looks soft, unlike anything I've seen before, and I notice Krew holding back a laugh while he stares at them. They must be something from his world, something I don't understand, but I can't imagine what.

Rekka is stunning in a short red dress that makes her skin look like it's glowing. One of the other women looks elegant in a flowing gown, though she'll have a distinct disadvantage if this challenge turns physical. The second woman is in a mint tuxedo that doesn't quite fit her.

"*Please choose your partner and move to the dance floor.*"

I look between Thoa and Krew, unsure what to do. Though in my heart I love Thoa, I also care about Krew. He's risking his life to be here with me, to protect me, and I can't just let that go.

Rekka steps up beside us and grabs Krew's arm, saying, "I'm taking this one. You Raiders will have to fend for yourselves."

Thoa smiles. "We'll manage."

He takes my hand and walks me to the dance area. With a bow, he says, "Lady Acconci."

A laugh escapes me. With everything that has happened since,

I'd nearly forgotten our time in Gearhaven when I'd pretended to be his wife. Rekka thinks she's abandoned us to a terrible fate, not realizing Thoa was a noble once, and with his guidance we'll be okay.

I curtsy, barely remembering the detail from the quick lesson I received before going to the Mayor's party. Thoa smiles and lifts my hand, putting the other on my waist. As the music starts up, he moves me through the room with such ease and grace, I almost forget where we are. I'm lost in his eyes, mesmerized by this man who has spent the last moon protecting me, loving me even when I didn't return his affections. He is more than enough to keep me happy all my days.

"It's strange to see you without a weapon," I say.

He nods, his eyes mischievous. "I still have a few things up my sleeves."

My eyes instinctively look to his arms, searching for a hidden weapon, but then he laughs and I realize he means his muscles. He says, "A shame I had to give up the whip before I got a chance to use it. I need the practice."

I laugh. "Practice? In the midst of the trials?"

He shrugs. "Nowhere better."

The music screeches to a halt, jarring me from my revelry. A heavy bass drops so hard into the music that now pounds through the room that the floor rumbles under my bare feet. Krew bounces past us with Rekka in tow, both laughing like they're at a party rather than in a death trial.

Thoa smiles down at me and motions for me to follow. We mimic Krew as he leads us around the room in a kicking, arm-flailing dance that is like nothing I've seen before. I catch on after a minute and do okay, but Thoa never misses a beat. I find myself laughing at the ease with which he catches on. He never participated in the festivities in the Raider camp and I didn't know he had it in him.

The music winds down and comes to a stop, leaving us all

breathless and panting. Thoa extends an arm to me and escorts me to the dining table. Each seat has a nametag on it and we sit accordingly. I sit between Thoa and the woman whose name I don't know, Heinrich beside her. Across the table is Rekka, Krew, and the others from Rekka's original team.

Behind them the wall slides away, opening to reveal a waitstaff dressed all in black. As the wall moves, they file out carrying silver trays. They place a tray in front of each of us while others fill our goblets. I glance to Thoa who shakes his head, confirming my thought that we shouldn't touch either thing offered.

When the speakers come on, I hear clapping in the background before Baz's voice chimes in. *"Well done, players. We couldn't choose who danced the best, because there's no fun in that, but we did choose who was the worst. Heinrich and Marleah, please stand."*

My breath catches as I watch Heinrich rise to his feet. The big guy lost his lover and has had no time to grieve, now he's stuck with a stranger for a partner and potentially facing the end. My heart breaks for him, for his loss, for what comes next.

"I pity Marleah's crushed feet," Baz says with a chuckle. *"But at least Heinrich has rhythm. Both of you were terrible, but one more than the other. Heinrich, Marleah, please take a drink from the goblet in front of you."*

Heinrich closes his eyes and takes a deep drink. I watch his face, holding my breath. After a few seconds, I see Marleah in my peripheral as she falls to the floor. Heinrich lets out a breath, dares to smile a tiny bit, winces at his own victory. I wonder if this partner's death reminds him of Morian.

"Sadly, Marleah will not be with us going forward. The good news is, with her gone and Borah drowning in the level you just left, there's only seven of you still in play. Great work, all of you."

I look at Krew, trying to question him without speaking. *Is it always like this? Does Baz enjoy commentating while people are murdered?*

A door in the side of the room opens and I lurch from my seat, but Thoa pulls me back down. They aren't letting us go through to the next level, they are sending someone in.

Two guards jog in and grab Marleah's body. They drag her out while a young girl enters the room. She looks to be around eleven, wearing a pale purple suit that is too large for her lanky frame. Her jet-black hair bounces in tight curls around her head. Her skin is dark, almost the same blue-black as Krew's, and they have the same nose.

I look from her to him and see the fear in his eyes. They're related, siblings I'd guess, and whatever is happening is not part of his plans.

His voice is quiet, his words clipped as he asks, "Zazira, what are you doing here?"

She frowns at him, her lips trembling, and I'm certain she's going to cry. "They made me come. They're mad at you."

Krew looks up at the cameras in the ceiling above the table and says, "She isn't part of this. Her life isn't tied to this game."

"Oh, Krew, so melodramatic. We're not going to hurt your sister. She's just there to make a delivery."

Zazira hands Krew a notecard. He puts his hand on her cheek and says, "Get back through that door and don't look back. Don't watch what happens. I'll be home soon."

"I'm scared," she whispers.

"Don't be. Nothing bad is going to happen to you."

She pushes a finger into his chest and says, "Not for me, for you."

He grips the finger pressed against him and says, "Go home, *petite sœur*. Don't stop for anyone."

Krew kisses the top of her head and she takes off towards the door. She casts one last look back to Krew, and in that moment the door closes before she can leave.

"Baz," Krew yells. The anger on his face is unlike anything I've seen from him. There's fire there. "Let her through."

"You know, that was the plan. But viewers are chiming in that they'd

like to see what happens with your sister in the mix. Will you betray your lover?"

"My sister is a citizen of Vaisseau, not a contestant."

"But that's the thing, pal: so are you."

Krew's grinds his teeth. "I chose to do this. She didn't."

"You chose, we chose, does it really matter? Either way, you're both there. Now onward to the next part of this level. Read the card and begin. If you survive, so does your sister."

Zazira moves to stand behind Krew's chair as he reads the note-card. His brows knit together as he checks the other side, but it's blank. He says, "All it says is to tell the truth."

The man next to Krew pulls the card from his hand and scans it. "There has to be more."

"There is," the woman next to him says. She points at the trays in front of each of us.

"What are you thinking, Clea?" the man asks.

"They don't do anything without a purpose. Whatever is on these trays goes with this trial."

I nod. "Makes sense. So who wants to go first?"

Without a word, Rekka whips away the tray lid from hers. There's a scrap of red cloth like the Chasseurs wear alongside a tuft of white-blond hair. Her jaw clenches as she stares at it and for a moment I think she might cry. When she looks up, her eyes go straight to mine.

"I already told you that my mother was murdered. I didn't tell you that it was your father who did it."

My heart skips and for a second I just stare at her with my mouth ajar. Finally the words rush back to me and I say, "I'm sorry. I had no idea."

"I know," she says. "I hate you because of him, and I don't think I can stop, though I know you aren't to blame. You barely know him."

My brows furrow and I ask, "How do you know that?"

She smirks. "You people talk too much, give away all your

secrets, and never pay attention to who might be listening. And I'm good at going unseen."

The speaker comes alive with Baz's congratulations. *"Bang up job, Rekka. You're on to the next level. Cheers."*

She picks up her goblet and takes a swig. We all watch, waiting to see if her drink was safe. When nothing happens, the whole room seems to let out a collective breath.

"That was easy." Clea says, lifting her own lid. She stares down at her plate for a moment and a tear falls beside the ring on the plate. She picks up a gold circle and holds it up to catch the light. There's a break in the metal. She looks up at the man across the table and says, "I broke our vows."

"What?" he asks, eyes going wide.

She opens her mouth to speak, her voice catching. Clearing her throat, she says, "I slept with Macy."

The man covers his face with his hands. His voice strains against the words as he says, "My mother?"

"Wow, that was a shocker," Baz says with a chuckle. *"Allon, do you want to go now?"* Allon shakes his head and Baz says, *"Yeah, we should probably give you time to digest that one. Buuuut that's not how things go. Pick up the lid."*

Allon picks up the lid. I don't recognize the item until Clea asks, "A bullet?"

He picks it up and weighs it in his hand. "Mom's husband said she was cheating on him. I didn't believe the old coot. They got into it and he hit her, bruised her up real bad."

"I remember," Clea whispers.

"Right or wrong about the affair, there's no excuse for him hitting her. But he was right, wasn't he?"

Clea nods.

Allon says, "Yeah, well. I didn't know. But even if I had known he was right, I don't think it would've changed what I did."

Clea's eyes widen. "The accident."

"Wasn't an accident," Allon says. "I shot him in the back of the head while we were hunting. No one is going to hurt my mom and get away with it. Brawling with someone is one thing—they know what they're doing and do it on purpose. But abuse..."

He trails off shaking his head. The rest of us sit in stunned silence. I stare at my fingers as I roll the tablecloth between them, queasy at the words being exchanged in such a public way. These confessions are not easy things, and the dread forming in my stomach reminds me that soon it will be my turn to confess something better left secret.

"Who wants to be next?"

The suddenness of Baz's voice surprises me and I jump. Sometimes it's easy to forget they're listening, watching our every move. Forgetting is something I can't do if I want to move past this tower and into their world—if I want to stop them.

I will stop them.

While I fantasize about defeating the star-people, Krew raises the lid on his plate. I don't know what the item is, but it seems like some sort of technology from above. He stares at it for a moment before blurting, "I lied about coming here for Ledwin. I came down illegally because I wanted to meet Nova."

He doesn't look at me. I don't know if I want him to. This isn't what I was expecting. He's already told me he knew my father, that he helped track me for the past few years, but I didn't think about it further. He told me once he came for adventure, that he didn't know what would happen when he got here. But now I realize he must've known. He knew I was a Raider, that I wanted to be a life-bringer, and he showed up exactly where I was hunting.

"Why?" I ask, my voice so soft I barely hear it myself.

Still, he doesn't look at me. "I've watched you on the cameras for years now. Part of me felt like I knew you already, like you would know me if we met. So, I came."

"You're leaving something out. Or someone, I should say."

Krew's eyes shift to the ceiling and he swallows hard. He looks to his sister's hand on his shoulder and seems to resolve himself to the words that come tumbling out. "My fiancé and I were fighting. He kept accusing me of being in love with you, said I spent more time with you than with him. I thought if I could see you in person, I could get over it and things with him would improve."

Thoa sits up straighter, clears his throat. "But."

Krew's eyes shift to Thoa. "I didn't mean to fall in love with her."

There's silence for a minute and then Thoa lifts his lid. There's a scrap of paper, cut in the shape of a star. "Do you remember what I told you in the woods? Before this mess, when we were still strangers?"

I shake my head. "So much has happened."

"After I killed my Raider father, after I became the Bonecutter, I wasn't allowed to play with the other children. They were afraid of me and the adults thought I was too violent to be around them."

"I remember now," I say, that moment coming back to me. "They wouldn't touch you."

He nods. "You came to camp after that, so you didn't know why I was alone. You would sit by me in the tent when no one else would, you offered me food from your plate by the fire, you smiled when you saw me. We didn't talk really, but you were kind. It made me feel like I had a friend."

His lips turn up at the corners, ever so slightly. He picks up the star and says, "I made this for you, but I never had the nerve to give it to you."

He places it in my hand. The paper is so old I'm surprised it doesn't turn to dust in my hand. "When?"

"When I realized I loved you."

I look from the paper to him and back again. "But this is..."

"Old?" he asks. "Yeah. I think you'd been at camp a few months. It was before I'd gone on my first hunt."

"We were just children."

He nods, shrugs. "I always knew. I just never had the nerve to tell you."

"But we didn't know each other."

Thoa smiles, but it looks sad. "You didn't know me, Little Star, but I've known you for a long time. I've watched you change and grow into a powerful woman, full of fire and strength and beauty, and all the while I've loved you."

Thoa's words seem to grow more confident as he speaks, but with each word I wither. I know who these game-masters are. There's only one thing that can be under my lid. I lift it and stare.

A piece of bark. A twig. A leaf.

Reminders of the forest and my time with Krew. The time while Thoa was being held captive. When I…

I look from my plate to Krew, to Thoa, back to my plate. Baz chimes in, "*Tell him.*"

"We took the children from Gearhaven," I say, my voice cracking. "You were stuck there, with Rego."

Thoa nods, looking from me to my plate. I continue, "Krew and I…"

The pause builds between us, making the words bigger, harder to get out. But he knows. It's written on his face. Thoa's voice is flat when he says, "Say it."

"We were together. In the forest."

"While I was getting the crap beat out of me to keep Nigel from killing your best friend, you were screwing Krew."

I reach for him but he jerks away. His eyes stare at the empty plate in front of him where the paper had been.

"Please," I whisper.

"Stop. Just stop."

"Look at me," I plead.

"I can't," he says. "All this time, I thought I was imagining this thing between you and him. I thought your feelings for me were growing. When we kissed on the way here…" He trails off and looks up at the cameras. "Are you laughing at my foolishness? Are you happy to show me who she really is?"

His words send a fire flooding through me. "You will not shame me for this. We are Raiders, Thoa. We commit on the solstice. I was not committed."

He laughs, but the sound is bitter to my ears. He turns to me and asks, "You think I'm upset because you had sex?"

I flinch under his gaze. Why else would he be angry?

"You do what you want with your body, Nova. I will not judge you for such things. But don't toy with my heart. Don't lead me to believe you love me, that you feel what I do, when you're also doing the same with Krew. You can't have both of us."

My mind flicks back to Ivy, to her two lovers, to the life she said is above. I realize now that is exactly what I want. I have feelings for both of these men. My heart is big enough to love them both.

"Why not?" I ask, letting the words tip out before I can stop them.

Thoa shakes his head. "I'm not wired that way. I know the Raiders choose as they wish, changing with the solstice as they desire, but my heart has always been only yours. I don't want to share you with someone else. I won't."

The table sits in silence until Baz says, "*Well, color me relieved. Glad that everyone is on the same page. Though there was a tad more cursing than I would've liked for* civilized *conversation. Oh well. I guess that just leaves Heinrich and you're free to move to the next level.*"

Heinrich lifts his lid. His plate is empty.

H einrich clenches his jaw. "I won't."

"What is it?" I ask.

"It's from when I met Morian."

"Tell us," Thoa urges, his voice soft.

Heinrich shakes his head. "No. It's a memory just for us. I won't tarnish it for these people."

"But Heinrich," I say, "if you don't tell us, they'll kill you."

"I know."

"Is that your final choice?" Baz asks. When Heinrich nods, Baz says, *"Very well. Krew, kill him."*

"What?" Krew asks, eyes going wide. "No."

"Kill him and your sister returns home."

Krew looks between Zazira and Heinrich. "I don't want to do this."

"It's okay," Heinrich says. "I'm ready to join Morian. Even if I won these games, it would mean nothing to me now."

Krew turns to his sister and says, "Zir, don't watch this. Please."

She nods, but her eyes never leave him. He walks towards Heinrich, but stops midway and says, "I need a weapon."

"No, you don't. You have everything you need."

Krew's eyes dart to me, fear and uncertainty at war on his face. I say, "Don't worry. I can walk you through this."

His face sours and he winces as he turns from me. "I don't want to be walked through it. I shouldn't have to do it at all."

"But you do," Heinrich says. "I couldn't save Morian, but you can save your sister. Let Nova teach you how."

A shiver runs up Krew's body, but he gives a nod. I stand and walk to the end of the table. I move Heinrich to the floor while I instruct Krew how to kill, showing him the easiest way to do it. Heinrich is a big man, and I worry that brute force will only hurt him, so I advise Krew to cut off his oxygen supply to incapacitate him. It isn't a pleasant death, but none are.

Heinrich sits on his knees on the floor with Krew behind him. I ask, "Are you sure you won't tell us about your empty plate?"

"No, I won't. My time is done."

I put my hand on his shoulder and say, "Goodbye, Heinrich."

At my words, Krew wraps his arm around Heinrich's neck and pulls back just as I showed him. I watch Heinrich gasping for air; even with the knowledge that he's dying, even wanting to die, instincts kick in. He bucks against Krew, trying to get air into his lungs.

"Hold tight," I say. "Just a little more."

Heinrich throws himself back towards Krew, landing on top of him. Keeping his arm tight on Heinrich's neck, Krew wraps his legs around his waist and holds as tight as he can. His face is shattered, broken, tears flowing down his face even as he chokes the life from Heinrich. Just as the big guy starts to lose his fight, Krew lets go of his neck.

"I can't," he says.

Heinrich looks up at me, his voice raw. "Please."

Thoa is there before I can blink. He wraps his big hands around Heinrich's head and twists so fast, so hard, that I hear Heinrich's neck snap. I blink up at him, surprised by the violence of the moment. But I shouldn't be surprised. He has been gentle with me, unexpectedly soft these last few weeks, but he is the Bonecutter.

Yet even now there's sadness in his eyes. This was a mercy kill.

I hear boots pounding down the stairs behind the wall. Krew sits crumpled on the floor on hands and knees, sobbing quietly over Heinrich's body. The guards appear and move straight towards him.

"No!" I yell.

Thoa wraps an arm around my waist and picks me up. I flail against him, screaming curses at the guards who drag away the crying star-boy. He doesn't scream, doesn't panic, just lets them pull him out of the room. One of them picks up his sister and slings her over his shoulder. She pounds away at his back, giving more fight than her brother, but there is nothing she can do.

I fight against Thoa, begging to be released, but he holds firm. The doors close and I slump against him. Anger and grief war inside me. I want to fight and I want to cry and I want this to be over. I look up to Thoa's azure eyes, soft moments before when he killed a man, hard now that he looks down on me. He releases me and walks back to his seat.

I'm suddenly aware of the silence in the room, the lack of sound rushing around my ears like a strange echo. I look up and realize the room is empty aside from Thoa and myself.

"They're gone," I say.

Thoa nods and points to the wall on the other side of the room. "Through there."

He picks up the paper star from the table and puts it in his jacket pocket. Without another word, he pushes past me and heads through to the next level. Tears well up, but I can't let them come. He's allowed to be hurt. And I'll try to give him space to feel what he needs, after we're out of this place. But until then, I'm resolved to protect him, even if he doesn't think he needs it.

Clenching my fists at my side, I barrel up the stairs and into the next level. There's a narrow corridor with red walls, several doors on each side. I run past all of them until I reach the end. I skid to a stop when I find the others sitting in a circle on the floor in front of me. Behind them is a white wall with a shiny black box in the center, with no indication what the box is for. Above the box is a large black rectangle that reminds me of the window at Hoshi's place.

Finally, Thoa waves his hand towards the circle and says, "They told us to sit."

I sit across from him in the empty spot by Rekka. I try to catch his gaze, but he won't look at me. Instead I look at the others. Rekka smiles back at me when I look at her, but the other two are also avoiding looking up. The space between them is wide enough for at least two more people to sit.

I hear Allon mutter, "I can't believe you had sex with my mother. Of all the people."

Clea winces. "I'm sorry."

"Why her?"

Clea opens her mouth to answer, but Baz cuts in. "*We've been asking the same question, Allon. In fact, it's the top trending topic of the hour. Congratulations!*"

Allon scowls and I wonder if Baz is trying to provoke a stronger response to entertain his audience. To us, his words mean nothing.

"*I thought you'd celebrate that more, but okay, whatever. I guess you're still reeling from finding out your wife has been having an affair with your mother. But hey, that plays right in with our next challenge. Are any of you familiar with the old game called Truth or Dare?*"

No one answers, but I'm sure by the name we all know what it is. Rekka says, "We tell you the truth or we have to do something. A challenge?"

"*Look at you, brawn, beauty, and brains. In our game, if you choose truth, you walk to the white wall and draw a card from the box. The card will ask a question we're all dying to know. Once you've told the truth, another door is taken out of play. If you choose dare, you move to the first door in the line and face whatever is inside. Sound good?*"

"No, it doesn't," I say. "We just did this downstairs."

"And look how well that turned out! Ratings are through the roof. So we've altered the game we were going to play so we can continue the fun."

"Come down here with us and I'll show you fun," I say.

"Now, now, don't get cranky. You're nearly to the end of our journey together. You don't want to ruin our fun."

I grit my teeth together but say nothing else. These people know me, my secrets, and my weaknesses. I can't risk their wrath when I'm this close.

"Right then. We're going to go in reverse order from the last level. Since Heinrich is lifeless on the floor below you, that leaves Nova going first. So, Nova, truth or dare?"

I look at the people before me, the illustrations of the disastrous effects the truth can have. I say, "Dare."

Baz laughs. *"Very well. Go to door one."*

I walk towards the corridor and look up at the doors. The one on my right has a ten on it. On my left is the number one. I put my hand against the door. The wood feels cool, grainy, unremarkable. With a deep breath, I turn the handle and step inside.

I sink into the floor, my bare feet surrounding by a squelchy wetness. The smell hits me before I realize what I'm looking at: earthy, pungent, with a hint of decay underneath. Thick, black mud fills the room, creating a miniature bog.

There's a box on the wall at the end of the room. I set my eyes on it and try to push myself forward. The mud suctions against each step, preventing me from moving with any haste. The farther I go into the room, the deeper the mud gets. I'm not quite halfway and already it reaches my knees.

Another step, but this time my foot brushes something in the mud. At first I worry they've filled it with snakes to torment me yet again, but no, this mud is too thick for such a thing. I reach my arms into the bog and grab hold of whatever it is. The weight of it is almost too much for me, but little by little I lift it through the mud.

With one last pull, it flops out of the bog and lands on top of the mud. Bile rises in my throat and I empty my stomach in the mud beside me. An arm sits in front of me, covered in filth and dried blood. I close my eyes for a moment to recover. Once my stomach has stopped doing flips, I survey the limb in earnest. Though it is covered in dirt, I can almost make out something on the wrist. I spit on my fingers and wipe away the grime.

A flower and sickle tattoo. The mazulla fighter I killed on the first level.

I look around the room and wonder how many others are buried in the mud. Is Morian here? Borah? Krew?

No, I think, *he's not here.*

Not because I think he's alive, but because there hasn't been enough time for them to dismember him and use him against me. If anything, his body waits for me in a later room, there to taunt me for failing when I thought we could win. He said they would honor my citizenship, if it came down to it, but I don't believe it. They didn't honor his.

I push past the arm and through the rest of the bog. There are things in the water pressing against me as I slosh through. I know it is body parts under my feet, grasping at my ankles, reaching towards me from the confines of death. But these things do not frighten me; no, it is the living who cause harm. The dead are only reminders of the decisions I've made.

There are steps leading up from the mud and I climb on them with dirty, dripping legs. I walk to the box on the wall and open it. Inside is a towel and a note. I sit on the floor in front of the box and wipe my legs with the towel. Most of the wet sludge comes off, leaving streaks and splatters of dirt. I do not mind that they are not clean. I'm certain there are worse things in these rooms that I will face soon enough.

I look over and see something black sticking up from the mud. I crawl over to the edge and realize it's a boot. I grab hold of the boot and pull it towards me. The limb doesn't budge an inch. *Because it's a whole body*, I think.

I climb back down into the mud, holding onto the boot so I don't lose it. I run my hand down the leg until I find the laces. I untie it and slide it up from the bog. I toss the boot towards the wall. It smacks and slides down, leaving a dark streak down the white wall.

Following the leg deeper into the water, my fingers graze against some sort of wet cloth. It feels like...Marleah's dress. I shiver, part of me wanting to release her. I've scavenged from dead bodies before, but something about this feels wrong to me. Nevertheless, I make my way to her other leg and untie the laces of the boot. I toss it with the other and climb back out of the mud.

The towel is so thoroughly soaked with mud by the time I'm finished that I'm pretty sure I'm getting dirtier by using it. I toss it into the bog and slide on the boots. They're snug around my toes, but better than nothing. As I tie the strings, something in the right boot digs into my skin. I flip out the tongue and find a tiny finger-sized blade sown into the leather.

"That crafty bitch," I say. It was smart, but not enough to save her in the end.

I pull out the knife and slip it into the underclothes they gave us in the last level. After one last moment of rest, I rise to leave the bog-room. I take a step and the notecard sticks to the mud on the bottom of my shoe. I'd almost forgotten it. I flip it open and read, "Ask Thoa what happened with Nigel."

The blood drains from my face. Without asking him, I already know. The Mayor hadn't been subtle with his interest in Thoa. I can ask him, or I can let it go. Maybe I would feel better if I didn't know the details. Or maybe I have to ask to pass the level.

I take a deep breath and grit my teeth, ready to face whatever these bastards throw at me next.

CHAPTER
TWENTY-EIGHT

R ekka is alone in the circle. She tips her head back in greeting
and says, "They're all in rooms. Buncha cowards."

I laugh, the sound surprising both of us, and Rekka smiles in
return. She pats the ground beside her and I join her on the floor.

"I guess you told the truth?" I ask.

She shrugs. "Went well the first time, why not try it again."

"So five doors are clear and another five remain." We sit for a
moment in quiet before I finally look up and say, "Can I go ahead
and take my next dare?"

"*Patience, Little Star,*" Baz says.

Fire boils in me. I clench my fists and grit my teeth, trying to
hold back my retort, but I can't. "Don't call me that."

I hear the smile in his voice when he realizes he's angered me.
"*Is that your* special *nickname? And here I thought we were becoming
friends.*"

"I'm going to rip your throat out the first chance I get."

"*I believe you would, if given the chance. Luckily for me, that chance
will never come.*"

Rekka perks up, saying, "Unless she wins."

Baz's laughter echoes around us. "*Oh good heavens, no, child. No* matter who wins, you won't mix with the general population until we've conditioned you to live with us. Even then, you won't be permitted within range of celebrities and public figures like myself."

I look at Rekka and mouth, "What's a celebrity?"

She shrugs. "So we go from the prison you've created here to a prison off-world?"

"Darling, it hurts that you would say such a thing. We've given you the whole earth as your playground and now you have this opportunity to live with your world's creators. How can you view it as anything less than amazing?"

"You know we're people, right? Do you viewers give two shits about the humans down here entertaining them?" she asks.

"I'd let you ask them, but our cameras are on the dares right now, so they can't hear you. And if I'm being honest, that sounds boring anyway."

Rekka shakes her head and sighs, pulling her knees up in front of her chest. I put a hand on her arm and whisper, "There's a way to fix this. We just have to figure it out."

"We?" she asks, looking down at my hand on her arm. She pulls from my grasp and says, "There's no 'we,' princess."

I shift away from her and watch the corridor, my foolishness making my cheeks burn. I didn't expect to be friends with Rekka, but we share a common enemy. Part of me hoped we could find a way to defeat them together. She'd make one hell of an ally, if she didn't hate me.

The others rejoin the circle within a few minutes. Thoa has a strange faraway look in his eyes but says nothing. Allon is dirty and Clea has scratches on her cheeks, but other than that they both seem intact.

Once they're settled, Baz says, "Welcome back daredevils. I see our challenges weren't enough to slow you down. One more round and you'll be on your way to level seven. I think we'll go in reverse order this time, so Rekka, what'll it be?"

"Truth," she says.

She hops up and practically bounces to the box on the wall. She pulls out a card and reads it quietly, then laughs. "Is this a joke?"

"Read it aloud, please."

"Have you thought about screwing one of your competitors?" she says with a smirk. "How would you even know if I was lying? I could say anything,"

"Honor system, Rekka. Now tell us the truth."

Rekka drops the card on the floor and she walks back to the circle. When she sits down she says, "Yes."

"Care to elaborate?" Baz asks.

"No," she says. "The card didn't ask me to name them."

"She's got us there," Baz says with a chuckle. *"That means door six is now out of play. Up next, to clear door seven, is Clea. Truth or dare?"*

"Are all the questions that easy?" she asks, eyeing Rekka.

Rekka shrugs. "Mine have been. But I'm not one for keeping secrets anyway."

Clea taps a finger against her tooth, weighing her decision. Finally, she says, "Truth," and walks across the room to the box. She pulls out a card, reads it, and her head droops. She says, "Are you in love with your significant other?"

Allon's head jerks up, his eyes searching her every movement as she stares at the card. He says, "Tell the truth."

She looks up and swallows hard. "No."

"Are you in love with someone else?" he asks.

"Yes."

The word hangs in the air. The brokenness between them is so sad, so lasting, I wonder if I'll ever hear laughter again.

Then the grand asshole from above chimes in, *"Wow, that was brutal."* There's laughter over the speakers as if the pain Allon and Clea are feeling means nothing.

Allon jumps up and says, "Dare."

He starts for the door, but Baz says, *"Not so fast. Door seven is a special one. You'll need a helper. We choose..."* Baz pauses for effect before saying, *"Clea."*

"But I cleared my door. I told the truth," she says.

"*And you did a wonderful job of it,*" Baz says. "*Now you can assist your husband in clearing his. Teamwork makes the dream work.*"

Clea stomps after Allon and Thoa gets up to walk to the truth box. He pulls out a card and reads, "If you had one wish, what would you ask for?"

He looks up at me when he answers: "I wish I'd told you sooner."

Thoa drops the card and returns to the circle. Baz says, "*Heart-breaker, that one. That leaves one door. Nova, what will it be?*"

My eyes haven't left Thoa. There's so much pain on his face, I can barely breathe. I can't risk adding more to it. "Dare."

"*Before you go, don't you have something you want to ask Thoa? A 'bonus' card, if you will.*"

I pull the card from under my dress and toss it at Thoa's feet. He picks it up and reads it, then presses his eyes closed for a moment before he looks at me.

"You don't need to tell me the details," I say. "But doesn't it make it a little hard to criticize me when you were doing the same thing?"

"It wasn't like that," he says.

"No? What was it like then? Did him for old times' sake?"

"I was trying to win him over to keep you safe."

"Well that's one way of doing it," I say.

Rekka says, "I'm really confused."

I say, "Before anything happened with me and Krew, Thoa had sex with a guy he used to know who clearly had a thing for him."

"What happened with you and Krew is completely different from what happened with me and Nigel."

"How so?" I ask.

"Because I'm not in love with him!" he yells.

Silence settles between us, but our eyes stay locked. Maybe he's right. Maybe my feelings for Krew make things different. Or maybe it doesn't matter either way. We weren't mated, so there was no betrayal, even if it feels like it.

The moment passes and I start towards the last dare, but Baz says, "Ah, ah, there's a catch. This is another door where a helper is needed. So let's see—Thoa, Rekka, Thoa Rekka. You know what? Let's get crazy. Rekka, you're in."

"What?" she and I both ask.

Baz laughs. "Now that is the surprise I was looking for. Good luck in there."

We walk to the tenth door. I turn the handle and we step inside. The room is plain, no decorations, white walls and floor. Against the wall is a box just like in the other room. I walk to it and take out the card. "Give in to your baser instincts."

I turn to Rekka, but she's figured out what the card means a second before me. She shoves me against the wall. She's strong, more than I realized, and I struggle to free myself from her grip. She pins my arms back against the wall. Her mouth covers mine in a frantic kiss. My body responds to her before I can think about what this is, what it means.

I press into her, hungry for more. I let my frustration with Thoa bleed into my kiss, my grief for Krew seeks this comfort, and part of me just *wants* her. Her grip on my arms lessens and I swoop my arms around her, pick her up, and spin her against the wall. She wraps her legs around my waist and I hold her there with my hips while my hands roam over her.

Kissing Rekka is different than kissing Thoa or Krew. She is soft where the men are hard, comfortable in ways they cannot be. Her body is like mine; I recognize the mountains and valleys of her form, knowing when and how and where to touch instinctively.

After too short a time, I hear the speakers above crackle to life, reminding me that someone is watching even in our most intimate moments. Baz says, "I'm truly sorry to interrupt—truly, because you are giving us quite a show—but time for this level is coming to a close and

Thoa is getting antsy waiting for you. Please wrap it up and head back to the circle."

Rekka pulls away from me, straightens her dress. I find myself strangely self-conscious, unsure where to look, how to act. She seems equally unsure as she moves past me to the door. She turns back to me, opens her mouth as if to say something, runs her hand over her shaved head instead.

"That was...ah..." She gives a half-laugh, half-sigh and turns away.

I follow her out in silence and we join Thoa in the circle. A moment later Allon walks towards us. His clothes and face are spattered with blood, his hands dripping with it.

I jump to my feet, but Rekka grabs my hand and pulls me back down. I look at her, brows furrowed, and she whispers, "Baser instincts. There were only two options."

Her words swirl through my head. She had the chance to kill me, but chose not to.

As Allon sits down, the black rectangle on the wall lights up. Baz says, *"Enjoy these highlights from our time in level six as we finish preparations for level seven."*

Pictures crawl across the screen: myself plodding through the mud, Thoa swinging from handholds on the ceiling while teeth snap up at him from a pit of creatures below. Clea faced a room of spiders the size of my head and I hold my breath for a second while I watch the fear cross her face. Allon's challenge was the worst of all. He was forced to eat the brains from the head of a competitor. The camera pans around in front of the body to show the man Rekka killed in the maze level.

My insides turn to stone as I watch the side-by-side split screen of Clea and Allon and myself with Rekka. We read the cards. Clea and Allon turn to fighting immediately. Rekka and I...don't. I try to see Thoa's face without looking right at him, but he wears a mask to hide his emotions. He sits motionless, the vein bulging in his neck the only indication he's even watching.

When both teams are finished in the room, the screen fades to black. Baz says, *"That was incredible. I'm delighted with the outcome. Now please, join us upstairs for level seven."*

Two doors open at the front of the room. Thoa and Allon both head to the one on the left. I call after him, but he doesn't turn. Rekka puts a hand on my shoulder and says, "He'll be fine. He knows you did what you needed to survive."

I wince at her words, recognizing the truth in them. Of course that's what happened. She did what she needed to survive. What did I think was happening?

As if reading my thoughts, she says, "But in the spirit of truth I should probably tell you that just because we *had* to do that doesn't mean I didn't enjoy it, or that I hadn't thought about it before." She winks and heads through the door.

I stand there looking after her. My insides roil with a strange mix of emotions and I can't help but question what's wrong with me. I came here to protect Thoa, so he wouldn't have to do this alone, but the rift between us grows with every level. Krew came for me, but he's gone. And now I feel some strange satisfaction because of the words of my enemy—my very sexy enemy, but still.

If I manage to make it out of here, what parts of me will survive? Will I like the person who emerges from this place?

CHAPTER
TWENTY-NINE

There's no one upstairs when I get there. I look around the room, my eyes taking in the slight scent of mango with each step I take across the coral-colored carpet. There are paintings on the wall unlike anything I've ever seen. One has a swirling background of blues and yellow stars. Another has a screaming person on a bridge. A third is full of melting clocks. Each inexplicably makes me feel homesick, though none are of my home.

There are frosted glass panels that stretch floor to ceiling, curving out from the wall. Something about them reminds me of the strange glass lift at Aeroport. The memory haunts me, reminding me of Aunt Rachel, of the family lost and returned, only to be lost again.

I shake my head to clear it and focus on the glass that bubbles out into the room, trying to figure out what it may be hiding. I stare hard at it, but can't see what's beyond. I go to the closest one and press my face against it, cupping my hands around my eyes to try to see what's inside. I can just barely make out a shape inside—a person—though I can't see who it is. I check the other panels as well; two of them are full, but the third is empty and waiting for me.

I run my hands down the edges of the panel but don't see a way inside. The walls don't seem to have a lever or button to access the panel, either. With a sigh I ask, "Can you please let me in?"

I can almost hear Baz laughing, though the speakers don't come on. Something about this doesn't settle well with me. He has been so vocal through our past challenges, giving directions and harassing us, that the absence of his voice makes me uncomfortable.

Still, there's no other option. The panel parts in the middle, revealing a small closet-sized room. I step into the enclosure and the glass closes in front of me. As it does, a small drawer in the side of the wall slides open. There's a gadget inside, a tech I haven't seen before, that looks like it fits over my eyes. I pick it up and a note dangles off one side, saying "Put on head." I do as it says, the strap on the back adjusting to me as I pull the mask-device over my eyes.

A figure approaches from the distance, looking as if they're made of light. They stop in front of me and reach towards my face. The light from the figure falls away, leaving the smiling face of my mother.

"Mom?" I ask. "What are you doing here?"

"I'm here to guide you, darling," she says.

I reach my hands towards her but they collide with the cool, slick surface of the wall in front of me. I swallow the lump in my throat. She's not here. This is only in my mind.

"It's good to see you," I say.

"I'm not real," she replies. "I'm built from your memories."

I nod. "I know. Still…"

Even knowing she is built from the part of my mind that remembers her, it still feels nice to see her whole and almost tangible.

She tilts her head and her red hair cascades over her shoulder. "Are you ready to begin?"

"Yes," I say, though I'm not sure what I'm agreeing to.

She turns away from me and waves her hand into the darkness. A village materializes before me and I watch a child chasing a figure as they walk down the path away from the huts. The scene zooms in to the child's face as she asks, "Do you really have to go?"

"I do. But when I come back for you, everything will be better."

She begins to cry. "I'm scared."

"Don't be afraid, Echo. I will win the trials for you. I love you."

I watch as a hand settles on Echo's shoulder. On the wrist is a flower and sickle tattoo. The camera pans to the face of the mazulla fighter who didn't make it past the first level. My stomach churns at the sight, knowing that I'm intruding on one of the last happy memories for Echo and the fighter whose name I never learned.

My mother turns to me and says, "You killed them."

I nod, unable to speak.

"Was it worth it? Would you do it again?"

The question eats at me and it takes a moment to find the answers inside me. "Was it worth it that the child will never see them again? Of course not. Would I do it again? In a heartbeat."

"Very well," my mother says. "Her death becomes yours."

Pain flashes through my gut and I double over with it. I run my hand over my body but realize I can't see the wound with the gadget on my head. I reach up to remove it so I can take stock of the damage, but mom shakes her head. "If you remove it now, you will not go to the next level."

My hand stops mid-air. If I remove it, I lose. If I don't, I may bleed out. Unless the wound is only in my mind. I don't know how much power this device has. It could easily be a distraction while the star-people destroy my body.

"But why would they?" Mom asks.

Her questions startles me until I remember that she is just a projection from my mind. It makes sense that she would know what I'm thinking.

The pain has subsided. It aches, but is nothing compared to the initial wound. Without the intensity, I'm certain this is all just part of whatever is happening in my mind. A wound like I gave the mazulla fighter would still hurt and would kill me quickly.

I nod to my mother and say, "I'm ready for what comes next."

"Are you sure?" she asks.

The scene changes and I'm watching two women sparring. One drops her sword, giving the other a chance to strike. The camera turns so I can see Borah's face as she hesitates. She knows she has the advantage, but chooses not to press it.

The second woman yells, "Strike me."

Borah shakes her head. "I've beaten you. There's no need."

"Do you think they will show you mercy in the games? No! They will strike you down at first chance. But you are strong, sister. You can beat them."

"I will win, but I will do it with honor," Borah says.

Her sister scoffs. "There is no honor in a city that thrives on blood. Kill them when you can and do not remorse. Your greatest mercy should be a quick death."

"Surely there are some among them with integrity."

"You cannot trust those strangers. Mark my words."

The scene fades and my mother asks, "Was her sister right? Are there any among you with honor?"

I ground my teeth together. Borah's time in the games was marked with betrayal. From the time she came to our team to her death in the maze, she tried to believe in others only to lose her life for her honor. When she came back for me in the maze, was it because she believed me to be worthy of her faith?

"We are all guilty of monstrous things," I say. "Borah showed faith when everyone else would've turned away. But to say we are all without honor would be wrong. There is honor, even among monsters."

Mom nods and my breath feels like it's sucked from my body. I struggle for air, gasping, but with each gasp it feels like something inside me is wrapped around my lungs, squeezing away the little air left in me. I start to convulse, my vision blackens around the edges. Just as I'm about to pass out, air floods back into my lungs. I gulp it down, greedy for each breath.

Mom asks, "Ready to stop?"

I shake my head. "I'm not giving up."

We continue through scenes of carnage, fits of death. Morian and Heinrich happy, in love, before they came here; I live both their deaths. I'm the man on level three who wanted a better life for his children, but died in a spurt of fire. I'm Marleah drinking poison, the man Rekka killed in the maze, Clea as Allon pummels her, tears streaming down his face the whole time.

"Last one," mom says.

I nod, but my body twitches in response. Though I know the pain only exists inside me, it doesn't stop the aches of my body in response to the trauma it is subjected to.

When Nigel's face materializes in front of me, my heart stops beating. If I'm seeing Thoa's before, does that mean…?

"You could stay," Nigel says, running a finger over Thoa's chest.

"I can't," Thoa says. "I love her."

The camera turns to him and I see the nobleman in his finery, his hair slicked back, living the life he was supposed to. He smiles at Nigel and it's clear that despite his words, part of him *wants* to stay. And why wouldn't he? His life would be so much easier without the Raiders, without the fighting, without me.

When the scene fades, I try to prepare myself for whatever pain they've inflicted on sweet Thoa, but I find the pain in my heart so great that I can't bear to consider what has happened. I clutch at my chest. The hurt I feel is far greater than any of the deaths so far.

"That hurt you feel," mom says, "was not the star-people's doing. That's what you did to him."

The words are a slap to my face, but I know they're true. I hurt him worse than the trials could. "Is he—"

"Alive?" she interrupts. "Yes. He's ready to move to the next level. The other remaining contestant has already gone ahead. But Thoa won't go without you."

My heart swells with joy and all the pain I've felt disappears. Despite the pain I've caused, despite his hurt, he waits for me. I smile and say, "I'm ready."

Mom puts her hand on my cheek and says, "Good luck, love."

She turns and walks away, her body turning back to light, then fading away to nothing.

I pull the mask off my head and the glass panel opens. Thoa is pacing the room. He turns when he hears my panel open and I run for him. He catches me and spins me through the air.

"I'm so sorry," I whisper, over and over and over, knowing it will never be enough to fix the pain I caused him.

I don't regret my decisions, the things that led me here, what happened with Krew or Rekka. But I do regret the way it made him feel. Whether his reaction was right or wrong, fair or not, I'm still sorry he had to feel the way he did.

"I'm sorry, too. I was hurt, but I treated you unfairly. You aren't mine, as much as I want you to be. I had no right to disrespect your choices. The star-people showed me the pain I gave you."

He puts me down and places his massive hands on each side of my face. "I was worried, Nova-du."

Life-bringer. The word sends a pang through me, reminding me of who I wanted to be, who I will never be. I shake my head and say, "I give death. Nothing else."

Thoa presses his forehead against mine. "You've given life to me. I only existed before, but you have changed it for the better. You breathed life into my lungs, gave my heart a reason to beat. You can't lose yourself in this place."

"I'm already lost," I say.

He smiles. "Then let me lead you back. We can finish this now. One more level and we can move on, move up, together."

I nod. He's saying all the things I need to hear, all the desires of my heart. And it almost breaks me knowing that the star-people are listening to us. Knowing what I do of them, I know this dream will never happen. They won't let it. One of us will die on level eight.

CHAPTER
THIRTY

A door opens and we ascend the steps together. I tie my hair back and take a deep breath, ready for the next battle. Before we reach the top, Thoa puts a hand on my shoulder and stops me. He withdraws the paper star from his pocket and hands it to me, wordlessly. I stare at the fragile thing in my hand, seeing it for what it is: Thoa's love.

We continue up the stairs and I hear Baz's voice echoing above us, but I can't make out the words. The speakers cut off as we step into the room. It is round with white metal walls, bare of any decoration, even the floor is plain gray concrete. There's a blue glass door across the room. Between us and the door, Rekka is waiting.

She whips her arm up and snaps her wrist forward. I watch something flying across the room as if in slow motion. Thoa pushes me and I fall to the floor. He stumbles past me, falling to his knees.

I push myself up and rush to him, though my muscles feel sluggish with each movement. It all happens so fast. I step in front of him and find a small knife hilt protruding from his heart. My mouth drops open and my eyes find Rekka's. It's the knife I pulled from Marleah's boot and hid in my dress. She must've taken it when we…

My eyes flick back to Thoa. "You're going to be fine. It's just a little thing."

His lips tip up at one corner. "You're a terrible liar."

"Promise," I say, kneeling in front of him. "We're going to get out of here."

"Kill her, Little Star. Live. For me. You have to live."

I nod. There's nothing more I can do. He starts to sink to the floor and I help him lie down. He's facing the middle of the room, like he wants to watch the fight.

So be it. I'll give him a show.

I stand and start towards her. Rekka backs away, walking around the circle with her arms up in a defensive position.

"I didn't want to kill him," she says.

"No, you were aiming for me."

She shakes her head. "I knew he'd jump in front of you. It was the only way I could beat him. If I'd have killed you, he would've ripped me limb from limb."

"That's what I'm going to do," I growl.

She smiles. "You might try. But I think I can take you."

"I guess we'll see."

I lunge forward. She dodges left, spins. She's quick. But I'm motivated.

She defends for a minute or two before making her first move. When she swings at me I dodge, but I don't see her leg as she sweeps it against my knees, knocking me down. I scurry back from her as she dives after me. I manage to gain my feet again, only to be knocked back down with a kick to the chest.

Rekka is on me in a flash. She sits on my hips, pummeling me with her fists. I block my head as best I can, but she gets in several hits before I finally buck her off. I throw my weight against her, trying to knock her off balance. She's smaller than me, lighter, and I need to use that against her. I've fought stronger opponents than her while training with Raiders. I can take her.

We're both on our feet again, circling one another. The next opening I get, I feint left with a punch. When she dodges, I dive towards her. I catch her shoulders with my hands and shove her against the floor. I flip her over so I can see her face as I kill her.

She tries to wriggle free, but I clamp my knees against her body. She throws her hands towards me, trying to catch me anywhere she can. Her fingers jab towards my eyes and I almost lose my balance, but catch myself before she can get loose.

Her arms go up as I swing at her head. The most I can hope for is a few good hits, evening us up. There has to be something else.

I grab her by the shoulders, pull her up from the ground and shove her back down with all my might. Her head cracks against the floor and her eyes roll back in her head.

As I grab her to drop her again, she whispers, "Nova, please."

I stop. This has to be a trap. But there's blood on the floor beneath her and my hunter's instinct tells me she's close to death.

Her voice is so soft I can barely hear her. "Don't let them win, Nova. It's up to you now. Ruin them."

I nod. Holding her there, about to kill her, instead I pull her against me. I whisper in her ear, "I'm sorry, Rekka, for what they've made us. For what it's worth, you made these games a helluva lot more fun."

She smiles and says, "Do it, Raider girl."

I slam her back onto the concrete. It takes six hits before her body finally goes limp. The ground is a bloody, pulpy mess. As much as I would like to have a proper goodbye with Rekka, I don't have time.

I run to Thoa's side. He's still breathing, but it's shallow. His face is pale and he doesn't respond when I try to talk to him.

I jump to my feet and scream, "What now, you bastards?"

The blue window on the other side of the room slides open. I walk towards it and see a black bracelet sitting on an elaborate gold stand. I pick it up, turning it over in my hands. It's like the one Krew, Ivy, and my father wear.

"What is this?"

"Congratulations," Baz says. "That is your reward. Place it on your wrist and we will bring you home as a citizen of Vaisseau."

"What about Thoa?"

"Unfortunately, there can only be one winner."

I hear his words, but just barely. There's yelling in the background. I hear my name, and something else. Baz is still talking, but I've tuned him out, focusing on the voice.

It's Krew. He's alive.

"You're already a citizen, Nova. You already belong here," Krew says.

The speakers cut out for a few seconds, and when Baz comes back on there's no longer noise in the background. "Put on the bracelet and join us, Nova. You've won."

I look down at the bracelet in my hand. Krew said it wasn't true about one winner, that he had a plan. While we stood in the maze he told me to remember, no matter what, that I am already a citizen.

"You didn't kill Krew," I say. "Because he's one of yours."

I lift Thoa's wrist and snap the bracelet into place. It seals around him, tiny wires coming out of the metal and burrowing into his flesh. The little light on the side turns from black to flashing yellow, then solid green.

"What do you think you're doing?" Baz asks. "You can't just give that away."

I force as much confidence into my tone as I can, hoping they don't hear my bluff. "Yes, I can. I don't need it. Thoa is yours now. He's still alive, so he won the games. Now help him before he dies."

The speakers come on as if Baz is going to speak, but in the background, I hear a voice say, "You heard her."

Thoa's body seems to disappear in front of my eyes. Little by little, parts of him fade as if to dust, and then the space in front of me is empty. A door on the side of the room opens and guards in black fatigues flood inside. One of them walks towards me with a black box in his hand that glows on one end.

"I'm a citizen of Vaisseau," I yell. "You can't kill me."

The guard stops as if he isn't sure what to do. Baz's voice comes over the speaker and says, "*You made your choice when you gave the bracelet to Thoa. There can only be one winner.*"

"I don't want to be the winner. Give the prize to Thoa. He is your winner. I want what is mine by birth. I want to come home."

Home. The word sticks in my mouth. That place means nothing to me. The thought of spending my life with those monsters makes me sick. But I'll do what I must to save Thoa, to honor Rekka and Borah, Heinrich and Morian, all the nameless ones I never knew, all the lives lost over the years to satisfy the bloodlust of the wannabe gods in the space outside our world.

Boots pound on the stairs. The guards and I all turn to see four people in red come through. They surround me, face the guards, and pull out weapons that crackle like lightning. The guards in black look to one another, unsure what to do.

When Ledwin Kennedy walks through the door, the guards seem shocked. A few of them actually kneel, while a couple others remove their hats in deference. He pays no attention to any of them, his eyes locked on me.

He moves across the room with such ease it's like he's floating. The Chasseur part to allow him to pass. He enters their protective circle and wraps his arms around me. He shakes against me—no, not him, that's me. *I'm* shaking and crying as he holds me, as he keeps me safe. He's been missing all these years, absent when I needed a father, but in this moment, I couldn't care less. He's who I need right now.

He pulls back and looks me in the eyes. "What the hell were you thinking? I thought I was going to lose you again."

Instead of letting me answer, he pulls me against him again. We stand there for several minutes before he finally releases me. He turns back towards the stairs and takes my hand. We walk together, the Chasseur escorting us, though the other guards haven't moved from whatever position they assumed when they saw my father.

"It was smart," he says as we climb the stairs. "They couldn't argue with your logic, even though they tried. They can't kill a citizen without a trial."

I remember what Rekka said about her mother being murdered on-world at my father's hand. She didn't have a trial and they killed her. But I dare not say anything about it. From this moment on, there is no one I can trust. Not if I'm going to destroy the sick system the star-people have developed.

Instead I say, "Thanks, Dad."

At the top of the stairs we emerge into the night. The stars shine above us, shimmering green through the column of light shooting above the tower. *Green light, for victory.* Across the tower is a glowing outline of a door. Two of the Chasseur pass us and go through. As they do, the inside flashes teal and ripples like a pond when you toss in a rock.

I walk around the door and look at the other side. I can see my father through the door as he smiles at me. He beckons me back. I walk through the door, but nothing happens.

"Where did they go?" I ask.

"Up," he says. "It's a portal."

"But I walked through it."

"You were going the wrong way."

I nod, though I don't really know what's going on. "Does it hurt?"

"No, it just feels like going through any other door."

"Okay then," I say, stepping towards it.

"Nova," he says, grabbing my arm. "I'm not going to be able to help you when we get up there."

"What do you mean?"

"They're going to take you for conditioning. They'll keep you separated from everyone until they think you're ready to be part of Vaisseau. I won't be able to see you or even visit. I just want you to know it isn't because I don't want to. I love you and I'm thrilled you're finally coming home."

There's a catch in my throat, but I don't know if it's because of his words or my fear of what's about to happen. I nod and say, "Just take care of Thoa and Krew."

He presses his lips into a tight smile, but there's a slight twitch in his neck as he lies to me. "I'll do what I can."

I turn towards the door, take a deep breath, and step through. My forever waits on the other side.

EPILOGUE

The walls are white, the floor is black, when these guards leave, the man comes back.

I chant the rhyme over and over in my head, reminding myself of what comes next in the pattern. It's the only way to keep track of my time. The guard are on rotation for eight hours, I think. I guess they could be less or more, but eight feels right.

Every fourteen cycles a man in a white coat comes to visit me. He takes my temperature, looks in my throat and ears, then asks me questions where he tries to make me angry. He says he doesn't want me to be angry, but then he tells me that Thoa died. He reminds me that Krew is locked in a cell for the next year, more if he doesn't start cooperating with them.

If the doctor didn't want me to be angry, he wouldn't say those things.

Last time I saw him, I broke his nose. He skipped the fourteenth cycle after that. But he'll come today. I want his visit. I need him to tell me that Thoa is dead, that Krew is imprisoned, so I can touch my rage. It's the only thing I can feel anymore, and only when I hear him speak the words.

The walls are white, the floor is black, when these guards leave, the man comes back.

A buzzer blasts through my room, warning me to move away from the door. The first time I heard it, I didn't know what it meant. When the guard came in with my breakfast, I charged them. I made it thirty feet outside my door before they tazed me and dragged me back.

Today I move to my bed, the corner where the walls meet, feeling their coolness to keep myself rooted in place. I let my fingers dip below the edge of the bed to the paper star I keep hidden there. It sings in my fingers: love, love, love.

I didn't know what a taser was before coming here. Now I know I do not like it. All the guards keep them at their hips now when they bring me food. Sometimes they see me staring at their holsters and they chuckle. I hate it when they do that. Don't they understand I would rip them apart on even ground? I would bash in their heads like Rekka's. *Crack, crack, crack. Crack, crack, crack. Make their eyes roll back, back, back.*

"You're in a good mood today."

I turn to see one of the guards standing by the table. My breakfast sits there waiting, but I needn't worry that it will get cold. It's already cold when it gets here. Buttered toast, mushy oatmeal, a cup of water, and sometimes, if I've been really good, little red gel squares.

I glance at the guard's hip. They are not wearing a taser. I cock my head to the side, checking for where they're hiding it. I know it's there. This is a trick, or maybe a test. If I pass it, maybe I'll be freed from this place.

For the first time since I've been here, I look at the guard's face. Thin lips, small nose, a spray of freckles across her cheeks. She's a chubby thing, cute as a button, and part of me thinks that's why they sent her in. Maybe I won't charge at the girl who looks like a child.

And they're right, in a way. I'm not going to attack her. But I want to.

"Yes," I say, my voice strange to my ears. I haven't spoken to anyone but the doctor in weeks, and somehow it feels wrong to speak to this girl. "I am feeling better. I don't feel angry today."

She smiles. "That's good to hear. Hopefully that means you won't be here much longer."

I try to return her smile, but fear I'm only baring my teeth. "I hope to be free soon. I'm excited to explore my new home."

She laughs like I've said the funniest thing she's ever heard. She laughs until there are tears in her eyes and she's wiping her face.

"What's so funny?"

"Just you," she says, trying to calm herself. "You're really trying to play me like I'm one of the fools from on-world."

"I'm not," I say.

She shakes her head. "Stop. We both know you're thinking about killing me right now. It's part of you. And you're going to be stuck in this room until you can look at another human without thinking of all the ways you can hurt them."

I push away from the wall and off the bed. I lunge towards the woman, planning to show her exactly what I'm thinking. She whips her taser from behind her body and jabs it against me. The shock vibrates through me and I fall to the floor. I convulse long after she's gone.

The walls are white, the floor is black, when these guards leave, the man comes back.

The walls are white, the floor is black, when these guards leave, the man comes back.

The walls are white, the floor is black, when these guards leave...

But he doesn't come, doesn't come, again and again the fourteenth shift passes and he doesn't come. He doesn't come and I am lost to the walls of whitest white, the floors of blackest black.

WHEN THE DOOR OPENS AND THE DOCTOR WALKS IN, I'M CERTAIN I'M dreaming. A sob sticks in my throat, afraid to pass my parched lips. He is a mirage in the desert.

"Good afternoon, Nova."

I bounce from my head and run towards him. He calls for the guards, but before they can enter the room I'm on him, wrapping my arms around him and hugging him as tightly as I can. Part of me knows they will taze me if I don't let him go soon, the other part is so desperate for human interaction that I consider never letting him go. When he puts his arm on my back and pats it, I'm certain I've entered paradise.

"That's enough," he says after a few minutes.

I release him and step back, afraid that if I'm bad he'll leave again. I mutter, "I'm sorry."

"It's okay. It's good. You miss being around people."

I nod. "Very much. I didn't realize before how important it is."

He waves towards the floor and we sit down across from each other. He says, "You don't have a great record with people, Nova."

"I know. I've been awful. But I want to do better. I promise I'll make you proud."

He smiles and I'm certain his teeth are made of sunlight. "I'm glad to hear that, but I have to be honest, I don't know how willing people are going to be to trust you. You've only been here a little over two months. It usually takes three or four to make real progress."

Two months. I've lived in this room for two months.

"Are you okay?" he asks. "Where did you go just now?"

He watches me, my eyes, my mouth, the way I move my hands. I know he is reading me, and I know he is good at it. I have to tell the truth. "Sorry. I was just surprised when you said two months."

He nods. Smiles again. "How about we take a walk? It'll give you a chance to stretch your legs and will let the people in charge see how well you're doing."

"That would be wonderful," I say, letting my own smile match his.

"Before we can go, there's a few things we have to talk about."

I nod. I knew this was coming and I'm ready.

"Tell me what you remember after you walked through the door."

I close my eyes and take a deep breath. "There were screens and lights everywhere. Things were flashing and beeping and there was so much chaos."

"And you saw Krew?" he asks.

I nod, picturing him in my mind. "His face was bloody. His eye was swollen shut and his lip was busted."

"Why was that?"

"He disobeyed."

"That's right. And what happens to citizens when they disobey?"

"They're punished."

"Is that what we're doing to you?" he asks.

I shake my head. "Of course not. You're helping me."

"Is there anyone else you can remember us trying to help?"

I swallow, readying the words I've been practicing for weeks. "You tried to help Thoa."

"We did," he says. "What do you remember?"

I bite my lip, my eyes still closed, pretending that I'm trying to remember. I wrap my fingers around the hem of my shirt to stop them from twitching. "The guards took me from the room where Krew was. He was yelling my name, and I was reaching for him, but the guards pulled me down the hall away from the bad man."

"Very good. Keep going."

"They took me down a hall with big windows. I saw Thoa through one of the windows and there were people in green clothes standing around him."

"Doctors," he says. "They were trying to stop the bleeding. Do you remember why he was bleeding?"

I nod. "That horrible, terrible girl stabbed him."

"What was her name?"

I dig my fingernails into my palms, focusing on the pain. "I don't remember." I hear him make a small sound in his throat, as if he doesn't believe me. I press on, saying, "Reeva or Roma or something. I'm sorry. Will you please tell me?"

He clears his throat and says, "It's not important."

Inside I smile, though I can't let him see it. *Rekka, Rekka, Rekka.* She's my secret, my stabby girl, my spark of revolution, hiding in my heart.

He asks, "Do you know what happened to Thoa?"

"No," I say, my voice small.

"Nova, you know what happened. Say it."

"I don't want to," I say, and I'm telling the truth. Whether it's true or not, I don't want to say it.

He sighs. "I thought we were making progress here, but it seems you need more time."

"No, please," I say, reaching out to touch his leg.

My eyes open and find his, the moss green of them a comfort in this room of white and black. I watch his lips turn up slightly at the corners. Something about this touch makes him happy, happier than it should.

He puts his hand over mine and says, "You have to come to terms with what happened."

I take a deep breath and let it out slowly. "Thoa died. The doctors tried to save him, but he'd lost too much blood. He's gone."

He squeezes my hand. "I know that was hard, but I'm proud of you."

I smile at him, as sweet as the red gel cubes they give me, but in my mind, I think, *Crack, crack, crack.*

ABOUT THE AUTHOR

Shelly Jarvis began working on speculative fictions thanks to a writing assignment in Mrs. Bettijane Burger's eleventh grade English class, but her passion for writing developed at seven when she wrote a Halloween tale about a witch and a ghost who became best friends.

An avid science fiction and fantasy reader, Shelly spends a large portion of each new day dwelling in other worlds.

Shelly enjoys spending time with her wacky spouse, her wonderful nephews, and her rescue pups, Gimli, Butters, Fergus, and Pickles. She currently resides near Charleston, West Virginia, in the wild and wonderful mountains that have her heart.

Learn more about Shelly, including other books and how to contact her, at ShellyJarvis.com.

www.ingramcontent.com/pod-product-compliance
Lightning Source LLC
Chambersburg PA
CBHW052038240626
47153CB00006B/2134